IN THE LAMPLIGHT

L. JAGI LAMPLIGHTER

eBooks

Stratford, NJ

PUBLISHED BY
eSpec Books LLC
Danielle McPhail, Publisher
PO Box 493,
Stratford, New Jersey 08084
www.especbooks.com

ISBN: 978-1-942990-35-2
ISBN (ebook): 978-1-942990-36-9

www.fotolia.com
Cover Art: Follow Me © Atelier Sommerland
Interior Graphic: Vintage dividers and borders © Seamartini Graphics

Copyeditor: Greg Schauer
Art Direction and Production: Mike McPhail, McP Digital Graphics
Interior Design: Sidhe na Daire Multimedia, www.sidhenadaire.com

To Mom,
for all the fantastic stories
you told me when I was little.

Contents

Of Exotic Cocktails and Mulberry Wine

I SAT IN THE GARDEN AT PROSPERO'S MANSION REGARDING THE CARDS. A plague of bogies was ravaging the town; over a hundred people were dead, gnawed from the inside out, and three of them were our men. Usually, I did not get involved in the legwork myself, but this was getting personal.

Unfortunately, the cards were not speaking today. I toyed with them as I sipped my mulberry morath. No one makes a proper morath anymore, which is a pity. Of course, no one makes hand-painted tarot cards anymore either. Lately, I have found myself mourning the lost glories of past ages.

I particularly missed the grace and dignity of the Victorian Age. But then, back in the Victorian Age, I had missed the Renaissance; and during the Renaissance, I had missed old Milan. And in Milan, I had missed my father's island. I had longed for a return to the time when he and I had dwelled in idyllic calm, with only aerie servants and the horrible Caliban as our company.

For you see, Shakespeare did not get Father's story quite right. Father never drowned his books nor freed his aerie spirits. Nor did I marry that sap Ferdinand. At the age of five, my father, the great magician Prospero, consecrated me to the sacred service of Eurynome. Handmaidens of Eurynome received many privileges—among them immortality. Did I mention that Eurynome's other name is Monocerus, as in Greek for 'one horn'? As you may recall, unicorns only come to virgins, so there was to be no marriage for me.

I have never regretted my choice. Of late, however, I have found myself longing for fit companionship; someone who could appreciate the fading past and the wonders I have seen. Mortal men have such short memories and such narrow areas of interest.

Just as I was about to indulge in another bout of nostalgic reminiscing, Mab, the company's head gum-shoe, came stomping around the corner, disturbing my revere. Mab was the granite-faced, hard-boiled type. He had an intense dislike of all things arcane. Too many years of chasing supernatural perpetrators had cemented his preference for the human world over the world of fey. He might have passed for a human himself, had he not looked so exactly like a detective from the movies.

However, Mab was not human. True, he was currently inhabiting a solid body—a recent innovation of Father's, designed to help Prospero, Inc. move into this new technical age. Yet, in truth, he was an aerie spirit like Father's servant Ariel, and, like Ariel, he was bound by the spell my father had cast long ago to bind the Aerie One race to my family's service.

"More bad news, ma'am," Mab drawled in his thick Bronx accent. He took off his fedora and laid it on the wrought-iron table. "The bogies got Gooseberry."

"Got…as in killed?" I asked, startled.

Mab nodded grimly.

I was quiet for a time. The first three of our men who had fallen victim to the bogies had been human employees from Prospero, Inc.'s various mundane businesses. Gooseberry, on the other hand, had been one of our best supernatural agents. Like Mab, he was an Aerie One living in a fleshy body. I had never lost an Aerie One before. I had not even realized they could actually be killed.

Mab jabbed a finger at the tarot cards. "Miss Miranda, you really shouldn't dabble in filth like that," Mab advised dourly. "Mortals trucking with magic are just asking for trouble—even immortal mortals like you. Believe me, I know. Before I came to work for Mr. Prospero, I used to be one of those spirits who gave them trouble."

"Yes, yes, Mab, so you so often tell me," I said, ignoring him. I closed my eyes, prayed to my White Lady, then lay my cards out one more time. A sense of warmth and well-being filled me. I opened my eyes to regard the cards. Still nothing. Folding them back into a deck, I placed them in their cedar box.

"This once, you shall get your way," I said, "Not because I am unwilling to face a little supernatural danger to avenge Gooseberry, but because the cards are not answering. Something is blocking divination on the subject of the bogey infestation."

Mab rubbed his jaw. Like every tough guy from Bogart to Han Solo, he showed about a half-a-days growth of beard. He asked skeptically, "How do you know you just aren't reading 'em right?"

I rewarded his impertinence with a sharp look. "The average diviner doesn't have much faith in her abilities. When the cards don't speak to her, she just assumes she's not seeing clearly, and she makes up answers to cover for it. I know better. I trust my abilities. They come from Eurynome, the White Lady of Spiral Wisdom. If I can not see, it is because the truth is being hidden. Someone is deliberately obscuring the source of this plague from diviners, which is why all your two-bit witches and police fortune tellers have not been any help in this matter."

"So the cards are blocked," Mab said dubiously. "Is that bad?"

"Very bad," I said. "All supernatural leads are now closed to us."

"You mean we'll have to do our legwork the new-fangled way? On foot?" asked Mab with a grin, adding without the least hint of dismay, "Ah, what a pity."

I sighed and stood up, smoothing the satiny cloth of my high-necked, emerald tea dress with my white gloves. "Let me get my coat. We can begin at the morgue."

✦

Forty-five minutes later, we stood in the lab in the basement of Prospero's Mansion, looking down at the remains of our man Gooseberry. His stiff, cold body was stretched out on an examination table under bright surgery lights. The coroner, who had released Gooseberry under the impression we were bringing him home to be buried, had given us a copy of the official autopsy, but I didn't trust those county employees to understand what they were seeing. So, we were about to take a second look.

Most of Gooseberry was in pretty good shape. Only his stomach was dismembered. Mab tried to cover the wound with his hat, to spare me the sight.

"Better you not look, ma'am. Pretty obvious what happened here," Mab said. "Poor sucker was eaten alive."

I pushed him aside impatiently. "For Heaven's sake! I've walked across battlefields. What's a mere disembowelment?" I peered closer. "This wound was clearly made by a creature clawing and gnawing its way out from the inside. However, we still have no idea how the bogies are getting in. Maybe there will be something in the throat or intestines which will give us a clue. See what you can find."

"I'm on it!" Mab said empathically, pulling on a pair of rubber gloves. "I want to get to the bottom of this before we lose another man. I had not realized how vulnerable my people are, once we get into these fleshy bodies Mr. Prospero made for us. If we don't find out what's causing this, the next victim could be me…or even you, ma'am!"

Mab got to work immediately, with only a minimum of hindrance from my familiar, Tybolt, Prince of Cats. Under the pretense of trying to help, Tybolt had leapt onto the corpse's legs, and now sat batting at Gooseberry's intestines. Mab swatted the sleek black cat aside, and Tybolt stalked off—stiff-legged, his velvety black nose high in the air—to sit in front of the filing cabinet and wash his bruised dignity.

"Best as I can tell," Mab eventually reported, "The bogey emerged from the upper stomach. The police report suggests that there was remarkably little bleeding. In fact, from the evidence, I'd hazard a guess that Gooseberry was already in some kind of coma at the time that the bogey hatched."

"I hope that means he was spared the pain of feeling his stomach ripped open from within," I said. "Poor soul."

"Gooseberry was an Aerie One, ma'am," Mab said dryly, "Chances are pretty good against him have having had any kind of soul at all, rich or poor."

"Any clue as to how the bogey got in?" I asked.

Mab replied, "Remains show the victim to have eaten bread, tuna, cola, and what was probably once ice cream. Bogies in their larval stage are fragile and could be crushed by teeth. Bread and tuna are chewed. Ice cream tends to melt in the mouth first. A larval sac would be noticed."

"Cross reference cola with previous victims' reports," I asked my familiar.

"Who are you talking to? Me?" Tybolt asked, eyeing me with bright yellow eyes. "I'm a familiar, not an errand kitten,"

"Just check the references," I growled.

Tybolt bestirred himself enough to leap onto the table and push the button to turn on the computer, but then he returned to the painstaking task of washing. He was saved from any further indignities by Mab, who, snorting with exasperation, pulled off his gloves and stomped over to search the database himself.

An examination of previous cases available on record showed one cola, Pixie Cola to be specific, to have been present in all cases. Mab and I reckoned that the bogey larvae could be made soft enough to slide down a throat during a large gulp. If the bogies were in the Pixie Cola, a lot more lives might soon be taken. On the other hand, a lot of folk drink Pixie. It's presence in the autopsies could be a coincidence.

"Pixie's a big company, ma'am. If we break a story like this and can't prove it, they'll slam us for libel." Mab growled.

"Let them slam. I am a Handmaiden of the White Lady! I will not cower before the likes of the Pixie Corporation!" I exclaimed vehemently.

"Right, ma'am," Mab drawled, pulling his hat low over his eyes to hide his expression.

I continued more calmly, "However, let's be sure, all the same. Mab, you check the paper and find out whether this spate of bogey deaths is a local or national phenomena. I'll locate the nearest Pixie warehouse."

We reached the Pixie warehouse down by the docks just after midnight. Creeping up to a pile of old boxes and barrels, we hid and observed the security. Two guards passed our position, talking among themselves. Mab and I remained motionless for the twenty minutes it took them to make their rounds and return to walk by us again. As soon as they passed the second time, we sneaked out the other way and slipped in a side door, which Mab quickly opened with a lock pick he carried in his shoe.

Within, all was silent. Next to a pile of crates, a lone guard slept within a tiny circle of light from an overhead lamp; an empty bottle of Pixie Cola resting on the floor beside his chair. Mab and I crept silently by and examined the boxes and bottles.

"Pss. Miss Miranda, look here," Mab called softly, his voice hardly audible in the great cavernous warehouse. He stood pointing at the guard's neck. I crept forward. Just above the collar bone were two identical puncture marks. His face was pale as chalk. I reached out and felt his wrist. He was dead.

Mab raised an eyebrow.

"Curiouser and curiouser," I whispered back.

After a once around, we determined that the place was empty and pulled out our lights. Mab, who distained magic, was carrying a Mag Light the size of a bobby's billy club. I, on the other hand, made a point of avoiding technology any time old-fashioned reliable magic would serve. I wore a coronet set with a small sun sprite imprisoned in a crystal gem. Tybolt had caught the sprite last Mid-Summer's Night. My brother Erasmus had trapped it in a gem for me and mounted it onto a silver coronet. It served as a passable headlamp.

My sun sprite leapt about in the gem, casting dancing lights upon the rows and rows of stacked cartons. Mab ripped open a carton at random, pulled the cap off a bottle with his pen knife, and poured the contents onto the floor. Sure enough, a thin gelatinous sack was visible amidst the dark pool of spilt liquid. Mab went to squash it with his shoe, but I stopped him.

"Let's take it back and examine it," I whispered. "We might learn something."

Across the warehouse, the door creaked. We could hear the voices of the guards, wondering aloud why the door was not locked. Mab doused his flashlight. I stuck my coronet back in its black velvet bag.

"Quick, we got to get out of here! If they find us, they're going to blame us for the guard's death!" hissed Mab.

"Where can we go?" I whispered back.

"There was another door at the back," Mab whispered back. "If the guards are here, they can't be there. Let's go."

Slowly, Mab and I crept along the extraordinarily long row of boxes heading for the back door. At first, we could see the faint illumination from the dead guard's light and the flicker of flashlights reflecting against the soda boxes. We moved quickly, stepping between the isles, with our backs pressed against the soda to avoid being detected by the guards.

As we retreated deeper into the warehouse, however, even those faint lights fell away. Soon, it was black as pitch. While I was grateful because this meant that I was out of the current range of the guards' flashlights, it also meant that I had to creep forward, my fingers trailing along the stacked boxes.

Ahead of us, Mab and I both distinctly heard the sound of someone moving.

"The vampire who killed the guard," I hissed softly, "he may still be here!"

Mab never did get a chance to answer me. Instead, I heard a sudden strangled noise from just in front of me, and the sounds of a scuffle.

The next few moments were horrible. I stood still, petrified with indecision. I knew Mab was in trouble—I could hear him thrashing around—but I could see nothing. I moved so that my back was pressed against the shelves and put my hands out in front of me, hoping to stave off any attack. Should I move forward and try to help him? Should I flee and see to my own safety. If only I had even the tiniest bit of light.

And then it struck me. Vampire. Sun sprite. The idea was intriguing. On the one hand, the sprite was a tiny, weak thing. On the other, we were in total darkness with nothing to dilute its effect. Could work...worth a try.

Grabbing the black velvet bag, which I wore around my shoulder like a purse, I cracked it open very carefully, hoping that the light would shine toward Mab and his attacker and without alerting the human guards up front.

I saw a momentary glimpse of a tall figure with his large muscular hands encircling Mab's neck, and then there was just a pile of clothes and dust. I quickly closed the bag. Phantom images hovered about me, as my eyes swam from the momentary onslaught of brightness.

"Worked like a charm," I laughed.

"Thanks, ma'am," said Mab. I could not see him, but I somehow knew he was rubbing his neck. "Too bad we could not apprehend him. Might have been useful to question him."

I shrugged. "Oh well, he's dust now. Besides, his presence here is irrelevant to the case. Let's get out of here while we still can."

When we finally escaped the warehouse, it was a tremendous relief to breathe the open air and see the starlight.

✳

Back at the laboratory, we examined the larva, which turned out to be a Type-2 bogey, its terrible incisors still nothing but gelatinous goo. When we were done, I let Mab kill it. Tybolt wanted to play with it first, but I thought that path led toward nothing but disaster.

"What next?" asked Mab grimly.

"You find out where that Pixie is bottled," I said, "I'm going down to the library."

The restricted area of the library contained a complete set of Encyclopaedia Arcanium. Bright and early the next morning, I was down there to look up 'bogey, Type-2.' According to the Arcanium, Type-2 Bogies were bigger than your run-of-the-mill Type-1 Bogies (usually found on farms), but not as big as your Type-3 Bogies, also called nightmare bogies or 'boogey men', (which were found mainly in ghettoes and have been known to grow to over seven feet tall.)

Type-2 Bogies, the encyclopedia reported, were known for stealing eggs, garbage, and babies. They ranged from about a foot and a half to two feet in height and could grow from larva to full size in a matter of minutes, once the developmental process began.

Believe it or not, the effects of swallowing bogey larva on the human body was documented. The encyclopedia article reported that Type-2 Bogey larva was normally inert within humans, i.e. swallowing a larva did not cause the bogey to hatch; however, the larvae did release a chemical which produced a mild euphoric sensation in humans. Certain cults in the Midwest were reported to swallow bogey larvae to induce mystical experiences. No cases of larvae hatching in living bodies had been reported by these cults.

Something was going terribly wrong.

Further into the article, I located a list of substances known to trigger development in bogey larvae. The substances were all written in chemical codes, only about a third of which I recognized. I had to look up the rest of them in a medical reference before I had any idea what we were dealing with. It took me more than an hour, but eventually, I determined that all the substances were associated with decay or decomposing corpses. None would be found in healthy living bodies, or even in Pixie Cola.

So, what was causing the bogies to hatch in the living?

Up on the library roof lived one of my best informants, Balthasar the Gargoyle. When I arrived, he was expounding to a group of pigeons, reminiscing about his days as a coal demon in the pits of Hell. His duties had included heating the hot coals on the beaches around the pools of muck and mire where the Wrathful and Sullen were condemned to swim. Balthasar describing with blissful glee how the damned would howl and jump, flapping their bony arms, whenever they tried to escape; their water-soaked feet sizzling on the glowing coals of the shore.

"Those were the days, Lady Miranda. Before I got conjured into the stone of this library," he said gloomily as the pigeons departed in a flurry of beating wings.

My heart went out to him. He had the nostalgia bug even worse than I did. At least I could order an aerie servant to go find me an original Chippendale chair or whip me up a batch of authentic mulberry morath. Balthasar could do nothing but sit and remember. He could not even clean the pigeon droppings from his stone head.

I washed his head with a bucket and towel I had brought along for that purpose and told him the story he always liked to hear about the time some overeager vampire tried to take a bite out of me. Virgin blood is considered a delicacy by vampires, and this particular one had been tripping over himself to sample this particular delicacy. Unfortunately for him, the White Lady of Spiral Wisdom frowns upon creatures of the night mistreating her handmaidens. The moment my blood touched his lips, he writhed, as if aflame, and promptly turned to dust.

Balthasar loved that story. He hated vampires.

"They leave droppings on my stomach when they roost up here in their bat forms," he complained. "Bad enough having a pot belly of stone, without having a bunch of defecating vampires to decorate it for you."

I gave his stone belly a pat and figured it was time to get down to business. "I'm working on a new case, Balthasar," I said. "Have you heard anything about where this rash of bogies are coming from?"

"Heard, no, but I've seen. Look down there," said Balthasar. "To the right, next to the doughnut shop."

Below, a large white and green 'Friendly Poltergeist Removal, Inc.' truck was making its way down the street. The truck stopped, and the drivers got out and placed large flat traps laden with sticky sweet foods and silver trinkets in an alley between the police precinct and the court house. A group of bogies, hungry and skinny creatures with spindly arms and legs about the size of large rabbits, ran out almost immediately and were quickly captured by the traps.

"How bizarre!" I exclaimed, quickly scribbling down the license plate. "Either those are some extremely enterprising humans who have decided to make a living impersonating a popular movie, or there is another supernatural organization in town beside Prospero, Inc."

Balthasar watched them drive away with a melancholy sigh.

"Wonder where they bring those things? Sure wouldn't mind having a few of them to eat. Pretty hungry these days. This generation of pigeons is already getting wise about sitting on my head. Who would have guessed that pigeons could learn," he grumbled.

I fed him the crackers in my pocket and promised to bring something tastier next time I visited. Rough life, the metropolitan gargoyle's.

<hr>

Back in the car, we discussed what we knew. Mab went first.

"Here's what my research turned up: the bogies are coming in the Pixie Cola, being drunk up by decent people, hatching, eating their way out through their stomachs, and moving into the walls of the nearest buildings. From there, they steal food and shiny objects. They've also carried off two babies," Mab reported, gesturing with his lit cigarette.

"My guess," I said, "is that Pixie Corp is adding bogey larvae to their product for its narcotic value. Trying to compete with that secret Haitian ingredient in Coke, most likely."

"A dangerous thing to do," muttered Mab. "Especially considering the outcome."

"Did you find out if the spate of deaths was local?" I asked.

Mab blew a ring of smoke into the air. I coughed and fanned the smoke away from me with my silver fighting fan, an elegant and razor-sharp implement made by the Japanese god of the forge himself.

"Hey, careful with that thing!" Mab squawked. "I get the message. As to your question: not local, but not country-wide either. Seems there are a number of areas where the larvae are hatching. As you might imagine, they are the areas to which new Pixie Cola ships first."

"Could it be something in the water Pixie is using? Perhaps it runs through the graveyard and carries traces of rotting corpses?" I suggested, recalling the list of chemicals that triggered bogey development.

Mab shrugged. "Couldn't tell you, ma'am."

"What about 'Friendly Poltergeist Removal, Inc.'" I asked, "Ever hear of them?"

"No, ma'am, but they bear looking into. I'll have some of my men check it out as soon as we get home."

We entered the Pixie plant as part of a public tour, slipped away from the group, and hid under some machinery until closing time. Mab checked the rooms one by one, while I slipped into the office and rifled through the desk. I hacked into their system with very little effort and began copying their records. Then, I pulled out my mini-scanner and began scanning all pertinent papers.

The documents and electronic files confirmed what I had expected. 'Mildly pleasing gelatinous sacs' had been added to the product to increase its competitiveness against Coke. The sacs were being purchased through a company called Widow, Roderick, and Company. From email correspondence, it was clear that Pixie had not originally been aware of the true nature of these 'sacs.' The test samples their labs had been given had not included bogey parts.

Recently, however, someone had alerted the upper management to the presence of Pixie Cola in the corpses, and they now knew about the bogey larvae in the sacs. They had immediately stopped production of the new, 'more pleasing' variety; however, thousands of contaminated bottles were already on the market. (Records indicated that at least a hundred thousand such bottles had been produced, thirty thousand of which had already been shipped.) According to their internal communications, the executives at Pixie Corporation were frantic to discover what was causing the sacs to hatch before anyone else did.

In the meantime, the response to the new variety—from those customers who had not died because their innards were eaten out by bogies—had been phenomenal. Sales had tripled in two weeks.

Mab came stomping back into the office. "Found the supply room," he said. "Bags of bogey larval sacs from floor to ceiling."

I shared with him what I had found. He nodded grimly.

"They should notify the public," Mab grunted.

"Mab! Look at this!" I exclaimed, holding up a newspaper clipping that had been laying in the top drawer of the desk. Splashed across the front was a picture of the guard we had found dead in the warehouse the night before. According to the article, he had been found in the morning with his stomach eaten out. The emerging bogey was said to have rifled through the unopened Pixie cartons and spilled a bottle onto the floor.

"Huh. Son of a dog," said Mab, scratching his head.

"I could have sworn that guy was a vampire victim," I asked, "...do Bogey's leave double incisor marks like that?"

Mab shook his head. "That guy was definitely vampire chow. Bogies are messier, and they don't drain their victims. You saw Gooseberry's body, the poor sucker. The bogey must have hatched later, after we left. But as to whether there is a connection between the neck bites and the bogey, that I don't know."

<hr>

Back at the mansion, I sent Mab away with some excuse about making tea, then headed down to the lab, where I dragged Gooseberry's body out of the walk-in refrigerator. Usually, I did not examine corpses myself, but in this case I did not feel comfortable voicing my suspicions to Mab. Luckily the Water of Life that extends my natural lifespan—a gift from Eurynome—also makes me stronger and faster than I would normally be, so I had no trouble carrying the corpse to one of the examination tables.

Donning rubber gloves, I checked the one place Mab had previously not thought to look. Sure enough, amidst the wrinkled skin of Gooseberry's withered male organ were two dark bruise marks. A favorite trick of vampiric succubi that, takes advantage of a large supply of pooled blood. I shuttered. Oh, but I hated those blood suckers!

I cleaned up the lab and removed Tybolt from the examination table. He was batting at Gooseberry's manly parts.

"You get to do it, why can't I?" Tybolt sniffed, as he stalked away.

"I wasn't doing it for fun." I said.

Tybolt's bright golden eyes regarded me steadily, "Oh, then why did you chase Mab away first?"

Sometimes, it is just not worth it to talk to cats.

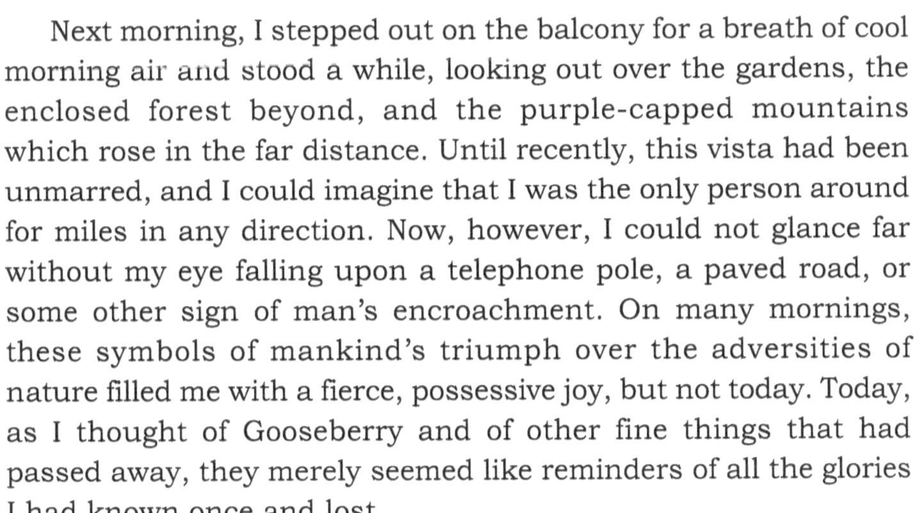

Next morning, I stepped out on the balcony for a breath of cool morning air and stood a while, looking out over the gardens, the enclosed forest beyond, and the purple-capped mountains which rose in the far distance. Until recently, this vista had been unmarred, and I could imagine that I was the only person around for miles in any direction. Now, however, I could not glance far without my eye falling upon a telephone pole, a paved road, or some other sign of man's encroachment. On many mornings, these symbols of mankind's triumph over the adversities of nature filled me with a fierce, possessive joy, but not today. Today, as I thought of Gooseberry and of other fine things that had passed away, they merely seemed like reminders of all the glories I had known once and lost.

Over breakfast that morning, I told Mab my conclusions.

"I may have discovered what's activating the bogey larvae," I said.

He raised an eyebrow. His mouth was occupied with a jelly doughnut.

"Vampire spittle," I said. "Gooseberry had been a vampire victim. That's why he was already in shock when the bogcy emerged. The man in the warehouse was also a vampire victim. When I looked over the other autopsy reports available to us, I found mention of twin puncture marks in more than half of them."

"At least, that means you were right that Gooseberry didn't suffer too much, the poor shmuck," Mab said, after swallowing.

I coughed discretely, and decided against sharing the details regarding the location of Gooseberry's puncture.

"So," Mab continued, "Pixie introduces a new ingredient to compete with Coke. That ingredient reacts badly with vampire spittle. What we really have, then, is a vampire problem, not a bogey problem. Pixie Corp can just tell its customers to wear crosses or carry garlic, and all will be well. Case closed."

"Not exactly," I said frowning. "We still haven't cleared up the matter of who is stopping divination into this matter."

"Pixie cola, of course," Mab said. "They don't want the deaths blamed on them."

I shook my head. "I don't think so. A ward strong enough to stop my gifts would require a substantial supernatural talent. It's not Pixie Corporation's style. Besides, there was no evidence of such a thing among their records. What about 'Friendly Poltergeist Removal, Inc.'? They could be involved in all this. Did you find anything on them?"

Mab shook his head. "They're not registered with any mundane business registry and their license number is recorded as belonging to a set of destroyed plates.

"Why is that hardly surprising?" I murmured.

"So, where do we go next?" Mab asked.

"Where else?" I asked, "Widow, Roderick, and Co. We can leave first thing after the funeral."

❧━━━✦✦━━━☙

We buried Gooseberry in the enclosed woods behind the house. Father officiated, and all the Aerie Ones came to mourn his passing. Their weeping was an eerie sound, chilling to the bone, and a storm rose, the likes of which had not been seen in many a year. Trees came crashing down, and cars were carried through the air. Gooseberry's passing would be remembered by mortals for decades to come.

As soon as the funeral was over, Mab and I headed south toward the offices of Widow, Roderick, and Company. This mission, I feared, would not be as easy as breaking into Pixie Corp. Any company that dealt with bogey larvae and massive obscuration spells was likely to pack a pretty impressive supernatural arsenal. So, before I left, I asked Father for the keys to the Great Hall, where we kept our greatest magic.

Now, as Mab drove, I held in my hands the warm wood of the Staff of Wind and Weather, a four-foot flute made from the same pine in which the witch Sycorax originally imprisoned Ariel. Into its length, Father has woven all the magic from one of his great tomes. Whoever played the flute could command the winds, the weather, lightning, whirlwinds, and all the members of Mab's race.

In the interest of personal safety, I wore my emerald tea dress. Father had woven many spells into the garment. It could turn aside both supernatural dangers, such as ghosts, wraiths, and angry djin, and man-made dangers, such as knives, swords, and even small caliber gunfire. In addition, it was a lovely garment, which complemented my green eyes. Unfortunately, it was a bit out of style lately. To make myself less conspicuous, I had covered it with a white trench coat.

Mab, whose hands burned if he touched cold iron, had brought with him his trusty lead pipe, half-a-dozen wooden skewers, and his fists. He also brought a pair of earplugs that allowed him to be present while I played the flute without having to dance to its tune. It would do no good to have Mab, in his heavy material body, trying to obey a command to fly or brew up a storm.

The offices of Widow, Roderick, and Co. were located in the foothills of the mountains, just south of the river. It was a large estate with a nicely manicured lawn punctuated by old oaks. A ten-foot-tall barbed-wire fence surrounded the premises.

Mab handed me several wooden skewers, which I stuck in the pocket of my trench coat.

"In case you find yourself in the mood for vamp-kabab," he said, adding, "Did you think to bring that sun sprite coronet thing? That came in handy last time."

I shook my head. "It's no use during the day. Even a simple incandescent bulb would overwhelm it. It was only in pitch darkness that it could exert enough concentrated sunness to dust a vampire."

Mab glanced up at the barbed wire. "Any ideas on crossing the fence?"

"Certainly," I said, smiling my favorite superior smile. I raised my flute to my lips and waited. Scowling, Mab put the plugs in his ears, and I began to play.

The wind picked up in time to the music. As gently as thistle-down wafting on a summer breeze, Mab and I were lifted up, wafted over the fence, and set gently down on the far side. When our feet were firmly on the ground, I lowered the flute, and Mab removed his earplugs.

"Boy, I hate that oversized piccolo!" he growled softly. "Someday, that infernal instrument is going to meet an unpleasant fate! I just pray I'll be there to see it!"

"Shh! You'll alert the guards," I said surveying the establishment.

What I saw was sloping lawns dotted with massive trees leading to an honest-to-god castle which rose like an out-of-place ghost amidst the otherwise New World surroundings. It was a great heavy structure with gargoyles set upon the parapets.

"Looks like a real castle," whispered Mab.

"It is a real castle," I replied. "I recognize it. Whoever is living here must have transported it stone by stone from its original resting place in Northern Scotland. The gargoyles are new, though."

"You've been in there before?" asked Mab hopefully.

Ruefully, I shook my head. "No, I've only seen the outside. Back in the Seventeen Hundreds, my brother Theophrastus and his friend, Josiah Barrington, cleaned out a nest of vampires that had been roosting in this castle."

"I remember those two," said Mab, shuddering. "We used to call them the Demon Slayers. They were a force to be feared by supernatural folk. No spirit with any sense misbehaved during their heyday."

"I wonder if one of the original nest escaped to return and move the castle," I mused.

"Could be," Mab agreed. "But then, this heap of rocks is so gloomy it practically screams 'haven for angst-ridden creatures of the night.' Damn vampires," he spat. "They wouldn't be half so irritating if they weren't so consumed with self-pity."

"What do you see, as far as defenses?" I asked.

Mab looked. "Well, the gargoyles, of course. We won't be sneaking up to this heap unseen. And those statues lower down among the trees, the ones that look like great lion-dogs? They probably come to life and attack. Ditto for those statues over there, the soldiers with their swords drawn. Other than that? That vibration in the air, over by the far corner, suggests ethereal guardians. Maybe efreets or djin. Also there are some human guards by the main doors. Probably there is more out there, but that's all I can see."

"So, no chance of us sneaking in?" I asked.

Mab shook his head, "None at all."

"Ah well. When stealth fails, there is always the direct approach," I said.

Sliding my left hand into the pocket of my white trench coat, I grasped the handle of the forge god's fan, my flute clenched tightly in my other hand. Straightening, I strolled brazenly toward the wide, tree-lined walkway that led across the lawns to the transplanted Scottish castle.

I moved forward, a graceful smile on my lips, no doubt making quite a lovely picture; a young maiden with hair the color of moonlight on snow, garbed in an attractive emerald gown and a billowing white trench coat. Even from here, I could see the spark of interest in the eyes of the human guards.

The sight of the old Scottish castle reminded me of happier days, when I and my siblings, my father's children from later marriages, had still lived with him. We had been one large, happy, magical family back then. I remembered the 'Demonslaying Twins', Theo and his friend Josiah, how fierce and fine they had been. Back then Brother Theo had been one of my greatest admirers, and his friend Josiah had been a fine man, scholarly yet agile, able to discourse with ease on nearly any topic. He would have enjoyed sipping mulberry morath and debating the virtues of Descartes, or the evils of Kant, or the pleasures of a horse-drawn carriage over those of the automobile. Why were there no men such as he today?

As we came over the rise of the lawn and headed down the slope toward the castle, we could see the door guards more clearly; two burly men dressed in Highland uniform, complete with kilts of red-and-blue tartan. They stood alertly at their post, watching us curiously as we approached. When we were within easy earshot, one of them called out in one of the most atrocious Scottish accent to which I have ever heard tongue give utterance, "Halt! Who goes there? State your business!"

"Upstart Yanks!" I murmured under my breath. Mab, who liked to consider himself an American, frowned at me disapprovingly.

"Good evening, gentlemen," I said, lowering my lashes and smiling at them sideways. "I seem to be lost. I wonder if one of you could help direct me?"

I had learned this particular look from my sister Logistillia, during one of her few moments of sisterly affection. I seldom used it, and frankly suspected that I did it very badly; but that never seemed to dim the enthusiasm with which it was received. The fake Scotsmen were no exceptions. The two kilted blockheads practically tripped over themselves to hurry to my side.

And kept on tripping, as Mab kicked one in the head and knocked the other one across the temple with his trusty pipe. They both fell with a thud.

As we stood over them, congratulating ourselves, the eyes of both guards glazed over. They jerked directly to their feet, without stopping to bend at the hip or knee, and lumbered forward, arms outstretched, groping like blind men.

"Damn Zombie spell!" groaned Mab. He kicked one of them in the face again. It jerked its head but continued forward. Mab backed away, crying, "Quick, stab them with something silver."

I drew my fan and struck. The guard's flesh parted like butter before the enchanted fan. Continuing my spin, I sliced open the second one's neck. His head rolled way from his collarbone. The two guards collapsed into heaps.

I stared down at them regretfully; a shame to kill them just because they were possessed, even if they did have atrocious Scottish accents.

From behind us came the grate of stone on stone.

"The statues!" I cried. "Mab, get the door open! I'll try to hold them."

Mab pulled at the great oak door. It did not budge. He raced back to grab the ring of keys from the belt of one of the fallen guards, while I turned to face the huge stone soldier. He stepped from his granite pedestal and came forward, each step leaving a huge, deep gouge in the soft green grass.

I surveyed the stone bully thoughtfully. The bulky statue was far too heavy for a light wind. Holding my flute above my head, I began to swing it around in a circle. Wind whistled through the open holes making an angry screeching noise. Within moments, a whirlwind danced atop the spinning flute. Like a baseball player at bat, I swung my flute and pitched the whirlwind directly at the stone soldier. The slim tornado picked up the animated statue and carried it away across the lawn, smashing it into the great trees as it went.

"Quick, ma'am! I've got the door open!" called Mab. I ran toward him, aware that the two dog-lion statues on the lawn were now rising from their pedestals and preparing to lope toward me.

Something invisible and fey swept by, trying to grapple me. A shower of green sparks erupted from my enchanted tea dress followed by a long mournful moan. Grinning, I made a mental note to thank Father, yet again, for his handiwork.

I reached the door, and Mab slammed it shut, barring it with a heavy wood bar that was apparently intended for just that purpose. Behind us, the heavy oak of the door groaned as stone paws crashed against it, but the door held.

Mab and I looked around. We were in a long hall punctuated by thick, marble pillars. Several tasteful Grecian statues added an air of elegance to the somewhat dark and dour chamber. By silent agreement, Mab slunk to one side and I to the other, and we began making our way down the hall.

Too late, I noticed the scratch marks on the base of the statue of Poseidon, marks which should have warned me that the statue could move. By that time, thick stone arms, like iron vises, had seized me and lifted me from the ground. I am unusually strong for a member of the fairer sex, but not as strong as solid marble. I writhed and kicked my feet, to no avail.

Across the room, Mab had troubles of his own. He had noticed the scratch marks in time to dodge the initial lunge of the animated statue of Apollo; however, the statue was now pursuing him. He managed to break one of the stone god's arms with his trusty lead pipe, but that only made the statue angrier. The heavy marble statue leapt atop Mab, pinning him to the ground.

A moment later, human guards came, more Americans in kilts. At least, this bunch were not trying to pretend they were Scottish. One of the guards, a large, bearded lout leered at me.

"What's this we've got here? Surely, the boss won't mind if we keep this one for ourselves."

"Careful," Mab growled. "The dame's still a maiden. You know how vampires value virgin blood."

Mab was taking a chance, of course. There might not be any vampires here, or even if there were, the guards might not be in the know. However, his gamble paid off.

The leader of the guards, a tall sandy-haired fellow, pushed the bearded one away from me, saying, "Back off, now. You know the price of screwing up. A bottle of Pixie and a sore neck."

The bearded guard scowled. "Very well, but I want to hold her when we pour in the juice."

In the end, it took the statue plus four guards to hold me down and open my mouth while they poured the bottle of Pixie Cola down my throat. Only three held Mab. Consequently, he was able to squirm more than I. Eventually, they left us bound and tied on the floor in a side alcove.

The moment the guards left, Mab spit out the gelatinous sack.

"Jeepers! But that was vile! What about you, ma'am? Manage to outsmart them?" Mab asked.

I sighed. "No such luck, I fear. I'm afraid I'm in for a 'pleasant titillation'."

"Geez, that's rotten. Just hope that vampire doesn't get us before the effect rubs off. Hate to see you go that way, ma'am," said Mab, shaking his head sadly.

"Thanks, Mab. How comforting," I replied dryly.

He asked, "Can you scoot over here and get the knife out of my shoe? I keep it right next to the lock pick."

"With all those gadgets in your shoes, it's a wonder you can walk," I marveled, as I wriggled closer to him and awkwardly fumbled the knife out of the back of his shoe with my bound hands. "Ah ha! Got it!"

A moment later, we were on our feet. A quick search turned up my flute, the fan, the pile of skewers, and Mab's trusty lead pipe, all of which the guards had left lying in an umbrella rack around the corner.

"Okay, Mab," I whispered, "we need some kind of a plan. Something better than my hare-brained frontal assault plan. What was I thinking?"

"You were thinking that you and I are both tough customers, and that there are few powers that can take us both out. Unfortunately, our host here seems to be one of them. My suggestion: kiss our arses good-bye."

"I bet you there are secret passages here," I said, ignoring Mab's pessimism and his inappropriate language. I examined the stone of the wall. "A lot of moody old castles had them. Originally, they were meant for escape in time of siege, or even for servants to use, so that they stayed out of sight of the gentry. What is more, I think I remember Theo and Josiah talking about one in this castle. Josiah found a female vampire, the last of the nest, hidden in a secret passage. I remember he mentioned how eloquently she had plead for her life before he staked her. Given their description, and what I know about secret passageways, I would expect one to be about…here."

With a soft groan, the wall swung open. Mab and I stepped quickly into the darkened interior and shut the stone door behind us. Inside, it was dim and dusty, but peek holes every forty feet or so allowed enough light for us to make our way.

"Which way do we go?" I asked.

Out of his pockets, Mab pulled a bag of apple blossom petals and a device much like a sextant. He squatted, dropped the petals, and squinted, taking a reading with his device. Detecting the supernatural was Mab's specialty. With the right gear, he could detect the breath of a passing phoenix or the trace of a faerie's wing upon the air.

"Magical energies break down physical laws, so the more magic in the area, the more the natural path of the falling petals is disturbed. This device allows me to measure the degree of deflection and gauge the direction of the biggest supernatural disturbance. In this case, it's that-a-way," he grunted, pointing to the left. "Might be the vamps. Might be the spell. Might be anything. Sorry, I can't be more specific, but conditions are not optimal. If I had more light, I might be able to get a more accurate reading."

"It's the only lead we have," I said. "We might as well follow it."

As we continued, a vague sense of giddy excitement filled me. We were on a tremendous adventure, sneaking through secret passages to fight a terrible monster. How handsome Mab seemed in the dim peephole light. Why had I never noticed before?

"Feeling any effects from the sack?" asked Mab, as we crept along.

"None at all. Everything is fine!" I said primly. Giggling, I added, "You know, you didn't have to blab in front of everyone that I was a virgin."

Wisely, Mab kept quiet.

Footsteps sounded in the hall beside us. Through the nearest peephole, we could see a group of men in white and green make their way across the floor. They were carrying large, rectangular boxes. I recognized their insignia immediately: Friendly Poltergeist Removal. Balthasar had been on to something when he wondered where they were bringing the bogies.

We walked softly beside them until the secret passage forked. Following the inner fork, we moved around a wide chamber containing large mesh cages filled with bogies. On one side of the chamber, males and females bogies copulated in enormous cages containing hundreds of the beasties. Smaller cages stacked on the other side of the room contained female bogies in various stages of pregnancy.

"Their larvae factory," Mab whispered.

I nodded and continued to stare. The happenings in that room seemed fascinating to me. Mab had to drag me along by the arm.

"Mab," I whispered, as we continued. "I seem to be losing control of my reason. You are going to have to make all the important decisions."

"That's too bad, ma'am," Mab replied glumly.

"Why is that?" I asked cheerfully.

"You don't listen to me when you're rational," he said dourly. "I have little hope of your remembering to listen to me now. My prognostication? We're doomed."

"Nonsense," I said airily. "I feel certain we can do anything we set our mind to. We have only to find the vamp or vamps that are behind this, dust them, and depart."

"Riiight," murmured Mab.

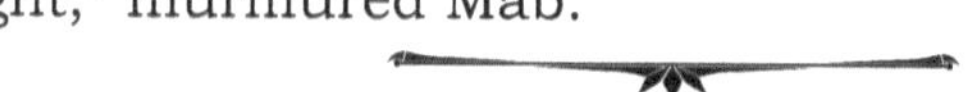

We came to a staircase, and Mab did his trick with the blossoms and the sextant again. This time, his results indicated that we should go up the stairs. So, we did. At the top of the short staircase was a door that opened up into a main hall again. Through the peephole, we could see a balcony overlooking a ballroom-sized chamber. The chamber walls were decorated with bas-relief of bat-winged succubi and dog-headed gods. A huge, flaming pentacle covered the floor below, surrounded by arcane circles and runes. Vast bat-winged shapes, chained at the neck, stood in each triangular arm of the star, tending the fires. At the five corners of the pentacle were five black pillars. Tied to each pillar was a naked young girl, hardly past puberty. A sixth girl was strapped to a huge, ornate table in the center of the star.

Mab averted his face and swore.

"A beastly thing to do to kids," he spat.

"The spell must require virgins. The only way to be sure is to get them young," I said. "This is it, though. This is the spell that is obscuring divination."

"What do we do now?" asked Mab. "I recognize this set up, but this kind of spell is difficult to undo. Each step must be undone in the precise order that it was originally cast or a disaster of untold proportions could ensue. Under ideal circumstances, I am pretty confident you and I could manage it, but it would take four or five hours, and we would have to see to it that we weren't interrupted."

"Or you could undo it the short way," I offered.

"What's the short way?" Mab asked.

"You won't like it," I grinned. The thought was vaguely pleasing. If this is what bogey larva can do to people like me, no wonder the sale of Pixie tripled in the last week.

"Spit it out, already," Mab growled. "It can't be that bad."

I blithely pointed out the obvious. "This spell requires virgins. If you were to go down and deflower one of the girls, the spell would be broken. Sort of the darker version of 'Love's first kiss'."

Mab just stared at me. "Ma'am, I sincerely hope you avoid bogey larvae from this day forth!"

He was still glaring at me when I smelled it. Clear and sweet came the scent, like an old friend, calling to me.

"Mulberry morath!" I cried with delight. Flinging open the door, I stepped boldly out of the alcove and onto the balcony.

"Ma'am! No! Wait," Mab's voice was saying somewhere behind me, followed by a muttered, "Knew she wouldn't listen to me." Poor Mab, he sounded so unhappy. I wondered vaguely what could be bothering him.

I tripped happily along the plush scarlet carpet of the hallway, oblivious of any danger. The scent of morath wafted from an open doorway just beyond the secret passage. Within was a cozy library lit by an oil lantern. A man dressed in a lace shirt and dark brown britches sat in a large, ruby-colored easy chair swirling a glass of familiar liquid. A buff long coat, of the sort gentlemen wore back when Napoleon was a threat, hung from an oak coat hanger.

He looked up, a handsome man despite his pallid face and his long pointy incisors, handsome and hauntingly familiar.

"Josiah Barrington!" I cried, astonished.

"God's teeth!" he laughed. "Miranda Prospero!"

We stood gazing at each other for a time. Sitting there, with his boots propped up on an ottoman, I thought Josiah had grown even more handsome that the rather fine figure he cut in my memory. This could be an effect of the larvae, I realized, but somehow, I did not think so. He had always been an attractive man, immorality as a blood-sucking leech had been good to him.

"But...but," I sputtered, regarding his long, slender fangs, shining like fresh ivory and as pointy as the incisors of a wolf, "You hated vampires!"

"Certainly, when I was young and hail," replied Josiah, whose authentic Scottish accent was a pleasure to hear. "Then, I grew old and weak, while you and Theo and all your family remained as youthful and strong as you had ever been. And I began to wonder why I had to die, if you and Theo could live."

"But...Vampires?"

"What other option had I?" asked Josiah. "Theo would not share your wondrous Water of Life with me. There was no other option for me, except death."

"You never did stake that vampiress, did you?" I asked. "The one who begged so piteously?"

"No," Josiah admitted, smiling sadly as he reminisced. "My heart softened, and I let her go. I made up the story that I had slain her to protect her from Theo's wrath, for he knew one had escaped him. Years later, when I was old, I crept back to this castle and begged her to return the favor I did when I spared her by adopting me, so to speak, which she did."

"This is...amazing," I said, dazed.

"Perhaps," he smiled at me, his blue eyes sparkling like sapphires. "Or maybe it is fate! How have you been, Miranda? Still young, I see, and still a maiden? What a cold, lonely existence you must lead. Perhaps this was meant, so that we might have this second chance together." He leaned forward and, taking a second glass from a rack, poured me a glass of his sweet, fragrant morath.

I cannot say how this would have sounded if I had not been hopped-up on bogey larvae, but at the moment, it sounded terribly inviting. Had I not been wishing for a companion? Someone with whom to reminisce about the old days? Someone with whom to sip mulberry morath?

I took the glass and sipped its contents. "Ah!" I said softly. "Now this is the real thing!"

Our eyes met and locked, my emeralds falling into his deep sapphire pools.

"I am so pleased to see you," his voice was as soft as a whisper. "You are even more beautiful than I remember."

"All right, break it up," said Mab, stomping into the room.

"And who is this?" asked Josiah.

"This is Mab," I said, "My company gumshoe. Mab, Josiah Barrington, of the Demonslaying Twins."

"Apparently, not anymore," Mab observed wryly, noting Josiah's fangs. To Josiah, he said, "Quite a spell, you got out there. A real piece of work."

"Thank you, I'm rather pleased with it, myself," Josiah smiled. "Keeps our current business quiet. Not quite strong enough, I gather, as the two of you made it through. Pray, tell me how you found us?"

"Pure, old-fashion gumshoeing," Mab said gruffly. "No magic."

"Really," Josiah arched a perfect brow. "How quaint!"

"So...what is this all about? Why the bogey larvae? Trying to ruin the good name of the Pixie Corporation?" asked Mab.

"Bogey larvae are a delicacy to the living, but human blood infused with the larvae's influence is a far greater delicacy to vampires. It is far tastier than any wine, even morath," he smiled at me. Time stopped as we gazed at each other. "It is ambrosia."

Mab growled, "Are you telling me, our man Gooseberry and the others, died to become a vampire cocktail?"

Josiah leaned back and put his fingers together, forming a steeple. "I suppose you could put it that way, though that makes something sublime sound rather crass. It is a pity the process wakes the bogey. I have no particular desire to see the human host die. Given my druthers, I would rather keep the cocktail, as you so bluntly call it, alive and be able to go back for seconds—for you know how humans are about intoxicants, once they have sampled the bogey larvae, they would most certainly go back for more.

"Some vampires," Josiah continued, "on the other hand, do not feel as I do. They feel that it is the very fleetingness of the delicacy which makes it so...precious. A lost thing that will never come again, like the past," he smiled into my eyes, his blue eyes wise and sad. "Like proper morath, or the smell of saddle wax, or wide, unspoiled vistas, and all the fleeting things we used to love that have passed away and will not be seen again."

For no particular reason, I began to giggle. "You'll have to excuse me," I said, "Your guards force fed me a bottle of Pixie."

A hunger came over Josiah's handsome face as he contemplated the taste of an immortal virgin on Pixie. He looked at me with such longing, I could hardly bear it. I wished I could do something to sooth him.

"Join me," he whispered. "Let us entwine our lives together. Let our future be one future. We can live together as companions, or, should we desire more, and you wish to leave the service of your Goddess and cleave to me, I could offer you an immortality of another kind."

Mab snorted in disgust and turned to me. "So what now, ma'am, do we stake him, or what?"

I hesitated, torn. Staking an old friend, even one who had become a monster, seemed a horrible thing to do; especially, such a handsome old friend and one who had done so much for our cause in his youth. Surely, it would not be so bad to let one vampire live?

I imagined my life if Josiah were to become part of it. How pleasant it would be to sit and chat with him. To speak of days gone by, of pleasures we both knew, to sip a wine only we remembered and talk of glories lost and of wonders yet to come.

On the other hand, even dazed as I was, I could never forget that, when push came to shove, I was with the good guys, and he was not...but was that really reason enough to stake him?

"No, I said softly. "I have a better idea." I stepped toward Josiah, who looked good enough to eat. My lashes lowering of their own accord...so this was how that look was supposed to be done. "Drink of me," I whispered. "Sup of the nectar so sweet it has no compare—not even among the sweetest of wines."

"No, ma'am! You're mad!" cried Mab, leaping forward. Josiah knocked him aside with an impatient arm, hardly even trying. Mab went flying out of the room and smashed into the banister. A quick glance in his direction assured me that he was all right, then I had eyes only for Josiah.

He came toward me, and I swayed toward him. His strong hands caught my shoulders, and he lowered his polished fangs toward my neck. The sting of their needle-like bite was with me for only a moment. Then, I could hear his sigh of contentment as he began to swallow.

"Sucker!" I laughed aloud.

Josiah lifted his head. From the horrified expression on his face, it was obvious that he had just remembered the story Balthesar so enjoyed hearing. Then, his sweet, handsome face contorted in horrendous pain. He writhed, crying out once, and crumbled away, a pile of dust upon the handsome Arabic carpet.

Mab looked so relieved when he arrived back at my side, I thought he would kiss me, "Thank god, ma'am! For a moment there I thought you were going soft."

"Never," I said, dismissing the very idea impatiently. "I live beyond my normal span of years because I have been granted extra life from above; not by robbing it from the helpless. And while I admit I might wish for a new diversion from time to time, I won't' stoop to murder to get it."

"So, why didn't we just stake him? Rather than risk your life with the vampire spittle and all?"

"I feared we could not take him," I said dismissively. "He was too strong for you, and I am in no condition for a fight."

Mab looked at me carefully. Finally, he nodded, "Riiiight, ma'am."

"Hmm?" I asked, arching a brow impatiently.

"Sure you thought we couldn't take 'em," Mab scoffed. "You just didn't want to stake an old friend. Rather let him go out with a bang, so to speak. Not that I blame you...entirely."

As I turned away to hide my smile, my head swam. Mab's words about spittle and bogies suddenly permeated the mist of my thoughts.

"Mab, guard me. I must pray, and hope that the Lady of Spiral Wisdom, the purifier of all poisons, will cleanse me before Josiah's spit hatches the larvae in my belly. While I might survive having my stomach eaten out from within...I'm really in no mood to find out."

I knelt and prayed until Her warmth came to me, moving through my limbs and clearing my head of all giddiness. As soon as I felt pure and whole, I pulled out my cell phone and called for backup.

Within an hour, Father, a few of my more annoying brothers, and some company bully boys had arrived. We cleaned the rest of the vamps out of the castle, slayed the bogies, bottled the guard djin, petrified the gargoyles, and banished the demons that were maintaining the obscuration spell, which allowed us to free the young girls. By the following morning, the castle was so free of supernatural stench that even Mab could not find anything about which to complain.

The young girls were all returned to their parents. Pixie Cola Corporation finally admitted their part and issued free crosses and garlic to all their customers. They were being sued, of course, but they had managed to convince a large part of the public that this whole incident was a smear campaign by Coke; probably the same part of the public who were still giddy from drinking Pixie Cola.

As for me, I had lost a friend who, under other circumstances, could have become the fit companion I so desired, but I was not left entirely bereft. I took home Josiah's entire supply of mulberry morath—to remember him by.

He would have wanted me to have it.

The Poppet

MY POPPET LAY UPON THE GROUND TRAMPLED BENEATH THE HORSE'S hooves and scarred by the wheels of the carriage. I was too old to cry with all my cousins looking on. I turned away as if it did not hurt. My Uncle Albert saw through me. There was pity in his eyes.

Devastated, I returned home and sat in the winter parlour. My poppet was gone, her fragile head caved in. I did not remember how I had felt when my mother died. However, I was sure that at the age of four, I could not have suffered as I suffered now. Surely, no one could suffer such pain and survive.

It was thus, staring into the flame, that my Uncle Albert found me. He held his hands behind his back, and he was smiling.

"Come, Kitty, m'love," he said. "I've brought you a present. Here's a brand new poppet!"

I wanted no new poppet, but Uncle Albert was so kind that I could not bear to disappoint him. Uncle Albert was a guard at London Tower. Father said that he led a dismal life. So, I looked up and attempted to smile.

"Thank you, Uncle Albert," I said meekly.

Uncle Albert came close to me, adjusting his breeches, so that he could crouch beside me.

"Can you keep a secret?" he asked conspiratorially. I nodded, solemn in my sorrow.

He brought a small blue figure from behind his back, about a third bigger than his hand.

"This is no ordinary poppet," he whispered, his eyes gleaming merrily in the firelight. "But the favorite poppet of the wrongly accused Queen Anne Bolyn, dead these seven days by the condemnation of her royal husband, our good King Henry VIII. I found it in her prison chamber. She was a kind and gentle woman. Not a word of what she's been accused of is true."

I leaned forward, amazed despite my sorrow. Hesitantly, I touched it's tattered dress, worse for its stay in the Tower. It was a sweet-faced doll, and delicately made.

"The Queen's very poppet?" I asked.

"Her very poppet," my uncle answered. "Now, as you have lost a poppet, and this poppet, she has lost a girl; perhaps the two of you can comfort each other."

He placed the poppet gently in my lap, then winked at me and strode from the parlour.

Queen Anne Bolyn's poppet was light in my hands. Her dark locks were soft as real hair. A scent of candle tallow issued from her, along with another familiar smell, sweet yet salty.

Her smock was of bits of blue cloth. Around her waist was knotted a pretty velvet ribbon, of black and midnight blue. She was quite different from my lost poppet, who had been a robust and cheery doll, but I took pity on her. I brought her upstairs and set her on the trunk by my side of the bed.

That night, I had many dreams, all murky and troubled. In the morning, there was only one that I remembered. I dreamed an archer came to my door and aimed his arrow at my heart. The arrows feathers were blue and jet. Afeared, I held up Queen Anne's poppet and cried that its face was not my own. The archer went away, but his laughter remained, hoarse like the cry of wolves or ravens. When I awoke, my stepmother's baby was yowling.

By the morning of the royal wedding of King Henry and Lady Jane Seymour, three weeks later, Anne's poppet and I had become good friends. I brought her along to her usurper's wedding, tucked in a carry purse. She was too delicate, and too scruffy, to travel beneath my arm.

The crowd was ecstatic and the streets were packed. All around, people praised the Lady Jane and denounced Anne Bolyn; "adulteress" and "witch". I petted Anne's poppet and whispered that we knew the truth, she and I. We were an island of sensibility amidst the raucous throes of ignorance. In the crowd were one or two other solemn figures. I wondered if their secret was the same as ours.

The royal couple rode from the cathedral in a gilded and bejeweled carriage. King Henry stood, hands upon his hips, his wide grin visible for all to see. Often, he stooped and kissed his new bride. I strained to see her, this seductress who stole Anne's husband and her life. Jane had been Anne's maid-of-honor, before she betrayed her. I imagined her as dark and sly. To my delight, Henry finally moved away, and I caught a glimpse of Jane's face. What I saw gave me two shocks.

The first was that Queen Jane Seymour looked to be a shy, sweet-faced young girl. The second was that her face was the face of Anne's poppet.

That night my dreams were wrought with horrors. Twice, I woke screaming. The first dream had been of the black-cloaked archer. I dreamed that he ripped Queen Jane's wedding bodice. His hand came away soaked in blood.

In the second, Anne Bolyn herself came to stand by my bed. Only, in my bed, her daughter, the tiny Princess Elizabeth lay. When Anne tried to reach for her, a wind blew Anne away. Without Anne, Elizabeth broke apart, as my poppet had beneath the wheels of the carriage.

I was out of breath when I reached London Tower. My rapid flight must have disturbed the resident ravens. They wheeled and cawed above.

"What troubles you, Kitty, m'love?" my uncle asked when I found him.

"It's very important, Uncle Albert!" I cried. Then I whispered. "It's about the poppet."

Solemnly, Uncle Albert led me to a quiet corner in the gate house. He sat me on a wooden trunk, then squatted down before me.

"Uncle Albert," I began. "Do you think it's true that Anne Bolyn was a witch?"

Uncle Albert was taken back.

"I think not," he said. "If she were a witch, why would she have let her husband kill her?"

"Uncle Albert," I asked softly, "Is it true that you can kill a person by making a poppet of them and hurting the poppet?"

Uncle Albert's eyes widened. His face lost some of its ruddy color. "You'd better tell me all about it, Kitty-love," he said slowly.

With shaking hands, I drew the poppet from my bag.

"Today," I said, "I finished a new bodice and skirt for the poppet. When I cut away the poppet's old dress—it was starting to smell bad—I found this."

Carefully, I lay the poppet on the trunk beside me, and pulled away her tattered smock. The little poppet was made all of candle tallow. She had a full bosom, a navel, and other womanly parts. The wax of her chest had a rosy hue, as if there was actually a heart beneath her little bosom.

"By God's head!" my uncle swore.

"Look! At her chest!" I whispered, my voice catching in my throat.

Over the rosy spot on the chest was scratched the words *Sagitta fari hic.* Uncle Albert looked at it, frowning.

It came to me that Uncle Albert could not read Latin. Sorrow and pity welled up in me. I wondered if Uncle Albert could read at all. I said, "It said, 'Arrow strike here.' And I keep dreaming of an archer whose arrows are the same color as this velvet tie." I held up the poppet's black and midnight blue ribbon. "What does it mean, Uncle Albert?"

It had never occurred to me that adults could be scared. My uncle's face was very white. He swallowed three times before he spoke.

"I think we have a problem, Kitty," he said. He didn't even call me "m'love". "If we harm the poppet, it may hurt Queen Jane, who is a decent girl. However, often the ghosts of those who are wrongly accused are trapped here in the world, forced to wander in torment until Judgment Day, unless they are avenged. From your dreams, I gather Anne Bolyn is such a one. Not a happy fate for any soul, much less an innocent one. No, I think our only course is to bring the poppet to a priest and have Anne's unhappy ghost laid to rest."

I spoke in a very small voice, "Uncle Albert, isn't that a Papist ritual? I don't think that the king's new religion allows exorcism."

Uncle Albert was silent for much longer than I wanted to wait. The wind howled outside the window boards. I heard the ravens. I kicked my feet against the trunk. Finally, he spoke again.

"Wisely or foolishly, we have taken the poppet into our keeping. Perhaps it is God's will that we judge its fate."

"Us?" I squeaked. "Oh no! Uncle, not us! Why if we choose wrongly, our very souls would be eternally damned. Can't we get someone else? A priest? Another little girl? Let her solve the problem."

"The poppet has come to us," he said, and he lay his large and weather-beaten hand on top of mine. "It is our responsibility. If we passed it on and the new owner chooses wrongly, the sin would still be on our heads, for we could have prevented it. Better to go to Hell for our own lack of judgment, than for someone else's."

"But, the Bible says, 'Judge not lest ye be judged,'" I said.

"Solomon was a judge," my uncle said, "and the Bible called him wise."

From then on, as I walked, kicking stones, or sat, poking at my needlework, I thought about life, and justice, and Solomon, and death. 'Judge not,' Jesus said. Yet, Solomon was wise. I puzzled at it, reading ancient Latin texts and studying the Bible with my father's chaplain.

In my most private moments, Anne Bolyn pursued me. She dwelt in my thoughts by day and hounded my dreams by night. I saw her standing above Princess Elizabeth, staring longingly, or kneeling in prayer in her prison chamber, weeping. In my minds image, she wore a simple black mourning gown, like I had seen my Aunt Mary wear to her husband's funeral, and a velvet choker of the blue-black ribbon her poppet wore. Her face was always solemn and sad.

At first, Anne's poppet sat in a place of honor upon my birchwood trunk. Several times, I determined never to harm her. Yet, so touching were the pleading looks Anne gave me from my dreams, that once or twice I awoke and lifted my comb to rent the doll, before I realized what I was about.

So, I locked the poppet in the trunk and hid the key downstairs, beneath the loose flagstone in the winter parlour. Once or twice, I thought of choosing once and for all, but the fear of eternal damnation, should I choose wrongly, paralyzed and tormented me.

However, on the day that King Henry issued the royal proclamation announcing that Queen Jane now carried the crown's heir, the nature of Anne's visits changed. That night, I dreamed she came before me and stared with stern and accusing eyes. With one hand she removed the blue-black choker, revealing an angry red line across her neck. Her head then tumbled sideways, falling from her body. Only it was my head. On the ground lay the shattered Princess Elizabeth. There was a hoof print in her chest and the bloody indentation of a carriage wheel formed a crown across her brow.

With each announcement of the health of Queen Jane and the child to be, these nightly visitations grew more horrible Now, I was doubly glad that I had locked away the poppet. In the dim-lit early hours, when I awoke to haunting images of disembodied heads and ghostly memories of worms devouring my innards, it was hard to remember I had wanted to make a wise decision. Once, I actually padded to the door of the winter parlour and stood with my bare feet on the cold stone, staring at the spot on the floor which covered the key. However, I turned away and went back to bed.

For it occurred to me that there was no assurance that damning my eternal soul would take the nightmare away. What if Queen Jane were to haunt me?

Then, one night I awoke to see a lone figure hovering at the foot of my cot, lit by a glow like early morning. Only, it was still dark without. The figure wore a dark gown, through which the tapestries on the far wall could be seen. The rustling of the leaves outside seemed to take on a rhythm, like a voice whispering words.

"Kitty," it seemed to whisper. "Why do you hold me here?"

"I fear for my eternal soul." I said aloud, then felt ashamed. How foolish I was, speaking into the empty night. Again I heard words, as if whispers in the wind.

"Do you believe that you will escape the burden of my suffering, drawn on these many months by the hardness of your heart?"

"Surely," I said aloud. "God could not burden my soul both with Anne's suffering and with Jane's fate. That would not be just." I sat up and hugged my knees in the dark. The figure remained, and the unearthly glow.

"Just?" Came the whispered reply. "Do you still believe God is just? Ahh, the innocence of childhood. Not so long ago, I was a new bride, with beloved child and doting husband. Now I am dead. My husband sleeps with my chambermaid, while my headless body rots. My little daughter is no longer allowed the title Princess. They call her 'bastard' and 'Little Whore.' Is that just?"

"Perhaps Anne...you...brought this fate upon yourself," I said, eager for some other soul to take the blame.

"What if I did?" Came the whispered rustle of a reply.

"My little Elizabeth surely did not. She is but a babe."

"How does this touch on Elizabeth?" I asked.

"Ah, little one, you know so little of the world. Once Elizabeth was the hope of the realm. What future will she have once Jane's babe is born? She will be a discarded heir, fated to become the pawn of every petty noble whose wine-inspired whims tempts him to lust for the throne?"

"So you want Jane to die before her child is born?" I whispered, suddenly understanding.

The figure's head nodded once.

"What of Jane's child?" I asked. "Jane's unborn babe is as innocent as your Elizabeth."

"It is you who believe that God is fair, my child, not I," the whisper replied. "Each moment I remain here burns my soul as hotly as might the fires of Damnation. Yet, I am constrained to stay until Jane's death." The whisper grew silent, then came again. "Even until the last, I did not believe Henry would kill me. He loved me once. He told me so—so many times."

I lay quietly in the dark and closed my eyes. Sympathy for Anne welled up in me, and yet I kept seeing before me my stepmother's babe with its chubby hands and wide blue eyes. I imagined Jane's child would be like that, a tiny bundle with the poppet's sweet face.

"What would Solomon do?" I wondered. "He would wait until Queen Jane's babe was born and then stab the poppet. That way both women would be dead, and for the same crime. You stole Henry from his first wife, and Jane stole him from you. Yet both women would leave behind a child."

"So be it," said the rustling voice. I opened my eyes to protest, but I found myself alone.

I grew ill, so great was my fear. The words 'So be it' echoed in my delirious mind. I feared both Anne and Jane. My uncle came to sooth me, but his visit brought no resolution. I could not bear it. Even Heaven was not worth this pain.

"I'll do it!" I cried aloud, "Let me be damned by choice, at least, rather than by omission."

The day that the birth of Queen Jane's son, Prince Edward, was announced to the realm, I took the key from beneath the flagstones and unlocked the trunk. Anne's little poppet lay atop my hope chest quilt. I lifted her out and stripped her of the pretty garments I had fashioned her. There she lay, naked in the candlelight. I held her closer to the flame and read again the words upon her chest. *Sagitta Fari Hic* "Arrow Strike Here." Carefully, I took up my embroidery needle and thrust it through the rosy spot upon her bosom.

I expected some resistance. Instead, the chest cavity caved in and thick red blood gushed out, covering my fingers. I screamed, staring transfixed at my bloody hands. The room grew misty, then dark. There was a feeling of motion.

Rising from darkness, I beheld winged men rushing by, aback demon horses. Midnight wolves howled and yapped at the feet of the steeds. They followed the black archer with the blue-black arrows, whose trumpet blares were like the howls of the wind. The smooth wall against my cheek...wall? Floor!

I was on the floor. Blood was on my hands. Blood splattered all about. My shoulder hurt. My head felt light. When I could see clearly, I stumbled to the chamber pot, bent over it, and vomited. Then I went out to the well and drew water to wash my hands.

To my surprise, all the blood washed away.

When I heard the news, I ran all the way to London Tower. My uncle was in an empty chamber, bent over a broken wooden cot.

"Uncle Albert!" I cried. "Am I going to Hell?"

"So, she is dead then," he said. Then for a long time, he was silent.

I waited, wondering if those as unclean as I should treat with other men. Might my sins stain them as leprosy stains those who touch a leper? I felt infinitely apart from him, as if I could never again be what I had been.

Then, my uncle took me in his arms and held me. And I was again just a little girl.

"Ah there, Kitty m'love, ah there," he said.

I told him what I had done. He listened. His thin legs and gnarled hands trembled, though he tried to hide it from me. Yet, I saw relief in his eyes, relief that it was finally over. He stepped away and looked at me with new respect, as if I were a noble woman instead of just his niece. I repeated my question.

"Do you think I will go to Hell?" I said.

"I don't rightly know about such mysteries," he answered after a time. "None of us can know the Will of God. But if I were you, I would figure that you were not going to Hell, rather than otherwise."

"Why is that?" I asked, surprised.

"Think of it this way, Kitty Love," he said. "If you believe that you are damned, you will be likely to take other bad actions in your life. Hope of Heaven will no longer urge you to do good. Then, your later deeds will lead you to Hell, whether you are damned now or no. However, if you believe there is a chance and always do your best, you may still win your way to Heaven."

This made some sense to me, but I was not satisfied.

"This act alone, however?" I asked. "Do you think it is enough to send a soul to hell? If I died today, for instance?"

"I am not a priest or even a cunning man, Kitty m'love," my uncle said. "Such mysteries have not been revealed to me."

"But could God still love me, a murderess and a witch?" I cried.

"Ah now, Kitty m'love," he smiled sadly. "I'll not say what you want to hear. I won't tell you that you did wrong and watch the Devil strangle you on your own guilt and self-pity. You did the best a girl could do. The best a girl could do. Maybe a saint could do better, but the King's new religion does not allow for saints. So we must be satisfied with the mere best of men and girls."

"I tried to be fair," I wept, burying my head in his wool vest.

"Even Solomon could not have done better," Uncle Albert said. "Do you think God is less fair than Solomon?"

A Few More Bugs To Work Out

Harley leapt.

Behind her, the aeromobile exploded. An enormous blast of billowing smoke and flame bloomed out from the destroyed craft. The force of the explosion propelled her downward. As she fell, a faint, bat-like outline passed before the sun and faded again into the blue sky.

A stealth camohawk! What the hell? Supposedly, no working camohawk prototypes existed! But, then, officially, no working model of the Uplift aeromobile existed either. Of course, now—thanks to the boys in the camohawk—no such model did exist. All that was left was that fiery ball behind her.

Looking up over her shoulder as she fell, Harley yelled at the vanished plane. "Hey, you, that was stolen government property you just shot down!"

Now, what the hell was she supposed to do? The ground below appeared far away, but already it was growing nearer. The chute Sergeant O'Ryan had packed for her was florescent green, yellow, and pink. If she pulled it now, she would stand out like a painted bull's eye. The boys in the camohawk had just shot down the expensive Uplift VTHL aeromobile, with its prototype metal hydrogen drive, without even attempting to hail her first! Chances were they would not think twice about taking out the pilot.

Checking the altimeter built into the helmet of the Supersuit, Harley considered her options. The altimeter read approximately 11,500 ft. After ten seconds, she would be falling at approximately 120 feet per second. That gave her about 87 seconds of useful time before she absolutely had to pull her chute. She glanced back up at the seemingly empty sky. There was no sign of the enemy.

The air rushed by at an alarming speed. The slightest motion of an arm or leg caused Harley to spin wildly. She had been taught the basics of sky diving when she joined Force 13. However, her last jump had been almost three years ago. Damn good thing she did not have to rely on memory. She had the expertise of masters at her fingertips. She was the girl in the Supersuit.

First thing's first. If the camohawk spotted her, she was a goner. She had to hide. The Supersuit, or the Man-Trainer 9000, as it was officially called, was coated with Sun-Cloth, Sun Systems' new monitor cloth. It could be dialed to any of 256 colors. One touch of the mouse ball beneath her right index finger dropped the menu down on the inside of the helmet directly before her eyes. The layout was designed to make the Supersuit as easy to use as those robot suits so common in the movies.

So much for designs. In reality, the suit was hot and bulky, and the software had more bugs that a peonies garden. The LED menu was too faint for Harley to see. She twisted frantically in the air and finally brought her head around to face directly into the brilliant noonday sun. A millisecond later, the photosensitive plate darkened, and Harley was finally able to read the menu choices. She tongued the diode that started the log and announced.

"Log entry 452. Wearer should have manual control over lightening and darkening of face plate."

59 seconds remaining.

The control panel offered sixteen shades of blue and a setting called 'sky camo.' Harley stared at them, stumped. She had never studied air-to-air camouflage—did one try to match the ground or the sky? Unwilling to give this matter any more time, she chose the palest shade of blue. The color spread swiftly across the suit.

51 seconds.

Now, to get down alive. Harley wiggled her index finger and rapidly examined the menu under 'Activities.' 'Climbing', 'Driving'.... She scrolled faster, 'Marksmanship?'

Harley snorted. Now, that was a waste of hard drive space! She could shoot better than the hotshot green beret they had picked to model that program. —'Long-distance running'... 'Skiing'. There it was: 'Sky diving'!

The right middle finger glove contained the 'enter' button. Harley pressed it. Little images of sky divers played across the helmet-screen, offering her choices. 'Relative' and 'Accuracy' read the labels beneath the icons. Accuracy jumping required a target, and Harley did not have the time to program the GPS. She chose 'Relative' and was offered the options of 'full-stable position', 'frog position', and 'speed dive'. Finally, her own sky-diving training came in use as she recalled that full-stable was the slowest of the three. As she needed all the time she could get, Harley selected the splayed-limb icon for 'full-stable' and relaxed, letting the suit do its stuff.

Of its own accord, the suit assumed the correct positions. Within the limbs, the aluminum framework flexed. Minuscule Teflon plates rotated, making previously supple limbs rigid. Her helmet tilted; her arms and legs spread; her back arched. Within moments, she was stable and falling steadily.

Routine mission, indeed, Harley snorted. She would have a few words to say to Commander Ramsey when she got back to HQ—if she got back. That handsome devil had assured her that the security on the Uplift was so light, a civilian could have walked off with the aeromobile. Up until three minutes ago, she would have agreed with him. Her current situation, on the other hand, was so inane, it was suspicious.

Glancing up at the seemingly empty expanse of blue, Harley wondered what the chances were that the camohawk was also stolen—and perhaps not by someone so friendly. Either way, the camohawk pilot was certainly not Force 13. No member of the Special Ops elite security surveillance team would destroy government property without at least attempting to recapture it first.

The altimeter read 7,163 ft. 43 seconds to chute time.

Experienced sky divers usually pulled their chute by 2000 feet. Under the circumstance, Harley decided to risk waiting until 1000 feet. When she fell below 1000 ft., however, she was going to have to pull the chute, camohawk or no camohawk.

The day-glo parachute would stand out like a wake-up call. Harley examined the terrain below her. There was a large body of water just left of her current position. If she could position herself above it, she could lose the day-glo chute some hundred or so feet above the lake and let the suit dive for her. The world record for high diving—set by the guy who had modeled the Supersuit's expert system diving program—was 177 feet, 2 inches. There was a far cry between 1000 ft. and 177, but anything that would shorten the time she spent imitating a sitting duck was fine by her.

Harley wiggled her index finger paging through the 'Activity' menu.

'Diving' was not listed

36 seconds remaining.

There had to be a diving program! She had spoken to the guy who did the diving about the troubles he had beating the 1987 record. Apparently, it was so new, it was not listed on the main menu. Could she locate it on the hard drive and install it in time? Why hadn't she insisted that they upgrad the system to the apps model?

There was still one place that she could turn.

The military liked to think of this suit as their baby. However, the Supersuit had originally been designed by Industrial Light and Magic—as a way to cut down on injuries to stunt men. The military version had so many quirks, they had been forced to hire the original ILM technician as a consultant. Harley stuck out her tongue, pushed the diode that activated the direct cellular virtual link, and prayed that Johnny was online.

"Johnny, I hope you're there! I need to make this thing do a swan dive to end all swan dives, and I need it now," Harley said, when, after what seemed like an eternity she heard the click of the line being picked up.

"Harley! Slow down. The Supersuit is not water proof. You can't take it in the water," replied a shocked Johnny.

"Damn! Look, I'm going to have to chance it. It's the suit or me. And if I go, the suit might not make it either," Harley said.

"If you get it wet, it's liable to short out and electrocute you," Johnny warned.

"I'll have to take the chance. Can you get me a diving program?"

"I'm looking…There's a diving program there, in the Test directory, but it's not installed."

8 seconds.

"Can you install it virtually from where you are?" she added the time remaining to the time she would be likely to be hanging in the chute. "You've got two or three minutes tops."

"I can try," he said dubiously.

"Do what you can," said Harley. If Johnny could not help her, she might have to try the dive herself. Damn shame that she had never paid attention in swimming class back in elementary school.

Funny that Force training hadn't included swimming. They must've assumed that everyone could swim.

The altimeter read 796'. She had to pull the chute.

The plume of bright cloth shot up from behind her shoulders, flying upward and billowing. As it spread, catching the air, Harley jerked violently backwards. Her downward plunge slowed to a gentle floating descent.

She should have been hanging happily in the harness. Instead, her body was flailing wildly, arms and legs jerking outward. Harley examined the situation quickly, trying to determine what was causing the flailing.

The Supersuit was still on 'sky diving'. It was trying to return her body to the 'full-stable' position. Head upside down, Harley slammed her pinkie finger against the interrupt button. The suit went limp. Gravity righted her, and she found herself hanging comfortably from her harness.

The next step was to get herself over the lake. Luckily, she was hanging from the kind of ram-air chute a baby could have steered. She adjusted the brake lines and angled the chute until her descent began taking her toward the large purple lake. Then, she drew her gun and began scanning the skies above.

What little of the sky she could see beyond edge of the brightly-colored nylon canopy. Using her tongue, she hit the diode that switched the helmet display to infrared. Still, there was no sign of her pursuers. Could it be that she was home free?

Her heart hammering with relief, she rested her helmet against the nearest lead. What a relief! She had not wanted to die. For one thing, she loved her job. The unofficial motto of the Force 13 security surveillance team was: *Anything James Bond can do, we can do better!* Harley and her teammates lived up to their motto practically every day.

In the past six years, she had pulled off thefts of which real criminals only dreamed. She had blithely driven off with a truck packed with old dollars that were supposed to be on their way to the incinerator. She had fitted a delivery truck with a fake floor, so that one of her team members could steal the contents out of a box that was under constant observation. She had participated in a jailbreak, rescuing an American officer from an Iraqi prison.

Just last week, she had returned from her most spectacular mission of all. She and her immediate superior, the dashing Commander Peter Ramsey, had sauntered into Wright-Patterson Air Force Base and waltzed out with an A-bomb. General Lanier, the base's commanding officer, had been so disturbed by their success, he actually decided not to debrief them. Apparently, he had been frightened that if a record of their heist existed, news might one day leak out and jeopardize his career. Harley and Ramsey had laughed long and hard over that one.

Well, Ramsey would probably laugh even harder over this one. One of his best operatives shot down while testing the security on a secret air force prototype—by another secret air force prototype.

Scanning the sky once more to confirm that no one was firing at her, she tongued the diode that activated the special scrambled frequency that connected her with HQ. To her surprise, the line was already active.

Voices burst forth from the speakers to either side of her head.

"Commander, this is Captain Renfro. The pilot was not killed in the explosion after all. He just pulled his chute."

It was the camohawk! They had broken radio silence to report back, but to whom? And why were they on her channel?

"Shoot him down, Captain. That prototype contained an enormous amount of classified material. We don't know how much the pilot might have been able to photograph or memorize."

"Yes, sir. Will do. You won't be hearing from us again, sir. We'll be raising our jamming system again. We've just received orders to maintain radio silence."

"Very good, Captain. Carry on."

Harley hung limp in her harness, hardly able to breathe. That second voice, the one the camohawk captain called Commander. She recognized it. It was Commander Ramsey's voice. But, he knew she was the pilot in the aeromobile, he had checked with her only minutes before the camohawk attacked. Why would Peter want her gunned down?

Ice ran through her veins as she realized there could only be one answer. She knew about the stolen A-bomb.

How naive she had been! She should have known there was something fishy about a general who was too afraid of publicity to take the basic security steps. Was General Lanier in on it too, or had Ramsey actually never told him about the theft?

Her thoughts were interrupted by Johnny's cheerful voice coming over her radio.

"Harley, I've installed it. But, I can't guarantee how well it will work, it's never been tested."

"Thanks, Johnny, you're a life saver—literally," replied Harley, wondering what the hell was she going to do when she hit the bottom?

"Listen, Johnny, could you do me one more favor? It's urgent. Contact General Lanier at Wright-Patterson Air Force Base. Ask him if he knows that Special Ops Force 13 has one of his A-bombs."

"Huh? ...Are you kidding? Wait, that's code right? Sure thing, Harley, whatever you say," said Johnny, "Signing off."

If the general was in on it, then she had just written Johnny's death sentence, too. However, if she lived to reach the ground, she was going to need someone who out-ranked Ramsey to protect her. Only the general would be in a position to confirm her claim.

The shock of Ramsey's betrayal had not fully struck her yet. The yawning pit somewhere deep inside her had only begun to open. It hurt like hell to find out that the man she trusted most had hung her out to dry. However, she dare not give it any more thought until she was safe—if she was ever safe again.

Suddenly, she could see the camohawk. The bomber was almost directly above her, and it was firing. She could see the heat patterns of the missile as it launched. In the spray of infrared, she got a good look at the outline of the craft.

It was all she needed.

Harley targeted and fired.

The kickback swung her backward, but the drag of the chute kept her from going off course. As soon as she was upright again, Haley switched to defensive maneuvers. The proposal for the stealth camohawk had said that the craft would be carrying heat-seeking missiles. The average heat-seeking missiles were built to seek for the kind of heat produced by jet exhaust, not the minor warmth of a human body. Not willing to leave anything to chance that she could control, Harley rapidly dialed the Supersuit's external thermostat to match the ambient air temperature.

The missile passed her at a distance of three feet. She could have reach out and touched it.

Harley's shot fared better. Even without the infrared scope, she could see that she had damaged the bomber's skin. True to the specs, the craft maintained its camouflaged state because it was entirely coated with Sun-Cloth, the same stuff that coated Harley's suit. As Harley watched a familiar oily discoloration of concentric rainbows spreading across the underside of the craft, she was pleased to see that their Sun-Cloth did not keep its integrity any better than hers.

Cheering, she yelled, "Should have waited for the Sun-Cloth v1.5 with damage control before you took your toy for a joyride, sucker!"

With their protective coloring pierced, the camohawk was going to have to run home. It could not risk being spotted by civilians.

And run home it did. Only, it took a parting shot.

Harley swore softly. She knew that they would not make the same mistake twice. This missile would be computer aimed, able to change course in flight. Harley looked at her altimeter; 178 feet to go. Well, she was about to make the next world record. Taking a deep breath, she released the straps that held her to the chute.

The chute shot upward and to the left. Harley plummeted straight down. She had only fallen a matter of yards when the missile became tangled in her chute and exploded.

For the second time that day, Harley was propelled downward by the force of an explosion. Below her, the deep purple surface of the large lake grew closer at an alarming rate. She wiggled her index finger, clicking on the new diving icon. A warning flashed across the screen, informing her that this program had not yet been tested...and nothing happened.

Then, suddenly, the suit stiffened, tucked, throwing her head down and feet up. Her arms straightened before her. Her toes pointed. Her helmet tilted until she looked past her praying hands at the deep waters below.

Shouting triumphantly, Harley swore that if she walked away from this alive, she would look Johnny up and take him out to dinner.

The glassy surface of the lake rushed toward her. A recorded voice in her ear told her to relax and let the suit control her motions. She had one unoccupied moment to wonder how deep the water was.

Then, she struck.

The glassy surface parted before her hands, and cold water crashed about her. The impact shook her and jolted her body, but as she passed down through the darkening depths, she felt no wrenching pain.

"I've made it! I'm all right!" Harley shouted, exhilarated. Still rocketing through the black waters, she tongued the diode to...

In the darkness, she could see the little blue arc of electricity which leapt from the diode to caress her tongue. The jolt caused her limbs to quake. She tried to stop the diving program, but her index finger did not seem to want to obey her.

Frightened now, Harley tried to rid herself of her helmet—which housed the power pack. The suit remained rigid, in diving mode. She tried to budge it by sheer physical strength, but her recently shocked limbs would not obey her.

Water began shooting in through pores in the suit. She felt it pooling about her knees and rushing down her back. Again, she tried to force her arms apart from their diving position, to no avail.

Her helmet was nearly filled with water by the time her hands bumped against the bottom of the lake. Well, at least she had stopped moving. Nearly faint from lack of oxygen, Harley let out a single, mournful sob.

After all this, killed by the Suit hardly seemed a fair way to die.

Harley gritted her teeth and strengthened her resolve. By God, she was not going to give up now. She was going to make it back and see that Ramsey got his.

As she rolled about the murky bottom of the lake, her thrashing hands struck a rock. That was it! Eagerly, she rolled back and forth, using the force of her whole body to slam the outside of her hands against the rock repeatedly.

The pressure of the blows mashed her limp pinkie against the interrupt button. The suit went soft.

Exerting one final Herculean effort, Harley yanked off her helmet and shot toward the surface, desperate for air. Wearily, her limbs weak and trembling, she managed to float until she reached shallow water. The last thing she remembered was crawling onto the shore.

When she came to, it was early evening, and she was staring at two pairs of legs. Looking up, she saw a wiry-haired young man wearing thick glasses, and a vaguely-familiar, grim, old man with a full head of white hair dressed in gray.

Come on, she thought blearily, *are these the only guys Ramsey could find to take me out?*

The guy with the glasses squatted down beside her.

"Harley? Are you all right?" His voice sounded familiar and friendly, though she could not place it. Maybe these were not Ramsey's hit men after all.

"Yeah," she said, rising to one elbow and wiping her face. Her rescuer offered a hand, which she took, and helped her to her feet. "Who are you?"

He looked surprised, almost hurt.

"I'm Johnny Radcliff—from Industrial Lights and Magic?" he said. "I found you by following the homing device in the suit."

Harley had never been so glad to see anyone in her life. She laughed and threw her arms around him. He hugged her back. It felt good. Pulling away, she gestured at the Supersuit and demanded, "Get this thing off of me!"

The old man cracked a faint smile. It was only then that Harley realized that he wore a uniform—with stars on his shoulder. She straightened up. Embarrassedly, Johnny hurried to introduce her.

"Harley Weinstein, this is General Lanier," he said proudly. "I managed to reach him by hacking into his PC."

The general leaned forward and shook Harley's. His grip was firm.

"Good evening, Lieutenant Weinstein," he said. "I have a few questions I would like to ask you about a bomb."

Never Again the Same

M IST ROSE ABOUT THE OLD HOUSE. ITS GABLED PEAKS, OVERGROWN with moss, jutted out of the swirling gloom. Behind them, the tall oaks and maples were barely visible.

Patrick stepped slowly from the back door of his parents' car, gazing apprehensively at the spooky old mansion. He had never been away from home before. Sleeping over at his friend Jason's house did not count, as Jason only lived two blocks down the street. The thought of spending the summer here, with no one for company except his creepy old great-grandfather who could hardly speak English, was too much for him to bear. Patrick burst into tears.

His mother came and wrapped her arms about him.

"Be brave, Paddy, you're a big boy now. You're nearly seven."

Patrick nodded and sniffled and wiped his eyes on his sleeve. As he did so, he noticed a strange little house barely visible through the mist. It stood by the curve of a little stream and had an oddly peaked roof that slanted downward and then rose with a curve. Curious, he left his mother's arms and went cautiously forward across the lawn to investigate.

As Patrick drew near the tiny Japanese temple, the door opened and out stepped a bent old man in a black, quilted robe. His snow white hair was drawn back into a strange bun. In his gnarled hands, he held a large iron key. Seeing Patrick, he quickly inserted the key into the small door and turned it, locking the temple.

Patrick halted, frightened. Then, he realized that this apparition was his great-grandfather.

"You no go inside. Forbidden!" his grandfather announced in his crackly old voice, glaring at Patrick from under unbelievably bushy white eyebrows. Patrick shrank back. He almost turned and ran to his mother and the car. However, the mystery of the forbidden little house won over his fear.

"What's in there?" asked Patrick.

"Very evil book," said his great-grandfather sternly. "Not for little boys."

A book? Patrick could not believe such an intriguing little house could hold anything so dull.

"That's okay," Patrick said disappointed, "I hate reading anyway."

As the two of them walked back to the car, however, Patrick could not help glancing back at the forbidden temple one more time.

Later, as he sat on the dark blue mat, hardly six inches off the floor, which his mother had explained was to be his bed for the summer, Patrick recalled the conversation he had had with his parents on the long drive to his great-grandfather's house.

"But why do I have to stay with Great-Grandfather? It's his fault I can't go to summer school with Jason!" Patrick had asked.

His mother had been sitting in the front passenger's seat. She had reached her hand back to take his, frowning sadly. "It is not your great-grandfather's fault that he is Japanese, Patrick."

"But why does that make me Asian?" Patrick had complained, his voice growing louder. "Why can't Asian boys go to Blackcourt Summer School?"

His mother had taken a deep breath; something she did when she wanted to yell, but thought she should not. "It's not that Asian boys can't go to Blackcourt, honey. It's just that your school, Great Mills, doesn't have enough Asian boys. So, they would not agree to letting you transfer over to Blackcourt for the summer. They said that they would be accused of being unfair if they had too few Asian children."

"But, now I'm not going to either summer school! And I can't stay at Jason's house while you go away, because *he's* going to Blackcourt Summer Reading School. And it's all because of I have Great-Grandfather's eyes. It's not fair!" Patrick had cried.

"You can say that again," Patrick's father muttered from the driver's seat.

"Now, Gregory, don't..."Patrick's mother had begun, but Patrick interrupted her.

"I'll show them! I'll never learn to read!" he announced.

Seated on the futon in the bleak room on the second floor of his great-grandfather's eerie mansion, Patrick repeated his vow.

"Never!" he declared fiercely.

That evening Patrick dined with his great-grandfather in the grownup dining room. Everything was wrong. They sat cross-legged on cushions at a table hardly as high as Patrick's knee. The food was weird, flat noodles and cooked vegetables. Patrick hated vegetables. There was not even a knife and fork–though Patrick rather liked that part. However, when he expressed his opinion of vegetables, his great-grandfather did not even offer him a peanut butter sandwich. Instead, he merely glowered from beneath his huge eyebrows and gestured at the table.

"All there is. Eat or no eat."

Glumly, Patrick picked at the unfamiliar food, while gazing around him at the many photographs that plastered two walls of the dining room. Most of them were old black-and-white photos in dark frames. A few smaller color photos in standing frames rested on the mantelpiece to either side of the large rusty key that his great-grandfather had used to lock the forbidden temple. Patrick wondered if any of the girls in those pictures were his mother.

One large color picture, however, caught his eye. It showed a smiling young Japanese man dressed in a Yankees uniform. Patrick loved baseball. He had never heard that anyone in his family knew someone who had played for the Yankees. When he stood up to leave the table, his great-grandfather did not object. So, Patrick wandered over to the picture and examined it more closely.

His great-grandfather's voice startled Patrick.

"That your great uncle Eddie. Good baseball player! Train very many years. Wanted to play major league. Once chosen for Yankees B team."

"My great uncle was going to be a Yankee?" Patrick asked, amazed. "What happened? Did he ever get to play?"

His great-grandfather slowly lowered his head. He was silent for a moment. When he finally spoke, he did so very slowly.

"He read book," he said.

"Book? What book? You mean the one out in that little house?" Patrick asked, his voice growing squeaky from his surprise. "How'd that stop him?"

"Once you read that book–you are never the same," said his great-grandfather, choosing his words with great care.

"What happened?"

"Eddie left team. He enlisted in army. Shot down in airplane," said his grandfather. He nodded toward another picture of the same man, now grim and humorless, dressed in an air force uniform.

"Oh, wow," whispered Patrick, awed.

His great-grandfather rose suddenly to his feet. His scowl caused pure terror to run in Patrick's veins.

"Not wow!" he commanded. "Book destroyed my son. Great-grandson, you are an idiot!"

Patrick bolted from the dining room.

For two days, it rained. Lonely and bored, Patrick stayed in his room playing with his Sega Saturn. He would have liked to go downstairs and watch TV or perhaps explore the house. However, he did not want to meet his great-grandfather. The old man's glowering eyes frightened Patrick, and his broken English caused Patrick to blush with shame. No, it was better to stay in his room on his hard mat of a bed, bored to tears, than wander out over the creaking floor boards of the old house and risk another scolding.

On the third day, the sky was clear, and Patrick ventured outside. He spent a magical day playing in the old cherry orchard and wading through the stream. Just behind the little temple, a wide, shallow area formed a little pool just perfect for the stamping of bare feet. Patrick remained there until his great-grandfather struck the gong, summoning him for dinner.

As Patrick came running back toward the house, his bare feet slapping against the grass, his shoes in his hand, his great-grandfather appeared on the front porch. He saw the direction Patrick was coming from, and his face darkened.

"You try to go into temple! You went to see book! Very bad!" he shouted angrily, brandishing his fist. Patrick stopped in his tracks, shocked.

"No! No, I was playing in the river. Look at my feet!" Patrick yelled back. He balanced on one leg and held out his wet muddy foot.

"Naughty boys get no dinner. You go near temple again. I smack your bottom!" his great-grandfather announced, and he stepped into the house and slammed the door.

"It's not as if I could read your stupid old book, anyway!" shouted Patrick. Then, he sat down on the lawn and burst into tears.

<hr>

Patrick cried late into the night. He wished he could have stayed with Jason and gone to summer reading school, like they had originally planned. He wished that he could have gone with his parents on their business trip. He wished that he could be anywhere but where he was; alone in an eerie old house with a crazy old man who was afraid of a book.

"I wish I could read that old book!" Patrick whispered, sniffling. "I wouldn't let it scare me!"

He was imagining doing just that when the door to his room opened. In the doorway stood his great-grandfather. Patrick shrieked and hid under his Winnie-the-Pooh blanket. His great-grandfather had known that he was thinking about the evil book. His great-grandfather could read minds!

However, no scolding came. Instead, his great-grandfather shuffled slowly into the room. Patrick could hear him placing something on the floor and leaning it against the wall. Curious, he peaked out.

The moonlight coming through the room's only window bathed his great-grandfather in dappled light. In his hands, his great-grandfather held two large poster boards. A third poster already rested against the wall.

Seeing Patrick emerge, his great-grandfather said gruffly.

"Walls very plain. Perhaps Great-grandson want poster to hang on walls?"

Patrick slithered across his futon to get a better look at the posters. They were movie posters. Nothing so cool as the posters he had at home, but after four nights in this dreadful bleak room, Patrick was delighted with anything that broke the monotony. He peered closer, examining the closest picture. It showed a man swinging on a cable and a pretty oriental girl in a fancy dress aiming a gun.

"That's Aunt Lily!" he cried, delighted. "Mommy told me that she was a famous actress!"

"Lily was very sweet girl, but, very weak and sickly. Spent much time in bed. Doctor did not believe she would live to be woman."

"What happened? How did she get better?" Patrick asked, looking up. His great-grandfather did not answer. Patrick could not make out his expression. "What happened to her?" he asked again.

"She read book," his great-grandfather answered reluctantly.

Patrick was thunderstruck. "You mean the book cured her? But I thought it was a force for evil!"

"Evil wear many faces," his great-grandfather said.

"How can getting healthy and becoming a famous actress be bad?" asked Patrick.

"Very sweet girl–grow up. Chose bad husband. Drink too much. Die young," he said.

"Very tragic," Patrick finished seriously.

In the dappled light, it was hard to make out his great-grandfather's face, but Patrick thought he saw the old man smile. Patrick peered up at him, thinking. There was a question he wanted to ask, but he was afraid his great-grandfather would just yell at him and call him an idiot again. Screwing up his courage, he asked.

"Great-grandfather?" he began. His great-grandfather cut him off.

"Great-grandfather no proper name. Better you call me Papa-san," he said. Patrick nodded.

"Papa-san," he asked, trying again, "Where did the book come from?"

"*Hmmphf,*" said his great-grandfather. He shifted his shoulders beneath his robes. Then, he sat down on the thick straw mat that covered the floor, upon which the futon rested, and tucked his white socked feet into his robe so that he was sitting in a position his mother called 'Lotus'. Patrick sat down and tried to sit that way too. It took some effort, but he did it. His great-grandfather nodded in approval.

"Story take place many years ago—Nineteen Forty-Two. Book come to me while at war camp," his great-grandfather said.

"Like a concentration camp?" Patrick asked. He had read about concentration camps in school. "I didn't know you were in Germany."

"Yes, like concentration camp, but here, in America. Camp for Japanese people," he said stiffly. "We put in camp because we were 'Yellow Peril.'"

Comprehension dawned on Patrick's face.

"You mean because you were Asian?" he asked.

His great-grandfather *hrumph*ed again. "Asian? Gandhi was Asian. I am Japanese!"

"But, you weren't helping the enemy, were you?" asked Patrick.

"No," said Papa-san.

"So it was like me–at school?" Patrick asked. "When they won't let me go to Jason's summer school, 'cause I'm Asian?"

He considered and nodded. "Yes, you and I both treated unfairly because of our heritage. But, you're unhappy because of overzealous people, not hateful people. After war camp, people passed laws—said 'no do that again.' 'Must be very nice to Japanese.'" he scowled. "Law cannot make people very nice. Laws only punish. So, when your school have too few 'Asians,'" he scowled as he spoke the word, "they fear American government will come punish them. When good American boy wants to change schools, they say no. Very bad!" He was silent for a time.

Patrick sat quietly too. He had been so angry at his great-grandfather for being 'Asian' and making him miss summer school with Jason. It had never occurred to him that it could have been hard on his great-grandfather as well. The old man looked up, frowning, "What was it you ask?"

"About how you got the Book," prompted Patrick.

"Oh, yes! Book! Old man come to me in camp–very old, older than I am now. He ask, 'Can you read English?' I told him 'No.' He said 'Good, then you will be safe. Take this book. It very old and very dangerous. To read it changes whole life.'

"So," his great-grandfather continued, "I asked, 'If book so very bad, why not burn it?' Old man shook head, weeping, and begged me not to harm book. He told me," Here his great-grandfather paused and took a deep breath, then continued. "'One man out of thousands who read book is changed for good. Becomes very great man.'"

With this, Papa-san unfolded his feet, rose, and began to leave.

"Papa-san!" Patrick called, jumping up after him and pulling on his robes "What about you? Did you ever read the book?"

Papa-san turned on Patrick, glowering from under his immense eyebrows. Patrick let go of his robe and cowered. But, then the fire drained from the old man's face. He shook his head sadly.

"Never found courage to learn to read English," he said.

⟞━━━✦━━━⟝

Alone in the moonlit room, Patrick lay on his futon, kept awake by wonder. Who would have thought that something as uninteresting as a book could have such power? Whole members of his family had had their lives ruined by just reading a book. Even more intriguing, however, was the promise—the hope—that that very same evil book might, just once, produce greatness instead of sorrow.

Patrick could not say exactly when the idea came to him, but after that, he could not sleep at all. He absolutely had to see the book—just to look at it. After all, he could not read it, so he had nothing to fear. But, what did an evil book look like? He had to know!

Very quietly, Patrick stole out of his bed. He put on a pair of sports socks, the best for sneaking across creaking floors, and made his way softly and silently down to the dining room where his great-grandfather kept the key to the forbidden temple. Carefully, one step at a time, he crept up to the mantelpiece. Sure enough, there was the key.

Upstairs, a floor board creaked.

Patrick stood stock still, frozen with fear. He remembered the terrible glower on his great-grandfather's face when he had been playing in the stream. The sadness with which Papa-san talked of Lily and Great Uncle Eddie. If his great-grandfather caught him now....

But, time passed, and his great-grandfather did not appear. Eventually, Patrick began to breathe more easily. He considered running back upstairs to the safety of his bed, but he did not. He absolutely had to see that book! Carrying a chair quietly over to the fireplace, he took the cold, heavy key from the mantel.

Slipping out the front door, Patrick ran across the lawn as quickly as his stocking feet could carry him. The door of the tiny Japanese temple opened without trouble. Patrick crept inside, shutting the door behind him. A round table stood in the center of the tiny chamber, lit by moonlight from the two side windows. On the table sat a single old lamp, with a red glass base and paper shade, and...the Book.

Patrick could smell the musky scent of leather as he fumbled with the light. Once it came on, Patrick examined the Book more carefully. The Book looked exactly as an evil book should, large, black, and very old. The gilded title letters had chipped off over the years and were now too faded for Patrick to read, but he stared in fascination at the intricate knotwork on the cover. It seemed to form a hedge and an arbor surrounding a swing, or maybe it was a sword.

Patrick was so excited, it was hard for him to breathe. He opened the cover with trembling fingers. Inside, an etched plate showed a knight on horseback facing a mounted skeleton. His mouth wide with awe, Patrick turned to the opening page.

The words were written in ordinary black print. Patrick felt a slight pang of disappointment. He had been hoping for something glorious, like dried blood. But, perhaps it was what the book said that mattered, not its ink. He peered curiously at the words written there.

They did not seem too hard. In fact, he recognized most of them. He really did know all the parts of reading, he thought with surprise. After all, he could understand the instructions in his video games, and the sentences that his teacher wrote on the board. It was just that when it came to books...well, everyone made such a fuss about them.

Peering closer, he began to puzzle out the first line.

Many hours later, Mr. Ishizuka put down the binoculars he had been using to look across the yard into the window of the tiny temple. He lifted the receiver of his phone and made a call.

When he reached his party, he said, "Trisha? This is your Grandfather. I call about Patrick. You can bake me cake any time now—I win bet," he said, grinning broadly. He was silent a moment, listening, then continued.

"Yes, he reading right now. Doing very good job! You have not more trouble with him at school."

Silence again, then. "No, no need thank me. But, I must warn you," the old man glanced back across the lawn toward the temple, a glint in his eye and a subtle smile on his lips. "Great-grandson may never again be the same."

Next Level

THE TOW TRUCK THAT CAME FOR THE CAR FOUND IT SUSPENDED PART way across the guardrail that separated Rt. 35 from the reservoir, as if the vehicle had attempted to leave the highway and drive the silver road cast by the full moon across the dark waters.

Nearby, the driver sat on the guardrail turning the snapped-off remnant of his rear view mirror in his hands. The headlights of the police car glinted off the gold rim of his glasses. As the officer approached, he rose, slipped the mirror into his pocket, and carefully brushed tiny splinters of broken glass from his suit.

"What happen?" The officer asked.

"Swerved to miss a deer," the driver replied. His voice sounded resigned, but youthful.

The cop shone his light up into the face of a well-dressed young man, perhaps twenty-four years old. His hair was dark, and his eyes, in the glare of the flashlight, appeared to be brown.

"Ain't it a little late for you out here? What, you coming home from some fancy party?" he asked, gesturing with his flashlight at the younger man's nice attire. The officer leaned closer, as if trying to catch a whiff of the driver's breath before he bothered pulling out the breathalyzer.

The driver shook his head wearily.

"I'm on my way home from work. I work at the hospital. I'm a doctor."

"At your age?" the cop peered closer, "Hey, I know you! You're Devin MacDannan, the boy genius! Graduated from medical school in the time it takes most kids to go to college, or something. We were mighty proud when you chose our town for your practice. You're a psychiatrist, aren't you?"

Young Dr. MacDannan nodded grimly.

"How do you like the work?"

MacDannan regarded the crumpled wreck that had only recently been his emerald-green Mercedes. He watched as the tow truck driver finish securing it to his truck.

"Not exactly what I was expecting," he said flatly.

The cop laughed and slapped the young man on the back.

"If you're as smart as they say, I'm sure you'll get the hang of it. Can I give you a ride anywhere?" he asked.

MacDannan shook his head and gestured toward the forest that ran along the reservoir.

"I live in Tanglewood Court, just the other side of the Ward Pound Ridge Reservation. I'll just walk home through the park. It's only about two miles, and the trails are well maintained," he said.

The officer frowned at the thick, black forest.

"Are you sure you don't want me to take you home in the cruiser?" he asked. "We get some...strange reports about those woods at night."

"I work with mad men," Dr. MacDannan said, smiling for the first time. "I'm hardly afraid of ghosts."

❦

After taking his leave of the officer and the tow truck driver, Devin MacDannan walked down Rt. 35 until he came to the front entrance of the park. As he turned off the main road, the moon was shining on the fields so brightly that he could make out each individual blade of grass. Across the far side, down by the band of trees that ran along the river, two deer grazed. Their delicate ears twitched warily to and fro as they lifted their heads. Devin passed by as silently as he could, but they raised their white tails and leaped away.

As he walked along a trail that wound through silence trees, he contemplated his last three months. Since coming to Mt. Kisco General, he had suffered one humiliation after another. The staff were jealous of his prestige. His superiors objected to his methods. He was as certain of the validity of his ideas as he had been three months ago. However, he had not yet had a single chance to demonstrate what he could do. He had not been allowed to treat one patient without some head doctor or battleship of a nurse meddling in his work. It had been so easy in medical school. He had not expected real life to be so different.

He was still in the midst of his revere when a voice called out of the darkness. Devin stopped and listened. Again it came, a low sound, like a woman weeping. Thinking it was the wind, he shrugged and pressed on. But, then it came again, sounding more human. Curious, Devin left the path and began moving slowly through the trees toward the source of the sound.

Ahead, the moonlight played across a small pond. Through the trees, Devin could see the early morning mist rising off the water. He made his way forward slowly. Branches caught his jacket and hair.

"Hello?" he asked. "Is anybody there?"

Silence. A shiver ran down Devin's spine. He pushed aside a pine branch and peered carefully between the remaining trees, trying to make out any human figure by the lake. He could not see one.

"I am here," came a soft, whispering reply. "I am here. Come to me. Join me...I am so cold."

Startled, Devin let go of the branch. It sprang forward, its needles screening his face from the woman's voice and the pool. The smell of pine resin was strong in his nostrils.

"There are three possibilities," he said softly to himself. "Either there is a real woman out there, standing by the lake in the wee hours of the night, complaining about the cold. Or, I am imagining this. Or, I have just encountered a supernatural entity." After a moment, he added, "Of the three, the first would be the easiest to live with."

Straightening his shoulders, Devin stepped out from behind the branches toward the shore.

"May I help you?" he asked calmly.

"I am here...Come to me...I am so cold," came the whispered reply.

A woman stood upon the lake, as if her soft green and gold slippers were upheld by the rising mist. She wore a gown of light green velvet embroidered with twisted gilt. Her long flaxen hair floated around her like a weightless thing. Her face and hands were so pale that Devin could see the far shore through them. She reached forward, imploring with dark eyes and transparent lips.

Drawing back in surprise, Devin murmured under his breath, "Well, possibility one is clearly out of the question."

The eerie woman began to draw closer, floating slowly toward him across the lake. A second shiver ran down Devin's back, but he ignored it.

What did one say to a supernatural entity? Devin wondered. He recalled words his mother had spoken to him once when he'd asked her the same question. The two of them had been exploring the ruins of an Irish castle, reputed to be haunted. They had come to stand on a half-disintegrated wall, overgrown with dark ivy, and gazed down at the ocean far below. Devin recalled his mother's laughter at his question and her fond caress on his wind-blown hair. "What do you say to the dead, my son? Why the same thing you would say to the living ... Any ghost you might be meeting is likely to be much more frightened of you than you are of it. After all, if it weren't frightened, it would be either in Heaven or in Hell by now, wouldn't it? 'Tis the fear that keeps 'em here. Fear and sadness."

Perhaps, his mother was right. There was only one way to find out.

Devin studied the apparition intently. He adopted her statuesque stance and her imploring expression. His superiors might object to him using modeling techniques to guess the minds of his patients at work—complaining that he was practicing pop-psychology—but they could not stop him here. While mimicking the pale woman's body language in every detail, he closed his eyes and contemplated the emotions such a posture stirred within him—deceit and hunger...no, deceit, hunger, and despair.

Coming forward to the edge of the shore, he spoke to her in the same, calm, even voice he used with his patients.

"It's cold here, and quite dark. Wouldn't you prefer to be somewhere else?" he asked.

"I am here...I am so cold," said the apparition, drifting slowly closer. As she came across the pond toward him, her hand outstretched, the air grew suddenly chilled. Devin felt strangely fatigued. He fought to keep his eyelids from closing.

"You don't have to do this," he said with studied calmness. He stared directly into the apparition's eyes. Her cold and lifeless face unnerved him, but he steadied his gaze and did not look away.

"I am as I am...and, as I am, shall you be," said the translucent spirit.

She had drifted all the way across the lake and now stood just off the shore, her hair floating about her like living tendrils of palest gold. Her long fingers brushed Devin's arm. His arm went numb. A terrible cold shot across his shoulder. However, he did not flinch. Slowly, he lay his other hand lightly on top of her icy sleeve and gently lifted her hand from his useless arm. Luckily, the horrible cold of her touch did not communicate itself through the cloth of her sleeve.

"It is okay. You don't have to be afraid," he said. From the pocket of his jacket, he drew forth the rear view mirror he had taken from his crashed car. "Behold yourself, and know what you are."

The woman saw herself in the narrow rectangular car mirror. She raised her hand and touched her pale face, patting her bloodless cheeks and running a finger along her colorless lips.

"I...I am dead," the lovely apparition whispered, her eyes widening. She looked up at Devin with wide, blank eyes. "I am a spirit. I am nothing."

Devin nodded.

"You are dead," he said softly, adding gently, "You can go now."

"You are not afraid?" the woman asked. She tilted her head and gazed at him with a glance that in a living woman would have been curious, perhaps even flirtatious. However, on her, it was lifeless and devoid of emotion.

"Are you?" Devin replied.

The apparition hovered uncertainly. She looked over her shoulder at the small reedy pool she haunted, hardly even a lake, then returned her empty gaze to Devin's face.

"Yes, I am afraid to leave these waters," she whispered. "Yet, without new life, I grow wan and hungry. Even the life in your arm renews me. Give me your life," she asked reaching her arms out towards him.

Devin shook his head. "No," he said. "But I will help you to leave the water."

Putting the mirror away, he took two large steps backward and extended his good arm toward her, mimicking the pose she used with him—only his expression was calm and serene, almost commanding.

"Come...come to me," he said.

"I...I cannot. I am afraid," she cried. Her cries were as soft as the night winds.

"Come," Devin said sternly. "Don't you deserve better than that tiny watery prison with only fish and frogs for company?"

"I...I cannot," she wailed. Her eyes fixed hungrily on Devin's outstretched hand.

Reaching into his other pocket, Devin drew out his Swiss-army knife. Holding it in his teeth, he managed to open it and cut the fleshy tip of his index finger. After slipping the knife back into his pocket, he pressed at the end of his finger with his thumb until a drop of blood glinted like a ruby tear on his fingertip. Slowly, he extended his bleeding hand toward the apparition's hungry gaze. Her eyes, fixing upon it, lit with an eerie gleam, reflecting some unnamable unholy need. She moved forward, reached the very edge of the water and wavered uncertainly, as if pained.

"You must leave the false protection of your prison behind, or you will never have what you truly desire," Devin said, "Don't you want to be free again? Don't you want warmth? All you need to do is leave the pool."

She nodded eagerly, mournfully, as Devin spoke; her eyes fixed on the gleaming drop of warm blood upon his finger. But, she did not come forward.

"Come!" commanded Devin.

The translucent woman lifted her skirts of gold and green, and stepped forward onto the earth. As her satiny slipper touched the dry earth, she turned suddenly, looking up over her right shoulder.

"I see a light. Do you see it?" she asked.

Devin peered through the trees, but he saw nothing. The moon was in another quadrant of the sky. The apparition continued to fix her eyes upon a thing Devin could not see. Her pale features became luminescent. Raising her arms as if in greeting or reunion, she smiled joyously and faded slowly away, disappearing like mist before sunlight.

Devin remained rooted to the spot where he stood, awestruck. A smile began to creep across his lips.

"I did it! I cured her!" he said and laughed aloud. Awe and victory mingled in his voice. "I knew I could do it if they would only leave me alone to try!"

His exaltations came to a sharp halt as he became aware of the swinging dead weight on the left side of his body. After licking the blood from his finger, he used his good hand to carefully examine the paralyzed arm. The skin of his fingers, and the flesh beneath his nails was entirely white, almost bluish.

Frostbite! Devin swore softly. In only a short time, he must return heat and circulation to his limb, or he would lose the hand. He tried massaging his hand and blowing on his fingers, but neither seemed to have an effect. Cradling his numb arm against his chest, he ran back the way he had come.

FACES AND ENIGMAS

T HE THING MIKE BOUCHER HATED MOST ABOUT HIS JOB WAS THAT HE was always either being boiled alive or freezing his buns off. It made sense—no one called a climate control technician when they were comfortable. Yet, understanding it was not the same as liking it.

Currently, he was wedged in an access tube off corridor Red-562, where he was trying to rewire the air blower on a cooling unit. The temperature in the tube was nearly 110 F, and he was sweating like a pig. Company legend said that a level-two technician named Ricky Hadley once drowned under just such conditions. Supposedly, the poor man sweat so profusely that the resulting liquid balled together and completely encased his body. He drowned in his own sweat—or so the legend went. Mike knew that without gravity to pull it away, water balled up close to the body. He had even heard of people drowning in showers because their air blowers malfunctioned. But death by your own sweat? He just didn't buy it.

At least, he thought, pushing the little balls of sweat from his eyes, he hoped it was not true. That would be a horrible way to go.

As he finished the rewiring job and slid out into the humid, yet cooler air of the main corridor, he could not help wondering whether he had been a technician three months ago. He was not particularly curious about his past. Pseudo-personas were designed to dull curiosity about the previous personality. After all, what would be the point of hiding your true identity and then spend all your free time trying to discover who you had been? Yet, he did wonder, in an idle sort of way, if his previous life had been substantially different from his present one...more meaningful? He could only hope.

He looked at his large hands hoping for clues, but the rough, fading calluses on his right hand told him nothing. His new persona could not bring to mind what he had done to cause them.

It might have been a tool he used on his last job, or merely some hobby he had once enjoyed. Mike frowned.

Speculating about his former self always led to the uncomfortable question of what had driven him to do something so drastic as to alter his own mind—not a good subject to contemplate; especially when he could be rushing home to his own personal suite where the pleasures of privately pumped oxygen and a personal cooling system awaited him. He had just finished the last task on today's shift roster.

Mike pushed off the bulkhead and maneuvered toward the steel transit cable stretching along the axis of the six-sided corridor. He caught the cable with the specially designed grip on his 'aft-gripper' footwear and began sliding along it toward his personal chambers. To either side, the rubbish nets lining the bulkheads were shiny and tattered from constant wear. In several places the ropes had frayed through and floating debris had escaped to bob freely in the corridor. Mike batted aside old squeeze containers and rancid fruit rinds, but hesitated as he came face to mug-guard with a floating mass of vomit. The brownish goo floated in lumpy balls. An undigested chunk of sausage drifted by, along with an individual green piece of what had once been lettuce.

Bobbing along the sweltering, stinking corridors, Mike could not help recalling the old drama-flats featuring grungy space stations which he—or perhaps his pseudo-self—had enjoyed watching as a kid. They had depicted the characters strolling— as if anyone would bother providing corridors with gravity to the pathetic nimps, low-life paugs, and riffraff of space—along decks lined with dull-colored girders and smudged with a little dirt. Those smudges of dirt were supposed to indicate filth and squalor. As a youth, Mike had though such places appalling.

Humph! he thought ironically, *the reality made the old flats look like paradise.*

The Up-halls of Ceres VI-D Space Station, as the station's inner zero-g service passages were known, were an abysmal place. They were stuffy and dim—where they were lit at all. Broken lights were seldom replaced. The air recycling conduits were perpetually clogged. Station Command could not be bothered to spring for new air filters more than once or twice a year. (In the air recycling conduits of the glitzy down-deck, the air filters were changed every other week.) Hence, the public air stank, and globules of murky condensation, composed of stinking sludge and human body fluids, clung to the bulkheads like a foul sweat, or worse hung suspended in the air. Only the very poorest—the paugs, the tragically hapless, or the absurdly brave traveled the up-halls without some kind of mug-guard.

Today, old Moggie was out with her nets. The agile old paug bounced easily from bulkhead to bulkhead, wearing one mesh bag over her face as a mug-guard and sifting the air with another. Her intentions were good, but Mike feared her mop of frizzy locks often caught more than her nets. Her bushy white hair glittered with tiny globules of red, brown, and black, shiny as beads. The effect was almost artistic, if Mike did not stop to think about what he was really seeing.

To his left, just beyond the mess, Mike spotted an unexpected sight—a bare face. Only this bare face had balls of water instead of eyes. Peering closer, Mike saw that the face belonged to a young woman who clung to a municipal sitting bar, her shoulders shaking. When she blinked, the balls of tears rolled onto her cheeks. However, as soon as she lifted her eyelids again, the water rushed right back into her eyes. Exasperated, she raised a shaky hand to wipe the tears away. The globes of water merely clung to her fingers, making her cry harder. Finally, she tried shaking her head rapidly like a spaniel. Tiny droplets sprayed from her face and floated away, glittering like translucent pearls. Silvery beads formed on each eyelash, giving her an exotic ethereal look.

As her gear was too shiny for a native, Mike pegged her for a newcomer and figured she must have been the one who puked. He felt sorry for the kid and hoped someone would have the decency to stop and give her a hand.

No one did, of course. From the tourists to the doughboy to the paugs, the present crowd was too busy or too apathetic. Yet, clearly the girl needed help. Mike thought of the fresh air, bright lights, and pleasantly regulated temperature awaiting him in his quarters and scowled. But, it could not be helped. Sometimes, if a thing needed to be done, you had to do it yourself.

With a sigh, he curled his toes to release his aft-grippers from the cable. Pushing off toward the nearest bulkhead, he bounced off the solid surface and maneuvered toward his destination. He ducked some floating trash and grabbed for the sitting bar to which the young woman clung.

"Close your eyes, ma'am," he said.

The young woman did so obediently. Taking his vacsorb from his tool pack, he dialed it to mild and sucked some of the water away from her cheeks. As she waited patiently, her eyes closed, Mike took advantage of the opportunity to look her over carefully.

Up close, he realized she was not quite as young as he had first thought. Her skin was the color of caramel candy; her lips were wine dark and overly full; and her hair was a fiery red, an odd combination. A close-fitting blue jumpsuit of the kind up-hall occupants wore in picture books covered ample curves. Between her knees was wedged a matching navy helmet. Mike gave her points for having had the presence of mind to remove her helmet before she got sick.

It occurred to Mike suddenly that he knew this woman.

"Gretchen Clark!" He blurted aloud. Her eyes shot opened and stared blankly at his mug-guard. "It's Mike. Mike Boucher."

The young woman's face lost all trace of expression.

"The Mike Boucher I knew is dead," she said, her voice cold and flat. "And you don't look anything like him. Before he died, he sold several templates of his personality to help cover his medical costs. So, who are you? One of those leeches who get off on borrowed memories?"

"...Shit!" muttered Mike.

So, Mike Boucher was not even his real name. Then, who was he?

The young woman's nut-brown eyes narrowed, scrutinizing him, then darted away. He watched her rapid change of expressions as she weighed her repulsion at this mockery of her dead friend against the likelihood that his affection for her, bottled though it may be, could make him a useful ally in this unfamiliar environment. He suspected that she dearly needed an ally.

Whatever her initial conclusion was, Mike never learned it. As she raised her tear-spangled lashes to regard him again, her face changed suddenly, and she sniffed. Sniffing again, she broke into a bright smile, tilted her head back, and began inhaling deeply.

"Where is this air coming from? It smells...clean?" she asked, a touch of longing in her voice.

Glancing down the corridor, Mike saw the tell-tale golden glow rounding the nearest corner.

"Angels," he said, smiling. "That's our station! The air stinks. The food sucks. But the law enforcement is the best in the solar system."

Fresh air sounded like exactly what he needed. Mike got as far as raising his hand to remove his mug-guard, before he stopped himself.

Mike could think of a number of reasons why someone might employ a pseudo-persona for a weekend or while attending a party. There was only one reason, however, for employing such a drastic measure over a long period of time...to hide from the Angels.

The Grigori Fraternity Arch Agents, or Angels as they were universally called, were inhumanely observant. Trained practically from birth in the gestalt arts; secret techniques which allowed them to draw correct deductions from the slightest clues; they could catch a criminal merely from his involuntary responses or subconscious reactions. Between this and their computer-enhanced intelligence, they could not be tricked or misled. No actor had ever fooled an Angel. The only way to successfully deceive an Angel was to acquire someone else's subconscious.

Up close, even Mike's untrained eye could distinguish pseudo skin from the real stuff. If the approaching Angel, with his gestalt training and computer-enhanced vision, caught a glimpse of his bare face with its pseudo-skin features, the Angel would most likely be able to deduce what Mike really looked like in an instant. This was, of course, the other reason Mike did not probe too deeply into his missing memory. Men did not hide from the GF for petty crimes. He did not care to know what he might discover.

The Arch Agent Raphael rounded the corner head first, propelled forward by micro-rockets imbedded in his boots. He slid among the fat doughboys and emaciated paugs like a sleek porpoise gliding among a herd of clumsy walruses. Meters of gossamer smart-mesh billowed about him like saffron robes, cleansing the dirty air as he passed through it. His pure white ocular mantle stretched from his shoulders like wings; its feathery surface gleaming with a hundred iridescent sensor eyes. A golden glow ring hovered above his head, providing illumination on numerous frequencies for human and mechanical eyes alike. In his right hand, his disrupter, which could disable a man without spilling blood, flashed like a flaming sword.

Despite his fears about his former life, Mike could not help but feel the same sense of awe and relief honest citizens felt in the presence of these glorious advocates of the law. All heads had turned to watch the splendor of the Angel's progress. Where their eyes were visible through their mug-guards, Mike saw a stirring of something akin to hope. Eager to catch Gretchen's reaction to her first glimpse of the glories of an Angel in zero-g, he tore his eyes away from the noble visage and glanced to his left.

Gretchen crouched in a ball, glaring at the GF agent. Her face had contorted into a mask of loathing, and her eyes burned with hatred. Startled, Mike averted his eyes and moved to his right, putting more distance between himself and her, lest the Angel think they were together.

As the Angel drew closer, the soft, melodic chimes surrounding him grew more audible. This was the sound of the ocular mantle's myriad of micro-interfaces interacting with every pocket tabular, clipbook, or micro processor within range. All computers in the corridor were being contacted and comprehensibly searched, their data parsed and sorted, by the Angel's augmented intellect. Anyone foolish enough to keep electronic records of evidence linking them, however indirectly, to a crime, would be instantly discovered.

Mike heard a soft ringing as the techpad in his tool pack interacted with the Angel's mantle. He was not worried. The tech pad contained only technical specs for the stations climate control equipment, nothing incriminating there.

The Angel came abreast of Mike and Gretchen and halted, hovering motionlessly before them, his face perpendicular to theirs. He stared at Gretchen, shifting his wings to fix her with several dozen of his augmented eyes. Gretchen met his gaze. Raising her chin indignantly, she spread her arms wide as if exposing her chest to his flaming weapon. The effect was slightly marred by the fact that this action sent her spinning.

"Go ahead!" she snarled. "Look all you want. There is nothing else for you to take!"

Mike, who was sweating profusely, inched nervously away, his eyes tracking the position of the glowing disrupter. Arch Agent Raphael remained motionless, his calm, inscrutable eyes locked with her hot hateful ones.

Suddenly, a faint smile touched the Angel's lips, and he saluted her with his blazing weapon. Then, turning away, he glided onward; leaving Gretchen clinging to the sitting bar again, panting heavily. She looked so red-faced and upset that Mike worried that she might begin to cry again.

Gretchen sat staring straight forward, her jaw set. Only after the Angel was gone from sight did she became aware of Mike's presence again. She turned on him and demanded.

"How long have you been Mike Boucher?"

"Three months," he answered truthfully.

"Three months?" Gretchen whistled, which required that she purse her thick, full lips. The move looked good on her. Mike wondered what it would take to get her to whistle again. "Hardly sounds like a weekend fling...What are you hiding from?"

"I don't know."

"Why don't you look like my Mike?"

"Probably asked for an unique face. Easy enough to program with these things. Guess I didn't want to be recognized by—" Mike shrugged. "—someone like you."

"I don't know a lot about it, but I once played an interactive which included a GF witness protection scenario. Aren't pseudo-persona usually programmed to turn off under some particular circumstances?" When Mike nodded, she asked, "Under what circumstance does yours revert?"

He shook his head. "I don't know."

Gretchen made a wry face. "So, at any moment you could suddenly revert to say, a rabid murderer or something?"

"That's about the state of things."

"Shit," she swore.

Mike waited, torn between his desire to get away from this possibly unstable woman and back to the comfort of his home, and a perverse interest in discovering why she despised the Angels and what had caused Arch Agent Raphael to show her a sign of respect. That bit of personal information was not part of his bottled memory of Gretchen Clark. Either it had been edited from the final version, or her dislike of the GF was a new development since her friendship with the real Mike Boucher.

Noticing her shift, grab her helmet, and cross her legs tightly, Mike grinned.

"Come on, I'll show you to the space john."

Gretchen raised her long red lashes, surprised, "How did you know?"

"Happens to all newcomers. Now that gravity is not pulling your blood down into your legs, the blood spreads out through your whole body equally, which means more of it moves toward you head. Your brain thinks there's too much liquid in your system and signals your kidneys to pull it out. So, your kidneys start thinning your blood and sending the extra liquid to the bladder. Results, you have to pee a lot, and you probably will feel nauseous for a few days."

"Great! It's worse than being pregnant! Do I have to go through something like this again when I go back down?"

Mike shrugged. "Some do. Some don't."

"Wonderful! Lead the way."

Mike showed her how to attach her aft-grippers to the transit cable and helped her negotiate her way to the nearest, reasonably clean facilities, where he explained how to use the tubes. When she eventually came out, she was wearing her helmet. Her face was now a shiny zone of darkened Plexiglas. Considering the dimness of the corridor, he wondered if she could see at all.

"I don't suppose there's any chance of getting some food?" Gretchen asked.

"Are you sure you want to eat? Swallowing in zero-g is an art in itself."

"That may be, but I left my lunch back in the other corridor. What I'd really like is a cup of coffee."

"We don't drink as much up here. We don't need as much liquid and liquids can get quite messy. Coffee is usually ingested in two forms; mocha bars or ice cream."

"Ice cream sounds divine. Where can I get some?"

"Several places. Cafeteria Red-590 is the closest, but it's no cleaner than this hall," Mike gestured at the oily stains along the bulkhead and the half-rotting vegetables twirling slowly by their heads. "Or, we could go to my private suite, which is slightly further but has the virtues of clean, cool, and breathable."

Gretchen's head moved, tracking the tumbling celery stalk.

"I'll risk your suite," she said.

They began maneuvering along the corridor, stopping a few times for Mike to give Gretchen pointers on how to travel more efficiently. He tried to think of a way to bring up the subject of her relationship with the Angels, but failed. What did one say under such circumstances? *So, tell me, a complete stranger who thinks I'm your old friend, what kind of insane bimbo snarls at an Angel?* Somehow, he doubted that would get the conversation off on the right foot.

"So, what brings you up here?" he asked finally.

"I'm here to meet a...business associate," she said, keeping her gaze straight ahead.

She was hedging, but not lying outright. Mike shrugged. It was none of his business. Maybe she had a lover's tryst. His bottled memory recalled that she had had a husband, but he did not see him here now. Watching her bosom strain against her tight-fitting bodysuit, as she waved her arms to recover from a sudden spin, he decided that whomever she was meeting, he was one lucky sucker.

To reach their destination, they had to travel from the five hundred zone of Red Sector to the one hundred zone of Blue Sector. When they came to the intersection with the passageway Mike usually used to connect Red Sector to Blue, he saw, to his dismay, that the transit cable traversing that corridor had snapped, making it useless for travel. Its severed ends snaked slowly about the nearly empty hall, stirring up the floating debris. Surveying the scene, Mike weighed his options sourly.

They could crawl along the disgusting, grime-covered rubbish nets, an unpleasant option at best. They could bounce from wall to wall, risking the dangers of a mid-air collision—not a good idea with a first-timer and a loose cable. Or, they could take a different connecting passage, which might add as much as twenty minutes to their trip.

From a round hatch in the wall leading to another corridor came the noise of a disturbance. Gretchen left the transit cable and awkwardly maneuvered to peek through the hatch.

"Mike, what's going on over here?"

Mike kicked free of the cable and joined her. On the far side of the hatch, several dozen people loitered, forming a loose globe around two men who were reeling around on the transit cable traversing that corridor. Both men had looped a thin scarf about the other's neck and pulled it tight. The larger man still wore his mug-guard, but the smaller one had lost his. His face was bloated and purple. As they clung together, limbs fluttering like an elastic toy, they did not resemble men so much as a fish waltzing with an octopus.

"It's a fight," Mike said gruffly. "Those strangling scarves act like ratchets. Once they're tightened, they maintain a constant pressure."

"How awful! Is everyone just going to stand around?" Gretchen's voice was muffled by her helmet, but Mike could hear her distress. "Why doesn't someone try to stop them?"

"Too dangerous," he replied, "The dynamics of two struggling bodies in zero-g are bad enough without trying to throw in a third body. Things could get bad. I suggest we get out of here."

"I can't go. See that smaller man? The one with the red scarf wrapped around his neck? He's the contact I came up here to meet."

"Shit!"

Mike and Gretchen slid through the hatch and joined the other spectators. They found an unoccupied sitting bar between a huddle of peddlers and a solitary wraith. The wraith was nearly eight feet tall and sported the long, snaky limbs and digits common to his kind; the result of having been raised in zero-g since birth. Mike nodded to him politely, all the while silently cursing the poor, unfortunate creature's parents.

From his new vantage, Mike could see that there were far more people here than he had glimpsed from the hatch. The rubbish nets and sitting bars on all six bulkheads were crowded with spectators and more floated free, willing to risk accidentally drifting into the fray. A few brave souls attached themselves to the cable that the two fighters were holding onto. Mike watched a youth get thrown face-first into a rubbish net when the violent motions of the cable proved to be too much for the cheap clamps on his aft-grippers.

The bulk of the audience were peddlers and shiftless paugs, though there were also a healthy number of technicians. Mike could tell an individual's social position and occupation by their mug-guards. Mug-guards were an essential piece of equipment up here—the sunglasses of up-hall life. Sunglasses kept unwanted glare out of the eyes, as mug-guards kept unwanted floating gunk out of the face, but they also made a fashion statement. More sophisticated mug-guards came with a personal air filter. Mike's mug-guard, a sleek black plexi number with a good filter, was standard issue for station technicians. Anything more advanced contained real breathing apparatuses and was usually called a helmet.

While a man's mug-guard might not reveal the inner workings of his soul, it often went a far way to revealing his rank and stature in up-hall life. As he glanced about at the audience watching the fight, he made guesses about his fellow spectators based on their mug-guards and felt that he learned much more than he might have from their bare faces.

Laminated cardboard mug-guards indicated vagrant paugs— the shiftless riffraff of the up-halls. Many of them lurked along the bulkheads. While others were distracted by the fight, they surreptitiously searched through the refuse trapped in the rubbish nets for anything salvageable. Across the hallway, another paug had covered his head with an old sheet. He floated sluggishly like a ghost from a Halloween party, as he watched the match. At least an old sheet was not lethal. Last week, one of Mike's fellow technicians had discovered a dead paug clogging up an air conduit. The poor jerk had made the mistake of trying to cover his mug with a plastic bag and had suffocated.

The group wearing tiny delicate breathers covering only their mouth and nose must be first-timers. Their air was probably of better quality than anyone else's—they did look more alert. However, no one with experience in the up-halls would come here with so little protection for their eyes and cheeks. Brown grime smeared their skin and many of them were blinking or rubbing their eyes. Their status as first-timers was confirmed when Mike noticed that they all wore the shiny, chrome aft-grippers offered at the rental shop.

A doughboy, bobbing like an apple, temporarily obscured Mike's view. An anchor line tethered him to a sitting bar where three bunnies sat, giggling together behind their floozy mug-guards. The fancy, custom-made helmet the size of a small beach ball fingered the doughboy for a rich man's son. It had to be custom-made. No normal helmet could cover that bulging corpulent head. But, then most doughboys were rich as Croesus—or at least rich enough to import delicacies. No one could get that fat on sponge paste and liquid protein. Watching the doughboy maneuver his huge, round body through the filth and debris floating in the corridor made Mike queasy. He wondered how long the pampered puffball would last if he had to lug his obese body around under any sort of gravity.

If the floating ball of human flab were not revolting enough, there were the bunnies. Mike could only see the head of the closest one. Her pert face plate displayed a picture of Marilyn Monroe, eyelids half-closed, lips half-parted. She had altered her body to give herself a larger chest and smaller waist than would be possible under the human body's natural conditions in a gravity well. She looked good, real good! However, any attraction Mike might have felt toward her was quickly killed by the idea of her and the doughboy doing...anything!

As the doughboy was blocking his view, Mike glanced farther down the hall and noticed a section of bulkhead coated with screen cloth. Currently, the screen was displaying a rotation of the latest GF wanted posters. The cloth was torn in several places and marred with rainbow distortions. The image quality was so warped that Mike could barely read the tag lines that appeared beneath the giant, grimacing visages of the solar system's Most Desperate. He was able to make out a few: 'Paulio Torres—wanted for the rape and murder of three young girls'; 'Bernard Kepler—wanted for last month's slaughter of the entire Pegasus 3 space colony'; 'Alvis Player—wanted for three counts of encryption smuggling and one count of murder.' Hardened criminals. The worst in the solar system....Was one of them Mike's true identity? Heavyhearted, he averted his gaze. The doughboy had drifted away again, and Mike was able to return his attention to the fight.

The combatants flopped like rag dolls, each trying to tighten the strangling scarf around his opponent's neck without letting his opponent do the same. The larger fellow had his aft-grippers firmly attached to the cable. However, the little fellow's grippers had come free, leaving him with only the other man's body for purchase. Had he been here on his own, Mike decided he would have rooted for the big guy, as his mug-guard placed him as a recycling technician. For Gretchen's sake, however, he rooted for the little guy, or at least, hoped the small man would survive in one piece.

He was hissing to Gretchen for the third time that there was nothing he could do, when he caught sight of a glimmer of steel. He swore.

"Damn, that little idiot pulled a knife! Do you have any idea how bad this place will stink if blood gets into the air processing system?"

Without a second thought, he lunged toward the combatants, springing off the bulkhead to propel himself forward. As he sped through the air, his hand automatically reached toward his hip…and grabbed air. Swearing at the absence of a weapon his conscious mind did not recall possessing, he twisted in mid-air to better position himself.

Mike sailed toward the combatants, approaching from behind the larger man. From his point of view, their feet would be in front of him as he passed by the cable. As he drew near, he grabbed the bigger man by the back of his calves and pulled sharply. The resulting motion simultaneously spun the technician backward toward Mike, while propelling Mike forward, around the cable. As Mike shot around the cable, he drew up his knees and waited.

All three men were now revolving around the cable. The technician revolved backward, his body fully extended. The small man flew forward, pulled by the grip of the larger man. While Mike curled around the cable like a ribbon curling around the stick of a party favor.

The big technician successfully seized the knife from the other man. When the motion of the cable unexpectedly flipped him backward, he released his hold on Gretchen's short friend and stabbed at Mike. This proved his undoing. As his center of balance drew closer to the cable, the speed of his spin increased dramatically. He went careening around, wildly out of control, and slammed the unprotected back of his head directly into Mike's waiting knees.

The blow jarred Mike's kneecaps and sent the big guy gyrating away from the cable. Panicking, the stunned technician tensed up, causing him to clench his toes and releasing the clips on his aft-grippers. He shot away from the cable and smashed chest-first against one of the bulkheads, where he was quickly surrounded by other bystanders eager to relieve him of the knife.

Twisting, Mike caught sight of the second man, still tumbling wildly down the corridor. From his erratic gyrations, Mike guessed he had initially begun tumbling backward. The human body did not form a stable system when spinning backward, however, so he had ended up rotating and spinning at the same time. The poor man was clearly suffering from vertigo, but the scarf around his neck was clenched too tightly to allow him to vomit. By the time several members of the audience intervened and stopped his flight, the little man had mercifully lost consciousness.

It was over.

Mike spread his arms and legs to slow his motion and drifted. As he relaxed, and the adrenaline left his body, he found his limbs were trembling. Where had he learned the zero-g mechanics needed to pull off a stunt like the one he had just pulled? He had no memory of learning such techniques; nor of why he would have wanted to know them. And what kind of weapon had he reached for so blithely? Surely not a gun, no one who lived in a tin can would risk putting a bullet hole through the wall.

A knife? Probably not, space men had a prohibition against shedding blood. There were a number of reasons for this. One, a tremendous amount of the stuff poured out whenever anyone was wounded in zero-g; two, blood could spread diseases and was unhealthy to breathe, even through a mug-guard; and three, it played havoc with the air recycling system. Blood would pass through the grates meant to stop solid stuff. Then, once it reached the air filters, it clotted, clogging everything. If the filter was not immediately replaced, it begins to stink to high heaven. Compared to dried, rotting blood, even the combined stenches of urine and vomit smelled like a rose garden.

So, ruling out gun and knife, what kind of weapon had he carried? A padded truncheon like the mobsters wore in the interactives? From the bulkhead before him, the giant, toothy grin of the rapist Paulio Torres leered down at him. Mike kicked off of Paulio's left eye and shot back the way he had come.

The bigger guy was being hauled away by a group of his friends, while Gretchen had found her way to the small fellow's side. The doughboy had departed when it was clear that the action was over, leaving his tether behind. As Mike approached, Gretchen was attempting to use the doughboy's tether to anchor the little man's inert form. The man's face was bloated and purple. His eyes bulged hugely, and his tongue jutted from his mouth swollen and blackish. It did not look good.

"Quick. Send for a medic!" Gretchen snapped, agitated. For his reply, Mike gestured toward the nearest of the ubiquitous, flat, black camera lenses embedded into the station bulkheads approximately every twenty yards.

"See that blinking red light just above that hawkeye? That means it's active. Security has become aware of what's going on here. They'll send a medic soon."

Gretchen turned her helmeted head toward the hawkeye. Her shoulders tensed, but her face was a black Plexiglas mystery. Returning her attention to her tethered patient, she yanked at the red scarf, trying to loosen it. Mike watched until he could no longer endure her ineffectual efforts.

"Here, let me at that!" he grunted. Bracing himself against the nearest sitting bar, he pulled off his tool pack, drew out a utility blade, and slit the spiny cloth of the strangling scarf. Then, loosening his mug-guard, he maneuvered his ear close to the little man's mouth. At the reassuring hiss of indrawn breath, he pulled away and muttered. "He's coming around."

"Good....thank god!"

"You can say that again! Have you ever tried resuscitating someone up here? Let's just say it's a task better left to professionals!"

The little man wheezed and coughed, causing his body to jerk and spin. The tether kept him from going too far, but the motion clearly was not aiding his recovery process. Mike, who was still braced against the sitting bar, reached out and steadied him. The coughing subsided. The little man opened his mouth to speak but was interrupted by a second coughing attack. This time, as he hacked, tiny red bubbles spilled from his mouth. Mike pulled a soft wipe out of his tool pack and caught the drifting blood droplets. Then, he held the cloth across the man's mouth, both to catch additional blood, and to act as a makeshift mug-guard to protect him against the general floating miasma.

"You know what I hate most about up-hall?" The little man said in a hoarse whisper when he could breathe more easily. "There ain't no down. You can't ever lay your head down, no matter how terrible you feel...." Focusing his eyes on Mike, he added. "Thanks for saving me."

"Why the Hell did you pull a knife?" Mike answered rudely. "You look like a guy who has lived up here a while. You know better than to let blood in zero-g!"

The little man gave a painful shrug and whispered, "I-I wanted to cut the scarf."

"Oh....guess that makes sense."

Gretchen pulled on the tether until she drew the wounded man's face near her helmet.

"Mackie Maloney, I'm the contact from Europa Station. The one you were supposed rendezvous with two days from now."

"Don't have it yet," the little man croaked back. "I was to meet the operative tomorrow at the junction of Red 520 and Red 506. You'll have to go instead."

"Red 520 and Red 506," she entered the coordinates into her pocketpad. "What's the operative's name?"

"Joe something. Haven't ever met him. He's new. Old contact cacked off last week."

"Have you checked this Joe person out?" Gretchen asked dubiously.

"Oh, yeah, yeah...he checked out fine. Clean as a whistle."

The man was obviously lying, Mike decided. Mackie had never checked on the new contact. Heck, he probably had not even thought of it.

Any response Mike might have made was interrupted by a high siren, and the painfully bright flashes issuing from the helmets of the approaching medics. Pedestrians moved quickly to get out of the way as the medics came skating into sight, pushing a deceptively light-looking gurney before them. In that aluminum frame, Mike knew, they carried as much gear as an old-fashion ambulance.

As the sirens died, the medical gurney's brakes could be heard squealing against the outer coating of the transit cable. Bystanders on the cable clenched their toes to release their aft-grippers and leapt away. Medical gurneys had a reputation for getting away from the medics and careening forward along the cable, crushing anyone in their path.

Gretchen moved to untie Mackie Maloney from the tether, but Mackie reached out and tugged urgently at her arm, drawing her back.

"One more thing…I must tell someone—in case I don't make it…."

"Yes?" Gretchen asked softly.

"Remember that big arrest last month? The Angels announced that they had arrested that crypto smuggler and kept some big new encryption program from being sold on the black market?"

Gretchen's helmet nodded.

Mike said, "Sure, I remember. A guy named Pete Graver was arrested by the Angel Sariel, down in Red 402. I saw him get taken away myself. Apparently, he tried to run, and the Angel struck him with his disrupter. I happened to be down that way on a job and arrived just as this Graver guy collapsed into a ball. Never actually saw an Angel use one of their weapons before."

"Pete was innocent," blurted Mackie.

"Impossible," Mike said evenly. "Angels don't make mistakes."

"I tell you, Pete was framed, and the Angel fell for it. Poor Pete. He wasn't even no smuggler!"

Mike started to object, but Gretchen's voice stopped him. Though her helmet did not move, Mike could feel her eyes upon him.

"There is at least one way of tricking an Angel," she said.

"Yeah!" the little man jumped in eagerly. "Those psycho-mask things! Like the fake Alvis Player used. I heard…"

Gretchen cut him off. "Mackie, the medics are coming. Quickly, before they get here...how can you be so sure Peter Graver was framed?"

Before he could reply, the medics were among them. With rapid, professional competency, they unfolded their light, collapsible stretcher-frame and snapped it around Mackie Maloney. A pull of a tab and both sides inflated, immobilizing Mackie's body. As Gretchen and Mike moved out of the way, one medic donned the harness straps while two others clicked the frame's sliding clips onto the transit cable. Just before he was pulled away, the little man hissed fervently to Gretchen. When she leaned her helmeted ear close to his mouth, he whispered loudly. "I know he was framed...'cause I'm the one they really wanted."

⚜

They reached Mike's rooms without further mishap. Once in the foyer lock, Mike stripped off his outer jumpsuit, placed his mug-guard in one of the sliding drawers and offered Gretchen a Dry-Wipe, so she could clean off some of the gook smeared on her jumpsuit after her trip through the corridor. Gretchen gave his naked face a hard look, then gingerly accepted the wipe. A chemical scent only partially obscured by perfumes issued from the large square of soft cloth as she unfolded it. She wiped off her shoulders and legs, spinning slowly head over heels as she did so. Meanwhile, Mike pulled open the laundry drawer and stuffed his dirty jumpsuit under the cover net.

Watching him, Gretchen asked, "What happens to laundry up here? Hardly seems worth the cost in imported water to clean them only to wear them again in the mess that is your corridors."

"Our clothes get spacers treatment," Mike replied.

Gretchen's head was currently in the vicinity of his feet. As she rolled toward him, her nose began curling up, as if she feared he was about to describe something unpleasant.

"Which is?"

"It gets temporarily spaced. Very little survives in the vacuum of space. Any stains which are or could be liquid—sweat, ketchup—evaporate instantly. The solid particles left behind become powder and can be easily shaken off with a quick beating like you'd give to a rug. Odor-causing bacteria die horribly and most viruses too. Stuff comes back cool and clean."

"Must be cheap!"

"Not really, you have to pay for the air that's lost when the air-lock cycles—our vacuum pumps aren't perfect, and air is not cheap! Also, some stuff doesn't come out—like lubricating oil or Vaseline. Stains like that require dry cleaning."

"Why don't they clean the station that way?"

"They did once, but proved too dangerous. A guy I know lost his grandfather that way. The old man lived in a rubbish net. When the call to evacuate came, he wouldn't leave his nest. Got swept out to space with the rest of the junk."

"Really? That's terrible! How could they...."

Mike chuckled. "You always this gullible? Or only when the blood is rushing to your head?"

"Let me guess...no one has been left to die during a cleaning?"

"Nah, are you kidding? They wouldn't waste the kind of money necessary to clean these halls. Do you have any idea how much air we'd lose? But, the story about the old man persists nonetheless...one of those legends old timers like me use to creep out new weenies like you."

Gretchen groaned. "You don't look like my Mike, but you sure have the same sense of humor."

"Hmm..." Mike stuffed Gretchen's used wipe under the cover net on the laundry drawer and cycled the door into the apartment itself. Fresh, cool air blew against his face. The pleasantness of the sensation helped take the edge off the ache caused by realizing that even his sense of humor might not be his own. He breathed deeply, then invited her to enter.

Mike's apartment consisted of a suite of three ovals connected by wide, round doors. Guide lines stretched across the empty spaces, making it possible to move easily from one room to the next. Each room had cabinets set into the walls, with pale grey Velcro covering the remaining wall space; except for the largest chamber, which was papered in screen cloth. The screen cloth currently displayed a kaleidoscope of moving, zagging, brightly-colored lines. Mike indicated the undulating display.

"Bought the program from a local peddler. If you don't care for it, it came with a dozen other settings. That patch over there is the controls."

He glided along one of the guide lines and slid up to the freezer, which looked from the outside like any other drawer. Once open, it revealed a burst of cold and a net which kept the frozen items from floating out. Fishing around, Mike located two coffee ices in rounded squeeze tubes. He handed one to Gretchen and showed her how to suck on the container's mouth as if it were a wide straw. A faint smell of coffee issued from the squeeze tubes as soon as they cracked them opened.

"When you're done, put the tube in the recycle drawer." He indicated another drawer. "They give these things an industrial cleaning and reuse them."

Gretchen took a tentative sip and followed Mike back into the main room. Bright lights swept over the screen cloth, dazzling her eyes. Numerous objects, including tools, minuscule computer disks in their round jackets, and a reproduction of sunrise on Jupiter, hung from the Velcro patches. To one side, a three-dimensional array of plastic-coated foam formed what could have been abstract sculpture, furniture, or a jungle-gym. Nearer hung a tangle of webbing and trampoline cloth. Gretchen pointed at this last object.

"What's that?"

Mike glanced up.

"A spawning net."

"What's it for?"

A wry smile played momentarily over Mike's lips. "Sex."

"Really! What's it like?"

"Madam...we hardly know each other," he said dryly.

"I-I didn't mean..." Gretchen stammered, but she was laughing. Mike grunted and turned away, only then allowed himself a smirk. *Play it cool, Mikey Boy*, he thought to himself, *and you may net her yet.*

Aloud, he said only, "Look around, I want to check something."

While Gretchen sucked on her frozen coffee and tried to get the hang of swallowing without the aid of gravity, Mike floated over to where his helmet and gloves hung and hooked his belt tether to a ring on the wall. As he donned the helmet and gloves, his virtual computer appeared before him. Most computers in up-hall were virtual. Typing on a regular keyboard required some sort of set up to keep you from continually pushing yourself away from the keys.

Mike's program imitated the real thing close enough to satisfy him. It even made a clicking noise each time he tapped a virtual key.

When the Stellar Search logo came up, he typed the address for GF's public database and hit the virtual 'Enter' key. The air hummed. Then, a blindfolded angel floated before him holding a balance and a flaming sword. Around the angel were inscribed the Latin words for the Brotherhood of Watchers: *Grigori Fraternity*

Mike tapped the balance and found himself surrounded by the database's 'title page'. Around him spun three-dimensional images of GF's Most Wanted. Seeing them filled Mike with a familiar sense of pride in the GF and their accomplishments. So efficient were the Angels that the forty-seven men orbiting him in holo-effigy comprised the entire Solar System's list of known felons not currently in custody.

ID tags around the felon's necks displayed who they were, the nature of their crimes, and how long they had been on the Wanted list. The majority had been listed for less than three months. The number who had been at large for over a year could be counted on a single hand. One of them was the infamous smuggler Alvis Player. His holo image sneered jauntily at Mike. He was clad in a blue-and-gold Solaran flight suit. From his left hip hung a padded truncheon of the kind favored by mobsters.

At the sight of the truncheon, Mike's good cheer evaporated. He thought again of the mysterious weapon he had reached for during the fight in the corridor. Was one of these floating felons him? None of them looked like the image in his mirror but that gave him little comfort. Several of them had his build; including Player and the gruesome Paulio Torres.

The word 'Caught' flashed in large red letters across the image of the colony murderer, Bernard Kepler. Mike cracked a grim smile. At least, he knew now that he was not Kepler.

"Go get 'em, Angels!" he muttered.

It took him about twenty minutes to find all the information he sought. Tipping up his goggles as he finished, he was amused to find Gretchen floating free about the room, asleep, still clutching her empty coffee tube. Some of her hair had come free of her braid and floated gently about her head like wisps of red ribbon. Mike grinned, then pursed his lips and whistled a few notes of a popular tune his canned memory told him Gretchen liked. She opened her eyes.

"Did I fall asleep?" she asked, wiping at her face. "I don't even remember feeling tired."

"It's easy to fall asleep up here. Under gravity, your head would drop forward and give you a warning. Here, you just conk out. We call it Astronaut's Peril. All zero-gers have to deal with it. Even the early astronauts back in the 20th Century used to have this problem. Since their bodies did not have to do the extra work of moving against gravity, they would stay awake far longer than on Earth; finishing in just a few days all the experiments NASA had provided for their ten-day mission. However, once they got tired, they were out like a light...even if it was in the middle of an experiment."

"Sounds dangerous!"

"Sometimes, it can be. Nowadays you can buy no end of products which promise to flash lights or ring bells if you start to fall asleep. None of them work reliably, though. There's just no alternative for getting a good sleep before your shift."

"You mentioned not needing as much sleep...is that why spacer's shifts are so long?"

"Yeah, we're up longer, so we have more time on our hands. That nonsense about us having longer shifts because they're working us like slaves is crap." Mike scowled. "I hate those political activists who don't bother to check their facts. But that's neither here nor there. Let me tell you what I just found out."

"Okay," she said warily. "Um...about what?"

"According to GF's records, that fellow Graver never recovered from the disrupter blow. Apparently, the blade was dialed too high for his body type. A very rare occurrence. Says here he had been smuggling a particularly insidious encryption program called "Blank Book"—which is now thankfully out of the halls."

"No it's not!" Gretchen blurted.

Mike gave her a hard look. "Is that what you're up here to buy?"

"I...No! What do you mean?" Gretchen's voice squeaked. Mike grunted in disgust. A kitten could have told that she was lying.

"You smugglers disgust me. You have so little appreciation of the civilization you're trying to destroy. We live in the best period of all human history. Crime is virtually non-existent. There is not a station in the Solar System where a sixteen-year-old girl carrying a bag of cash sticks could not walk naked around the entire promenade in perfect safety. Even here in up-halls, among the lowest of the lows, there is little crime. Sure, there are still fights now and then, and a few petty thefts. But, there are few murders and fewer rapes. And even here, such crimes seldom go unpunished. This kind of freedom from fear would have been unimaginable to our ancestors, who were always either afraid of their governments or of each other.

"And what is the terrible price we pay for this freedom from fear? Do we have to kowtow to emperors? Or obey the rigors of a fascist regime? No! All we have to do is agree to open our records to the Angels.

"But, you smugglers—you ingrates! If you succeed in your schemes, you'll destroy our entire way of life! You'll allow criminals to hide their wrong doings...and for what gain? What will law-abiding citizens receive from the increase in crime in which your efforts will result?

"I could understand risking imprisonment in order to spread encryption, if our police were corrupt or brutal. But, the Angels are polite. They are seldom wrong and never personally involved. What need do we have to hide anything from...."

"Cut the crap!" interrupted Gretchen

"I beg your pardon?" Mike asked, taken aback.

"Listen to this poster-perfect drivel your spewing. No real person believes that nonsense."

"Plenty of people believe it," Mike objected. "I believe it myself."

She shook her head, her body shifting in counter-rotation to the jerky motion. "No you don't. No one could. The real Mike never believed this kind of shit. It's probably a canned opinion, added deliberately to your pseudo-persona."

"Can that be done?"

"Sure. In the interactive I played, there was a guy who was known for being unusually frightened of dogs. When he went into the witness protection program, they altered his pseudo-persona so that he loved dogs—so that no one would suspect it was the same guy."

"That was a game," Mike said doubtfully.

"True, but it was based on the latest technology," Gretchen

countered.

As unnerving as it was to know that his memories were not his own, it was worse to contemplate that his opinions might not be his either. Mike was not sure he bought it.

"Why would I have deliberately altered my pseudo-persona to believe our society is worth defending?"

"Isn't it obvious?" she cried. "It's because you're hiding from the Angels! You didn't want to have any opinions that might bring you to their attention. So, you indoctrinated your new persona with respect for the status quo. Now, you're at ease in their presence—just like the guy who had been afraid of dogs."

"Okay, you seem to have an answer for everything. Tell me, why exactly am I hiding from the Angels?"

Gretchen smiled triumphantly. "Because you're really an encryption smuggler, of course!"

"And you've come to this conclusion...how?"

"Why else would you have gone to the trouble of making yourself believe that Unlimited Access bullshit?"

Mike frowned darkly. He found the idea that he might be an encryption smuggler distasteful. In his heart, he felt he sincerely believed in Unlimited Access and the blessings it brought to their society. He believed that the loss of privacy was more than made up for by the safety and security it provided.

Of course, he had no way of telling whether this belief was actually his or not.

After all, many of Mike Boucher's memories felt real—such as his memories of the night he and Gretchen had spent on a beach on Earth, the one time he had kissed her. It seemed real, yet that memory had clearly belonged to the other Mike. So, maybe Gretchen was right. Maybe, his beliefs had been faked. Well, better an encryption smuggler than a rapist or a murderer.

"You could be right," he muttered grudgingly.

Gretchen smiled with girlish delight . She was floating near the center of the room, doing slow somersaults around one of the heavier guide lines.

"I've figured out who you really are!"

"You have?"

"You said you'd been here for three months right? Three

months ago, Alvis Player disappeared. Now, I just so happen to know that Alvis Player is an excellent pseudo-persona technician, and you have his build. As to your face... that's pseudo skin, isn't it?"

"Yes."

"Do you have the restoration sequence?"

"Yes..."

"Run it!" she spun around the guide line a like a happy child. "We'll see what you really look like!"

"No." Mike crossed his arms, which caused him to drift backward.

"Oh!...Please!" she begged.

"No! And that's final." His voice cracking harshly. "How'd a nice girl like you get mixed up in something as shady as encryption smuggling anyway? You mentioned that you'd been pregnant. Don't you have a child to home to?"

"I have a child...a perfect child." Gretchen's face became a mask of pain, but as her back was currently to Mike, he did not see it.

"Every mother thinks her kid's perfect," he smiled kindly.

"In my case, it was the GF who thought he was perfect." Gretchen snapped back bitterly.

"He was chosen as Angel material!" Mike was impressed.

Gretchen voice grew flat with anger. "They took my son. Those bastards stole my little boy."

"Oh....How did it happen?"

"A routine scan of my pocketpad on the street revealed his medical records. They liked what they saw, so they just walked up and took him. If I had had even the most rudimentary right to privacy, I would still have my son."

"What did your husband say?"

"Ex-husband," she snapped. "He was flattered, the bastard! Can you imagine? They stole our son, and he was flattered."

Mike grunted. He would have been flattered too, but he thought it impolitic to say so.

"So, that's why Arch Agent Raphael saluted you. You're the mother of one of their future members."

"Yeah," Gretchen muttered angrily. Clearly, it galled her.

"Look, I understand you're angry...but how is smuggling

encryption programs going to help you? If your files had been encrypted, the Angels would merely have arrested you for possession of illegal software."

"That's why Blank Book's so important," she replied intently. "It covers up your data in such a way that a scanner won't know it even exists. It can be used by anyone, and it can't be detected."

"The Angels will have it cracked soon enough."

"Not if the Angels never get their hands on it. If what Mackie said is correct, Pete Graver was not actually carrying Blank Book."

Gretchen had been drifting slowly toward the wall as she slid along the guide line. As she gestured, her hand knocked into a small, leather-wrapped rod held in a Velcro clip. She pulled the rod from the wall and peered at the object, puzzled. A strange tightness gripped Mike's chest. The same uncomfortable feeling he felt whenever he picked the leather-wrapped thing up himself.

"Put it back!" he said brusquely.

"What's this thing?"

"I don't know."

"Then, why do you have it?"

"Only thing I brought with me from my old life."

"Have you unwrapped it? It could be a high-tech encryptor! I saw one once shaped a lot like this." She examined the rod, looking for the end of the leather wrap.

"Don't! Just leave it! Messing with that thing makes me uncomfortable."

"See…more pseudo-persona programming. If you kept it, and bothered programming yourself to leave it alone, it's got to be important. And probably illegal!"

Mike had no trouble believing this strange chest-tightening emotion was artificial. The shortness of breath and tension in the pit of his stomach he was experiencing felt like what he expected of neural programming. Resisting the sense of rising panic, he inspected the rod closely for the first time. The size and shape exactly fit the unknown calluses on his right hand. He turned his hand over, but there were no accompanying calluses on his knuckles. Well, at least he had not used the thing for punching people.

Gretchen reluctantly put the rod back in its clip. Then, she pushed off the wall and floated closer. Mike noted the curve of her bosom as her body arched effortlessly through the air, the pleasant color of her complexion, how long and thick her lashes were. As she drifted even closer, he could smell her perfume again. The sweet, heady smell went directly to his head…and other places.

"Come on, Mike. Show me your real face. You owe me that much. After all, you know my dread secret. You could get me arrested as a smuggler in an instant. If you show me your real face, we'll be even."

"What if I'm not who you think I am?"

"Then, you're not."

"What if I'm someone else you recognize—a wanted rapist or murderer?"

She laughed. "You don't strike me as the type."

"That's Mike Boucher's personality you're judging by," Mike reminded her.

"You're Alvis Player, Mike. You've got to be. The coincidences are too close."

Mike thought about the truncheon in the GF holo-portrait. He and Player did look something alike, he admitted reluctantly. Then there was the matter of the pseudo-persona. It would take an expert technician like Player to design a program as complicated the one Gretchen believed Mike was currently using. Could he be same arrogant bastard whose holo-image had so recently sneered at him?

"Isn't Player a murderer too?" he asked glumly.

Gretchen looked disgusted. "They call it murder if anyone dies in connection with a felony. I think they're stretching the law in Alvis's case."

"What happen?"

"About three months ago, the Angels caught Alvis Player, brought him in to go on trial. While on the way to the courthouse, Player tried to escape and was killed. After his death, they discovered the corpse was not Player—just some guy with an Alvis Player pseudo-persona."

"And they're pinning his death on Player?"

"They're claiming Alvis inflicted the pseudo-persona on the

guy involuntarily, which is a felony. But they don't really have any evidence to support this. The man could have been a volunteer, a member of our movement."

It took Mike a moment to understand. "You mean this interplanetary criminal Player is some kind of hero to this movement of yours?"

"He's a freedom fighter! He brings hope to those who suffer under GF's oppression."

"What GF oppression?" Mike asked.

"Those who don't believe that the Angels should have the right to violate our privacy," Gretchen replied haughtily.

"And how many of these people are law-abiding citizens like you? How many were just minding their business when they had a run in with the Angels?"

"H-hey, that's not..." "Gretchen stammered uncertainly.

"Very few, huh? Let me guess....most of them are petty criminals like Mackie Maloney, aren't they? People who don't fall under GF jurisdiction because they haven't committed a felony yet—but who are afraid the Angels will find out about some petty misdemeanor of theirs. Tell me, Gretchen, how many cases do you know of Angels abusing their position?"

"Other than taking my son?" she countered hotly.

"Angel's have 'right of recruitment' and you know that. Arch Agent training has to be started at a very young age," Mike said gruffly. "So, yes, other than your son."

"I-I can't think of one, off hand." She evaded his gaze and was silent for a moment. Then, she rallied her spirits and declared, "But, that's not what this is about. This is about principle. Just because Angels have never been caught abusing their power much doesn't mean they never will be. Our laws should be designed to protect us from unnecessary searches, from enforced self-incrimination. All we want is to go back to the same protections as the ancient Bill of Rights."

"And this has something to do with Player?" Mike asked dubiously

"Alvis Player believes all men should have the right against self-incrimination. To this end, he has broken the law, smuggled encryption codes, and risked his life numerous times. He's one of the few hopes people who desire privacy have. He even designed a special pseudo-persona, to help show the Angels why a decent, law-abiding citizen might want privacy. Unfortunately, he could only get one of them to try it, and nothing came of it...but it was a terrific idea!" Her eyes sparkled with emotion. It made her look very lovely. "It's one of the things that makes us admire him so."

"And you think I'm him?"

"Yes." Her cheeks and throat had grown flush with her enthusiasm. Mike liked the effect. He glanced surreptitiously at his unused spawning net. Women liked to give themselves to their heroes, or so he had heard. If he was Player...

"You could come with me to meet Joe," Gretchen was saying excitedly. "Think how excited he'd be to meet Alvis Player!"

"I'd be careful about this Joe fellow if I were you," Mike growled. "Mackie Maloney lied about having checked him out."

"How do you know? I don't think Mackie was lying...why would he? Come on, Mike....please let me see your real face! I promise, I won't tell anyone." She smiled sweetly, bringing a tantalizing life to her features that made her very difficult to resist.

"Not even me?" Mike asked sternly.

"You don't want to know?...then, not even you," she swore.

"Oh...all right."

Mike touched his face until his fingers felt the three, tiny, tension plates deep within the gel beneath the pseudo skin. He tapped in the restoration code.

"The stuff doesn't come off easily, but it will move to mimic my real features. Basically, I'll look like myself only heavier."

The pseudo skin began to slide. The sensation was odd, but not uncomfortable. Mike waited patiently, making sure that there were no reflective surfaces in his line of sight. Gretchen curled and uncurled eagerly, avidly watching his features as they changed. The pseudo skin crawled across his face for a time, then grew still.

"Sweet Jesus!" whispered Gretchen, her pupil's widening with horror.

"So, I'm not Player, eh?" he said, his heart sinking. "Do you recognize me then? Some murderer or rapist from the Wanteds?"

Gretchen was nodding wordlessly. She pulled herself along the nearest guide line, moving rapidly away from him. Mike touched his face and rapidly tapped in the masking code. The pseudo skin began crawling back to its former position.

"It's all right," he said, "I'm putting it back. You can forget you ever saw the real thing."

"I...I have to go!" Gretchen cried. She turned and began moving toward the door as rapidly as she could, using a guide line to aid her flight. Mike made no move to stop her. After all, he could not blame her. What woman in her right mind would want to remain alone in a room with a psychopath...even if that psychopath happened to believed he was one of her oldest friends?

✦

He drifted purposelessly for a while amidst the flashing colors emanating from his walls; unable to motivate himself. He wished he could turn back the chronometer and return to his previous state of ignorance. Knowing he was once a wanted criminal sucked.

Time passed, he slept a bit, forced himself to eat a tube of paste—a form of torture in itself—and called in sick to his next shift. The shift manager expressed concern, commenting that he had never missed a shift before. Mike mumbled that he would be all right and hung up. Then, he stretched out and faced himself.

So, he was the worst of men, and all his fine thoughts and civic impulses were borrowed from a better man. Because of this, he had lost the only attractive and charming woman he had met since coming to Ceres VI-D. He had been a fool to give in and let her see his face. If he had not, she might be in his arms right now. He should have never allowed her to talk him into changing his mind. He had gone soft.

The hope that he could atone for past sins by forsaking his former self and embracing his new personality presented itself temptingly. Surely, his moral actions were a matter of choice, and he could choose to reform. But, he knew it was bullshit. At any moment, some mysterious stimulant might trigger the eject command on the pseudo-persona and return him suddenly to his former, sordid self. Since he did not know anything about how his former self thought, he could make no predictions as to whether the improvements of his new personality would remain or vanish like smoke in an air recycler. That left only one option. Sighing, Mike pushed off the nearest wall and drifted over to his helmet and gloves.

It was time to do the right thing and turn himself in.

As the Stellar Search logo came up, Mike noted absently that it was already the next day. Gretchen would be meeting with Joe about now. Figuring he could put off his arrest a few minutes, he hacked into the hawkeye circuits, overrode the red-alert lights, and entered the coordinates for the corner of Red 520 and Red 506. It was an easy hack. Any station technician could do it. Then, he waited while the hawkeye became active and reported its image.

Sure enough, Gretchen, looking sleek and lovely in her blue jumpsuit and helmet, was talking with a tall man wearing black peddler's garb and a sleek 'smugglers' mug-guard. The two of them floated just inside corridor 520, an ugly corridor where someone had tried to cut costs by replacing the rubbish nets with Tacki-coat, a type of paint to which objects were supposed to stick. This Tackicoat was of a poor grade, however. Not only could it not hold the rubbish which had been pressed against it, but the Tackicoat itself drifted away from the bulkhead in long, taffy-colored ten-drils.

Joe was speaking. Mike found his voice syrupy and annoying.

"…was expecting someone else. Don't want to make any mistakes, you know. I'll have to take you to see my boss."

"Great!" chimed Gretchen. She still had her aft-grippers hooked to the transit cable and was slowly revolving as she spoke. Currently, her head was nearly ninety degrees away from Joe's. "I'd love to meet your boss. I'm always eager to make more contacts in our organization."

"Yes, of course. He's right this way. Believe me, he'll be delighted to meet you too."

Back in his apartment, Mike slammed his hand into his fist, growling. "Damn it, Gretchen, can't you see he's lying? That man is about to betray you! The bastard!"

The computer interpreted his motion as the disconnect gesture. As he went to login again, Mike found himself suddenly wondering: How *did* he know Joe was lying?

For that matter, how had he known Mackie Maloney was lying?

Or Gretchen? A great many memories rushed by; his attitude about encryption; how it differed from the obviously programmed reaction to the leather-bound rod; his zero-g fighting skills; the calluses on his right hand; Gretchen's expression when she saw his real face.

With a sudden burst of clarity, Mike knew what Gretchen had seen...and who Joe's boss must be.

Hesitating only to grab the mysterious rod from its clip, Mike tossed on his mug-guard and rushed toward Red 520, overriding the cycle lock of his foyer and letting precious private air spill into the stale corridor.

Mike reached the intersection where Gretchen had been speaking with Joe in record time. As he rounded the corner into 520, he could hear voices coming from the nearest hatch, which was slightly ajar. He avoided the writhing, putty-like tendrils of Tackicoat that drifted from the bulkheads, causing the corridor to resemble an underseascape, or perhaps someone's intestines, and moved toward the hatch. The corridor was cluttered with free-floating trash. Mike had to bat aside expended batteries, old squeeze tubes, and a shoe.

Ahead of him, coming directly toward his face, floated a globular ball of dark yellow liquid. He swore and grabbed the transit cable, throwing his leg around it so as to swing his body perpendicular to its former position. The bobbing ball drifted by him, leaving a faint acrid scent of ammonia, discernible even through his mug-guard. Mike pushed off toward the hatch, muttering in disgust, "Whoever is responsible for that should have their johnson tied off!"

Despite the poor quality of air, Mike removed his mug-guard and attached it to his belt. The stench was less than he had expected, as if the air had been cleaned recently. Tapping in the restoration code on the pseudo skin pressure plates, he felt the fake skin sliding across his nose and cheeks, restoring his natural features. Then, he carefully unwrapped the leather from around the rod. Beneath, gleamed a metallic cylinder with a dial at one end. Mike adjusted the dial and grasped the rod in his right hand. The cylinder fit perfectly, nestling snugly against his calluses. He slid one finger over the 'on' plate and waited, listening.

From within the hatch, he heard Gretchen. Her voice trembled with fear, but she spoke bravely, as if refusing to be cowed.

"You murdered Peter Graver, didn't you? So no one would ever learn that he was not the real encryption smuggler. And the fake Alvis Player? Did you deliberately kill him too?"

The answering voice was cool, melodic, and beautiful. Hearing it confirmed all Mike's suspicions. Normal men did not have such voices. It was the voice of an Angel.

"It is so, and now you shall join them."

"No! Please! I won't tell anyone what I've figured out. I swear!"

"Are you willing to turn your back on this cause and return to an ordinary life?"

"N-no!"

"Then, you must die. If you continue among the encryption smugglers, you will eventually be caught. You will be questioned by the GF, and the truth will come out–whether you wanted it to or not. Tell me, how much does this cause mean to you?"

Despite her fear, Gretchen's voice rang out confident and clear. "It means everything to me! I would give my life for it! Men must be allowed to live in privacy and peace!"

"If you believe so strongly in this cause, surely you wish it to prosper. Therefore, I ask you. Whom do you believe can do more for our cause, spread encryption more widely, and better protect those who wish to use it? You or I?"

"...You," Gretchen whispered, defeated.

"You have already said that you would give your life for our cause—that is all that I am asking. I would prefer it were otherwise. We should never have met. Had Mackie Maloney come as expected, Joseph would have gone ahead with the exchange. He believed he was part of a GF sting effort. When an unknown contact showed up, Joseph thought it would please the Angels if he brought you in right away. If you had not tried to resist arrest by revealing you knew of my connection to this matter, I would have seen that you merely received a slap on the wrist as a first-time offender. Unfortunately, that is not what came to pass. So, you must die to ensure our efforts remain secret."

"But, there is no point in killing me," Gretchen cried desperately. "GF already knows there is a traitor in their midst. They're onto you."

"What evidence causes you to say this?" asked the Angel softly.

Gretchen's voice grew defiant. "Why else would GF bother putting an Angel under cover?"

A slow, grim smile flickered across Mike's lips. That was his cue.

There was an intercom on the bulkhead beside him. He pressed the button and softly called for security, identifying his suspect and giving his real name. Then, activating the device in his right hand, he pressed the switch to swing open the hatch door.

***

Mike dove into the room head first, curling lengths of crimson energy leaping from the hilt in his hand to form the humming disrupter blade. The air within, recently cleaned by the Angel's layers of smart-mesh, was crisp and fresh. Breathing deeply, he spoke in a deep and authoritative voice.

"Agent Sariel of the Grigori Fraternity, I place you under arrest for the murder of Peter Graver, the attempted murder of Gretchen Clark, and for charges of encryption smuggling to be enumerated later."

The Angel Sariel floated effortlessly in the midst of the chamber. Layers of gossamer smart-mesh wafted about him forming indigo robes. To either side, his ocular mantle stretched from his shoulders like jet black wings gleaming with a thousand unblinking eyes. The glowing ring above his head cast a pearly white light, illuminating the small steel maintenance chamber. In his hand, his disrupter burned with azure fire.

Across the small chamber from the Angel, Gretchen clung to a steel sitting bar, her helmet in her hand. Her face was pale despite her caramel skin. A look of desperation and hope glimmered in her eye.

The Angel was oriented such that, as he entered, Mike found himself looking at him from beyond his micro-rocket studded boots. The Angel arched his wings, focusing a few of his myriad opticals on the newcomer. Upon beholding Mike, his perfect composure shattered momentarily.

"Arc-Arch Agent Michael!"

Mike regarded the other Angel coolly. His disrupter buzzed in his hand.

"What made you do it, Sariel?" he asked. "Why turn aside from our sacred precepts? Why destroy the system we know and love?"

Sariel inclined his perfect head and smiled. "We call ourselves the Grigori Fraternity. Do you know who the real Grigori of mythology were? Not angels of heaven, but fallen angels who loved the Earth too well to return to their appointed place in Paradise. When God called them back, they turned their backs on Heaven, choosing instead to remain in the world and teach humanity all the secret arts they knew—so that Man would prosper.

"I took a good look at our fellow man," Sariel continued, "and found that I loved what I saw. I felt pity for those who did not have what we have. I decide it was time we lived up to the true nature of our heritage and gave Man his secrets back."

Mike listened silently, eyes narrowing. When Sariel finished, he growled. "So, you decided to break our laws and start killing your own co-conspirators out of pity? Bah! Let me guess...you were the Angel who accepted Alvis Player's offer to see what it was like to live and think like a normal man?"

Sariel nodded solemnly.

Mike continued. "Did you check afterward to see if the program was entirely removed? Or did you leave your mind open to the machinations of Player, one of the few men who has ever routinely escaped the GF? Are you certain your current thoughts are your own, and not some copy of your mind installed by Player, after he tinkered with some of your basic opinions?"

The other Angel's face remained calm, but his voice betrayed surprise. "Can that be done?"

"Apparently, it can," Mike replied grimly.

"I did not know how to check....But, I take responsibility for all my actions, whether or not it turns out my mind was tampered with."

"Good man."

"All my actions—including this one." Sariel, his face still composed in inhuman serenity, floated toward Mike. In his right hand, his azure disrupter blazed. "The cause of freedom and privacy must live. Therefore, I fear you too must die, Brave

Michael."

From somewhere deep inside of Mike, cheerful, derisive laughter rose.

"*You* want to fight *me*?"

"It will be no contest. You may be the great Battle Angel Michael, but I wear maneuvering rockets and my mantel. You do not."

Mike considered. Without all his memories back fully in place, he had no way of knowing if the supreme confidence he felt was justified. Sariel's rockets might not give him any advantage in so small a chamber. On the other hand, he could not be certain that he would remember what to do once the fight began.

He said evenly, "Perhaps, you are right. Or, perhaps not."

Sariel pointed his toes and glided forward. The automated eyes on his outswept wings glittered with activity. His disrupter blazed with azure fire.

Mike, still gliding near Sariel's feet, was pelted with ice crystals from the cold, compressed air propelling the Angel's micro-rockets. As Mike was beyond his feet, the Angel was forced to come about before Mike would be in his striking range. Mike took advantage of the delay and let his momentum carry him to the nearest wall.

The room in which they were about to fight was a standard prefab plug, designed to work efficiently at any level of the station. The bare metal walls were equipped with both sitting bars and ladders. Four shallow alcoves allowed access to maintenance crawlways. Round doors, flush with the wall, concealed switch-boards and fuse boxes. At two places, large Velcro pads held vaguely dumbbell-shaped fire extinguishers. What dim light the room provided issued from strips of screen cloth. Most of the il-lumination currently lighting the chamber came from Sariel's shining halo and from the two blazing weapons.

Mike moved the nearest fire extinguishers, pulled it from its restraint, and hooked his arm about the middle of it. Out of the corner of his eye, he could see Gretchen moving from sitting bar to ladder to sitting bar in an effort to reach one of the shallow alcoves and move out of the way of the combatants. He waited a moment, until he saw that she was safely in the alcove, then launched himself away from the wall at an oblique angle to Sariel's current path.

Sariel moved his feet and changed course. His sable wings curved, helping to guide him as a sail or rudder might guide a ship. He came bearing down on Mike, his burning sword thrumming in his hand. As soon as he was in range, he swung at Mike and would have struck his shoulder, had Mike not successfully parried.

A shower of purple sparks erupted as the crimson and azure disrupters crossed, momentarily coloring the otherwise dim bare metal walls. Sariel's micro-rockets and ocular mantle quickly compensated for the force imparted by clashing blades. Mike, however, was not so lucky. The impact of his parry sent him spinning wildly.

Sariel tried to turn and come after him immediately, before Mike regained his bearings. However, the Angel did not have enough room to maneuver. There was a rackety sound as the delicate eyes along his sable wings brushed against the metal wall. He tried to use his micro-rockets to back away, but succeeded only in thrusting himself shoulder first into one of the ladders. Eventually, he was forced to reach out with his hand and push himself away from the wall, before he could make effective use of his boots again.

All of this gave Mike a chance to regain his bearings. He too had been thrown against a wall, though he managed to get a hand out in front of him, and to get his disrupter out of the way, before the collision. His wrist smarted, but he was able to successfully launch again.

Sariel came upon him just as Mike passed the room's midpoint. The Angel approached from behind, and Mike was hard pressed to parry behind his head. He blocked successfully, but found himself spinning again. With a skill he did not recall learning, he clenched and spread his limbs in a series of maneuvers that steadied his course.

This left him revolving in mid-air, his momentum slowing. Sariel was approaching again. The crackle of his weapon grew louder. Mike wondered fleetingly how many of his own victims had lost hope when confronted with that same crackle.

Out of options, Mike released the fire extinguisher with a

well-calculated push. The change in mass altered his direction and momentum. He veered off to the left, out of Sariel's path. In the narrow, confined space, the Angel could not maneuver quickly enough to cut Mike off before he reached the wall.

After a quick glance at the trajectory of the rebounding fire extinguisher, Mike sailed toward Sariel, swinging his blade horizontally across his chest. Sariel, swirling toward him in a vision of blue, brought his own weapon down from over his head, like a samurai. Mike adjusted his attack to block the other Angel's blow, and their weapons crossed in a shower of violet.

As he spun away, his concentration was momentarily disrupted by a sudden, returning memory from his real past—a glimpse of himself streaming through the vacuum of space enveloped in layers of vermilion gossamer, with his crimson disrupter crackling in his hand. Much as he desired to recall his real self, he could not afford to become distracted now. He concentrated on Mike Boucher and the battle.

As he had planned, the fire extinguisher, which had rebounded from the wall, now sailed toward Sariel's back. The glimmering automated eyes dotting the black wings saw the object coming, but even with his micro-rockets, Sariel could not swerve quickly enough to avoid it. The extinguisher struck him in the leg, sending him sprawling. As he spiraled away, Mike managed to grab the rebounding extinguisher again and bounced off the nearest wall.

The metallic chamber echoed with Sariel's calm, yet ironic voice. "Surely, you do not expect a fellow Angel to fall for the same trick twice?"

Mike did not bother to answer.

Sariel had nearly collided with the wall again. However, he was now back in the center of the chamber. He flew head-first toward Mike's chest, his sword stretched out before him, so that he looked down his burning blade. If Mike did not move, the other Angel's disrupter would impale him.

Mike waited until the Angel was nearly upon him, then briefly squeezed the trigger on the fire extinguisher, which he had carefully positioned near his center of gravity. The spray of white liquid simultaneously sprayed the Angel and sent Mike flying backward and away.

The cold liquid splattered over the Angel's face, causing him to cry out. His disrupter flickered, darkening briefly where the foaming fire retardant sprayed over it. Even with his human eyes blinded by the white foaming fire retardant, Sariel refused to be daunted. He continued toward Mike relying on his glittering ocular mantle to guide him.

Mike had been thrown into the nearest wall. There, he caught ahold of one of the ladders. Wrapping an arm around a ladder rung, he sprayed himself with the fire extinguisher. The biting cold of the liquid passed through his jumpsuit, numbing the skin on his arms and chest. As the liquid became foam, however, the coldness dissipated somewhat. Stuffing the fire extinguisher between two rungs, he launched his foam-covered body toward the blinded Angel.

The two men flew at each other, flaming blades poised. Their positions were askew, so that to Mike, Sariel seemed to be gliding on his side. Sariel maneuvered his boots to alter his position slightly, bringing him closer to upright from Mike's point of view.

Then, they were in range.

Both Angels swung. Only, as he did so, Mike thumbed his disrupter off and on. As the two weapons met, the field forming Mike's weapon dissolved, offering no resistance. A moment later, it crackled back to life, and Mike's disrupter was inside Sariel's guard.

Both blades struck their targets simultaneously, throwing the combatants apart. Mike's blow landed full across Sariel's indigo chest, causing the Angel to start violently, then sag. As Sariel's weapon entered the fire-retardant foam covering Mike's body, however, it flickered and went dark. Mike was sent sailing safely away before the disrupter recovered and flared back to life.

He had won.

Sariel floated unconscious, his jet-black mantle folded like sable wings about the indigo length of his body. Mike switched off his disrupter and clipped it to his belt, right where he had reached for it during the fight over Maloney's knife. After checking the other Angel's pulse, turning off the other disrupter, and wiping the fire retardant foam from his closed eyes, Mike secured Sariel to the wall and bound his hands with his belt tether. Then, he went to check on Gretchen.

She was hovering in the small alcove, watching with pale face and wide eyes. Her helmet had gotten away from her somehow and was floating freely in another part of the room. As Mike approached, she smiled tentatively. Mike rotated so that his feet oriented toward hers and met her smile with a cheerful one of his own.

"Thank you for saving me," she whispered, her smile widened fleetingly. Her wide, dark eyes reminding Mike of a frightened deer. "I'm sorry I ran away yesterday..."

Mike nodded brusquely, then asked. "Sariel claimed you accused him of being part of the smuggling when he tried to arrest you. How did you know he was corrupt?"

"It was a guess," she admitted, "based on two things. One, you said that Peter Graver's death was unusual—that Angels did not usually make mistakes with their disrupters. And two, your identity. I recognized you as the Arch Agent Michael right away. Why would one of the most famous Angels be hiding from the other Angels unless there was a traitor in their midst, one he was trying to smoke out?"

They were hovering close together. Gretchen moved her arm and she began to spin. She caught Mike's shoulder to steady herself. This close, he could smell the scent of her body, even over the pungent odor of the fire retardant still coating his clothes. He caught her head in his hands and kissed her.

With a little sigh, she wrapped her arms tightly about his waist, and they clung together in a tight embrace, unmindful of how their motions spun them or of the foaming fire retardant pressed between their bodies. Mike slid his hand over her soft jumpsuit, caressing her as he had wanted to do since he first saw her. Her hands clutched more tightly at him...pressing against his back. Through the fabric of his suit he could feel the pressure of the tiny disk hidden in her palm. His face hardened, and he pushed her away.

"Gretchen Clark," he announced sternly, his voice grave and impersonal. "You are under arrest for the crime of encryption smuggling."

Gretchen tried to pull away. Mike grabbed her wrist and held her in place. Twice, she tried to wriggle free, but Mike merely used her lack of training to aid him in securing her. Tears came into her eyes.

"I haven't done anything!"

"You accepted the disk containing the contraband Blank Book. That was enough. Or do you claim this disk contains something else?"

"Please," she begged. "Hasn't my experience taught you anything? Don't you understand how unfair our current laws are?"

Mike frowned. "I am an Angel, a guardian of the Law. Our laws are the fairest Mankind has ever known."

"But, my son..."

"You do not remember what life was like before the GF. You say you miss your son. Can you imagine what it would have felt like to lose him to a random shooting? Or worse, a kidnapping—where you might never know, for the rest of your life, whether he was alive or dead?

"Modern kidnap victims are recovered in a matter of days, if not hours. Because kidnappers cannot move their victims or provide for them without leaving computer records for the Angels to trace. Would you rather the Angels were unable to return those children to their anxious parents? That will be the result if encryption becomes commonplace. Before the Angels, kidnapped children were often never found. We are not talking about a handful of missing children, mind you; but about thousands upon thousands of children; ripped from their homes never to be heard of again. Is this the state to which you would have civilization return?"

Silver tears glistened on Gretchen's thick red lashes. Finally, she whispered. "But you said the other day that our system only worked because the Angels were incorruptible. What happened today proves that there are corrupt Angels. Doesn't that change anything?" When Mike did not answer, she cried out, exasperated. "Don't you Angels feel any pity?"

"We are servants of Justice. Only Fallen Angels feel pity."

⁂

He waited while the security guards bound Gretchen and the unconscious Sariel. As she was pulled out the hatch, Gretchen threw him a last anguished look over her shoulder. He met her imploring gaze with the coolness of a GF agent, impregnable and unapproachable. Defeated, Gretchen averted her eyes and let herself be led away.

Arch Angel Michael watched until Gretchen was no longer in sight. With his familiar disrupter back in his hand, Mike Boucher's life parted like a dream, and his own memory returned. His work here was done. He could go back to the cool, clean halls of GF headquarters and return to his proper life.

Yet, he remained, hovering in the empty chamber. Between his fingers, he held the tiny silver disk containing the Blank Book encryption codes. As he gazed at the disk for which Gretchen had been willing to give her life, the first faint hints of a troubled frown began to disturb his perfect, angelic face.

Foot-Sore Angel

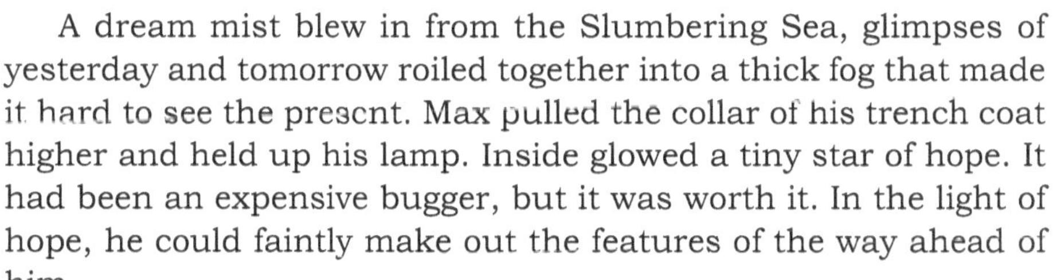

*This story takes place in the background
of Pathfinder's* Coliseum Morpheuon

MAX SHEFFIELD ROLLED HIS SHOULDERS, CAUSING HIS TRENCH COAT to rustle, and scratched at the stubble on his chin. He stared at the shimmering silver scroll in his hand. Above his head, his halo was on the fritz again. It buzzed irritatingly. Max slapped it twice. It flickered and then winked back on, its cheery neon glow a reminder of everything wrong in his life.

"Whatcha got there?" asked Sam Clam, the proprietor of the undersea cabaret where Max liked to hang out. Sam liked Max's company. Even more, he liked the fact that his bar stools did not scuttle toward the dart board and his dance floor did not morph into a swimming pool while Max was present.

Max held the gleaming document up for the bartending clam to see. "Celestial summons."

Sam whistled, no easy feat for a clam. "Not a place you'd normally go."

"That's the understatement of the..." Max made a vague gesture with his hand, "however we measure time here."

"Gonna respond?"

"Would you ignore one of these?"

"Good point."

A dream mist blew in from the Slumbering Sea, glimpses of yesterday and tomorrow roiled together into a thick fog that made it hard to see the present. Max pulled the collar of his trench coat higher and held up his lamp. Inside glowed a tiny star of hope. It had been an expensive bugger, but it was worth it. In the light of hope, he could faintly make out the features of the way ahead of him.

The dream stuff of the shores of sleep was hard to navigate. Certain landmarks remained the same, eroding and changing into something new only over centuries as the expectations and beliefs of whole cultures changed. The rest of the landscape changed daily, hourly, sometime by the minute.

The wakies where he grew up had a saying that went: "If you don't like the mountain weather, wait twenty minutes. It'll change." Here, if you did not like the mountains, you could wait twenty minutes, and the entire countryside would change. Of course, there was no guarantee that the new one would be any better. Difficult terrain often stayed difficult. All that changed was what made it hard to cross.

Ahead of him, out of the fog, loomed a landmark he recognized, one of those that the Winds of Change weathered only slowly. The Crossroads of the Wandering Ways marked the meeting of three major dream paths. The paths always went to the same places. How long or short it took to traverse them changed as rapidly as the whim of a spoiled child.

As Max approached, the Chimera of the Wandering Way hunched on its great basalt boulder, its three heads guarding the three branches of the crossroad.

"Who goes there?" hissed the dragon head. It would be the dragon head—the fire-breathing one—that pointed in Max's direction.

"Nobody in particular," Max murmured, wishing he had put on his hood.

"Oh. It's you."

Max drew out a cigarette. He pressed it against his buzzing halo until it lit. The chimera snorted in disapproval.

Taking a puff, Max blew a plume of smoke in the creature's direction. "Yeah. It's me. Good to see you again, too. Frolicked in any autumn mist lately?"

"You came here to make sport of me? To mock me?"

"Never, old friend."

"Have you visited the ruins of Dylathleen lately?"

Max ignored the dig. He gestured toward the other two roads. "I'm looking for the way to Dreamport."

"One road leads to Dreamport. The other leads to the floating palace of Madam Equinox."

"Any chance of you telling me which one is which?"

All three heads turned and regarded him. The lion roared. The goat snorted. Then, they looked away again, leaving him with the dragon. Smoke curled from its nostrils.

"Thought not." Max took another drag.

"You!" The dragon eyes glittered with hate. "You had the opportunity to free me from this boulder where I am trapped, and you did not. I will not help you."

"Great. Thanks. Be that way."

Max glanced down at his hand. It had only been moments for him, but the cigarette's time had passed more quickly. It was already burned down to a stub. Damn dream time. He dropped it and crushed it under his boot.

Max chose the road guarded by the goat-head. It seemed the least threatening of the three. As he walked, the curling horns butted him from behind sending him sprawling. As he climbed to his feet and brushed off his trench coat, he consoled himself with the thought that at least he had not been set on fire.

The Floating Palace of Madam Equinox was a sight to behold. It hung in the air like an upright egg, all swirling black and white against a pale silver sky. When he first glimpsed the palace, it revolved far overhead. Then, he made the mistake of taking a single step in its direction. Next thing he knew, he was standing inside its presence chamber.

Madam Equinox herself was as beautiful as she was mysterious. But that kind of dame only led to one thing—trouble. Max turned to depart, but she motioned him over. She wore an elaborate headpiece and robes of swirling leaves that obscured the throne upon which she sat. Half of her face was that of a sweet-tempered woman with dark skin and wide features. Her other half was pale, and the look in her blue eye was icy and disdainful.

"Sorry, ma'am. Didn't mean to trouble you." Max tipped his halo. "I'll be going now."

"No one comes here by mistake. Do you know who I am?"

"I have heard of you, ma'am, rumors and dreams—but nothing substantial."

"Really?" She flicked open her black-and-white fan, regarding him over the top of it. "What do they say?"

Max gave a nervous shrug. "Some say you are the opposite of the Solstice King."

She laughed, a sound that was part-melodious and part-bitter. The fan closed with a snap. "My opposite? True in some ways. The Lord of the Hunt is always in motion. I never leave my throne. He finds love but never seeks it. I seek love and never find it."

"That can't be. A nice-lookin' dame like you."

She smiled. Her dual lips almost matched. "There are men who love summer and men who adore winter. But where is there a man who would embrace both?"

"Er...I see your point."

"I am a Harbinger of change." She leaned forward. "Your coming here means a life will change."

"My life?" Max asked somewhat nervously.

"Not necessarily."

"Change for the better? Or change for the worse?"

Her laughter was like the tinkle of a rushing stream leaping over jagged icicles. "When is change ever for the better?"

✦

When Max finally arrived at Dreamport, he felt bone weary. That thought evoked from him a dry chuckle. Folks back in the waking world looked forward to sleeping so that they could rest. Occasionally, Max recalled his waking life with longing, wondering if a few hours of alertness might restore whatever it was that seemed to have seeped from his soul.

Dreamport was a land of flowing fire and burning waters spun together. Twisters of fire, blown in from the Slumbering Sea, ranged across it. At the center of each tornado, snug in its eye, traveled buildings: mansions, towers, cottages, even stores. From time to time, the storms winds blew in such a way as to bring all these structures together to form a city. If one followed the right road, one could usually find it that way, at least for a short while.

Max stalked into that city. Below the glassy streets of solid wind, the flaming waters had calmed to form a burning lake. The river Brightspark flowed through the center of it. Salamanders and flame nymphs cavorted in its multi-colored flames. Above, like amazing moonlight, the wavery fires flowed and waltzed together.

Already, the waters of the blazing lake were rising and the dancing aurora descending. When they touched, they would set off whirlwinds that would lift the various parts of the city away from each other, and the cycle would begin again.

Max strode quickly through the town. He peeked out from under his hood, a huge black triangle of cloth, such as universities once awarded to their graduates. Some whom he passed were True Dreamers, some oneirobound, some willful minions of the Khan of Nightmares here to visit the markets or carry messages on their master's behalf. Others still were phantasms: beings spun of dream stuff, who existed only so long as they were dreamt of. Then, they faded away, their pale faces contorted with longing and sorrow as they reached out one last time, as if their insubstantial fingers could grasp the existence forever denied to them. Max hurried past, ignoring their painful pleas.

"Yeah. I know," he muttered, even though he knew they were not accusing him. "Could have made you real. I didn't. Get over it."

He made his way to the docks, where torrents of solid wind and sleet thrust out into the Slumbering Sea. Aways farther down the shore, he could make out the Brightdocks of the Khan's city, its waters glowing faintly with the same light cast by his Hope Lamp. It took only moments to find the vessel he sought.

Captain Starkadder leaned over the rail of his ship, *The Heart's Caprice*. His horns curved high above his moon-white hair. His saber, Dreamkiller, hung at his side. Around him, his ship floated like a vision, its masts higher than Max could imagine. Even with the light of the Hope Lamp, he could not distinguish its voluminous sails from the billowing clouds above.

"Ho, there? Do you desire passage?" Captain Starkadder called. "We set sail with dreamtide but still have room for three."

Max craned his neck upward and looked into the captain's face. This turned out to have been a mistake.

"Oh, 'tis you, is it?" the captain spat.

"It's me. Long time, no see." Max gestured at a crow's nest, high among the rigging. "My handiwork is still holding up, I see."

Beside the mast, flags hung on a long line. Max spotted a worn banner displaying a laughing child on the back of a three-headed monster. Seeing it did not bring the joy it once had.

"I'll not have your kind here," barked the captain.

"My kind!" Max laughed harshly. "What kind is *my kind* that it doesn't include *you*, bro?"

"They say ten thousand died the day the demon Kadesh fell from heaven. They say he holds court in the crater created by his fall, eating from the skulls of those killed by the impact."

"Yeah. Right. Heard all about it."

"You had the chance to free the God of Hope, whose blood, seeping from the wounds made by his bonds, lights the waters yonder. But you did not. I will not help you."

"Yeah. Yeah. Yeah. I know the drill."

Max threw back his hood. In the glare of his halo, the lines of the ship became crisp. The docks grew still and solid. All this steadiness alarmed the locals, who scuttled away from the neon light. *Poseurs*, Max thought, *they would not last a minute in the light of the sun.* But it was a bittersweet thought.

To the captain, he said, "You know, if I had freed your sleeping god, everyone else would still be mad at me. No one seems to think about that."

"'Tis nothing to me."

"My point exactly."

⁕

In the end, Max had to swim. Or rather, he walked. So long as he could keep his halo burning merrily, he could stiffen the dreamstuff of the Slumbering Sea enough to stride across it. But whenever his halo sparked, he fell into the sea. There, the waves tossed him around as neon storms that cared nothing for the tiny glow above his head rained down upon him.

He traveled by the light of the orange-and-green lightning flashes that flickered perpetually over the Slumbering Seas, or, when they grew quiet for a spell, by that of his Hope Lamp. The creaking of trees and the lowing of cattle played in his ears, though his eyes showed him no such objects. Occasionally, islands and dwelling places rose amidst the torrent of the phantastic. Max avoided these if he could, as encounters with other beings would only delay him.

It occurred to him a number of times that if he pulled off his trench coat, he could get there in a flick of a dream. A mixture of guilt and sorrow held him back. Besides, somebody would see him. He had gotten enough grief as it was. If this was how people treated him now, what would his life be like if the whole truth came out?

He passed flotillas bathed in the light of strange suns, islands of unnatural forests where outlandish trees with tattooed leaves snatched their meals from passing squads of multi-eyed squid. Once, he wandered too near the tall, rocky, windswept islands known as the Ghoulish Cliffs. A pack of ghouls chased him across the foamy wave stuff. To lose them, he had to run in the wrong direction for an immeasurable period. He finally lost them by running three times around a floating island filled with dancing sharks. The ghouls apparently found the isle's inhabitants more interesting than prey they could not catch.

Not everything was nightmarish. For a time, he rode on the back of a sky whale, and he spent a night at Tirfu Thuine, the stronghold of the Sea God Mannanan. Great living walls of shifting fish weeds kept back the wilder ocean. Within, the only solid thing was a single tear-shaped palace of crystal. The crystal broke the light into a myriad of scattered rainbow parts, so that to dwell in Tirfo Thuine was akin to living amidst eternally dancing lights. Outside the crystal, delicate creatures came to be and passed away, lasting but moments. Visiting courtiers watched and clapped.

Max ate his fill and watched the show, but he found these creatures even more disturbing than the phantasms. They did not even know enough to be sorrowful before they were snuffed out like yesterday's candles. He pulled his hood lower and hurried from the viewing chamber.

❖

At the very end, he really did swim. The seas around the island he sought were as calm as glass. No storm raged there. No nightmares plagued the waves. The waters would not respond to his will or his halo. But even though his soggy trench coat hung heavily upon him, he found the swim soothing, even rejuvenating, as if he were bathing in liquid peace.

He clambered out of the ocean onto the warm sand. The water sluicing from his trench coat was the only noise. A short walk led through a garden so serene and refreshing that by the time he reached the huge hall of white marble that dominated the island, he no longer felt weary. An aura of peacefulness radiated from the landscape. Max paused, recalling the silent, cathedral-like redwoods through which he had once hiked in what seemed now like a different life. Breathing deeply of the scent of rose and honeysuckle, he passed through the line of august columns and entered the wide, double doors behind them.

Blue sky stretched away from him studded with winged angels and cheerful, fat cherubim who hung frozen in a strange, motionless splendor. Glorious mountains, breathtaking vistas, shining golden cities with four-square walls all spread out from where he stood.

He had walked into paradise.

Directly in front of him, a marble floor cut through this the holy vista. It stretched into the distance far beyond where his eyes could see. Peering down it, he saw robed monks erecting scaffolding.

Max's eyes adjusted. It was all painted, a painted paradisiacal landscape that continued infinitely into the distance.

A brown-robed monk with a rope belt approached him, bowing. Max thought he caught the man frowning at the puddle forming around the hem of his trench coat.

"Welcome to the Halls of Painted Heaven. Have you come to lend a hand in the work?" the monk inquired hopefully.

Max flashed his silvery summons. The monk nodded solemnly, sighing. He gestured for Max to follow him, murmuring softly, "So much work, so few to help. Will more never be sent?"

Following his guide, Max shuffled forward, soaking wet and dripping with seaweed. His boots squeaked. They walked for some time, passing the scaffolding where monks worked silently, brushes in hand, paint pots softly clacking. Beside the monks, other individuals who had been pressed into service painted as well. Near them hung scrolls upon which descriptions of the dreams of the righteous—those who long for a place of bounty and eternal peace—had been faithfully recorded. Occasionally, the monks paused and consulted these scrolls to confirm that they were portraying the visions correctly.

Beyond the last row of scaffolding, the monk would go no farther. He gestured toward the way ahead of them.

"The messenger awaits."

"Er…thanks," muttered Max.

"When you are done—if you survive—please consider joining us, if even for a short time. We are always short-handed and can use help recording the dreams of the faithful." The monk bowed again and departed, leaving Max alone amidst partial images of celestial blossoms and winged travelers.

Max looked around for the messenger but saw only a glow in the distance. The glow grew brighter until it was so bright, Max had to shield his eyes and look away. His back bowed as the borrowed weight upon his shoulders grew unexpectedly heavy. Then, without it growing dim, the light no longer hurt him. Max looked up.

An angel stood before him, glorious and shining. Everything around stabilized and became solid. It was like being in the presence of Max's halo, only a hundred fold. Max almost felt awake.

The angel spoke in a voice like beautiful thunder. "We have a message for a denizen of the Slumbering, but she cannot hear our voice. Heaven has chosen you to bear it to her."

Max struck a cigarette against his halo. To his surprise, the soggy length lit.

"Why me?"

"It was thought you would appreciate this opportunity for penance."

"Oh." Max puffed on the cigarette. "That."

"You may do Heaven a service by carrying this message. It is an opportunity for redemption."

"Greaaat." He blew out a long plume of smoke.

"Will you bear it?"

"Why don't you do it yourself?"

"I cannot come further in or those near me will start to wake up."

"Aw. Too bad for them."

The angel took a step forward.

The painted hall vanished like the dream it was, and Max began to see the sleep lab at the Lucidity Institute. The IV he had talked Dr. LeBerge into allowing him, dripped into his arm. His mangled legs were covered by a fluffy blue comforter.

Disappointment flooded through him. He did not want to wake up. *Not now!*

The thought of being back in his crumpled body was bad enough, but it did not stop there. The sensation of waking continued, growing stronger, more demanding. The walls of the sleep lab grew translucent. With a certainty entirely unlike that which comes in dreams, Max realized that he was about to awaken again, into yet another world: a larger, greater place that shone with light.

Terror slid through his veins like a thousand slivers of ice. That kind of awakening went by a name all its own, a name no one enjoyed speaking aloud.

"I'll do it!" Max cried, terrified.

✳

Still dripping and squeaking, Max tromped along the frozen, neon-colored waves. He should have asked who the message was for before he agreed. Even death might be better than this. Or rather, death by waking up into some glorious afterworld—even if he was not allowed to stay in that place long. He knew all about bait-and-switch—was preferable to death by some painful, degrading method.

And that was what was going to happen when he reached the person for whom the message was intended.

Finally, he reached Dreamport just as the lake of burning water met the falling wavery fires. Max grabbed hold of a general store and held on for dear life as it was encased within a tornado and flung into the sky. He managed to cling to the door for a time. Then, he lost his grip and sailed into the violent winds.

A great deal of tossing about followed. Finally, he managed to yank off his hood and slap his halo until it snapped on again. The neon light around him flickered and grew brighter. The winds holding him calmed.

There was no way to get his trench coat off in time. So, of course, he fell.

✳

He landed in a crumpled heap and lay, groaning, in a forest where every leaf had an eyeball imbedded in it. All the nearby eyes swiveled to stare at him, making him feel even more awkward. He wished his halo would wink out, so he could use the ambiguity of dream to rearrange his many mangled limbs. Instead, it showed steady and bright, almost regaining its original brilliance. Perhaps, standing so near to a heavenly creature had infected it somehow.

The pain was intense. Max relived the screeching tires and crunching steel of the accident over again. Then, slowly, by jerks and tugs, he began to pull himself together.

As he writhed on the ground, thunder rolled in the distance and trumpets blared. No, not thunder, hoof beats. Hoof beats and the baying of hounds. Nor was it in the distance.

Max groaned.

"Aw. Why me?"

Auberyon, the Solstice King, towered above him. He stood over ten feet tall, his lithe, muscular form radiating power and majesty. Mighty antlers crowned his head. His feet were cloven hooves. Deerskin trousers clothed his lower body. His bare chest bore intricate scarlet tattoos. His mere presence was said to cause even the most callous of women to swoon. It did not have any such effect on Max.

Tempest hounds milled around Auberyon's feet, sniffing Max. The largest of them, a magnificent beast, growled at him.

"Nice to see you, too, Lai Elderon," Max murmured.

The Solstice King spoke, "Bear not the message, or it shall go badly for you!"

Max sighed and jerked his head around so that he could see the antlered figure more clearly. Neon light bathed the dogs. Auberyon froze and peered down at Max, his face entirely devoid of emotion.

"Oh, it is you."

"Yeah." His own voice sounded raspy. "It's me."

"Bear not the message. No good will come of it. You have already caused harm enough."

Max chewed on the inside of his cheek. Redemption was not a concept this guy would understand.

"Have to." He coughed. "I am compelled."

"Ah," the Solstice King inclined his head. "A geas."

"You...wouldn't happen to know the quickest way to the Witch of Stolen Hopes?"

Auberyon drew back. "I will not help you. You could have clothed all the worlds in forest, and you did not."

Max opened his mouth. The words: "You should have raised me better," made it to the tip of his tongue before he wrestled them back into his throat. The big guy would not grasp the humor of it.

Max settled for, "I was young."

"I hold that as no excuse."

Max shrugged. "Have it your way, Father."

Without another word, the Solstice King turned. Leaving Max lying in a heap, he thundered off into the forest of eyes, his hounds baying at his heels.

Of course, Max mused as he lay there, Auberyon had not raised him at all. That had been left to his mortal mother, whom the Solstice King had abandoned without a backward glance. His father had not even bestirred himself to inquire after his son when Max had arrived, pale and broken, on the shores of the Slumbering Plane after his accident. To him, Max was no different than any other object that could not be bedded or chased, of no interest whatsoever.

Dragging his arm back into its proper position with a Herculean effort, Max bit back a scream. Forget the time after the accident, Max mused, just now, his father had not even bothered to help his son up.

"Whaaat!" hissed Lady Puzzledeep, the Witch of Stolen Hopes.

She loomed above him in the alley behind the market where illicit dreams were bought and sold. The opened message dangled crumpled her hand. Slithering forward on the serpentine length that ran from her waist to the ground and continued on behind her, the lovely lillend spread her green and blue wings and bared fangs at Max.

Max drew back. He had not known she even had fangs. Good-looking chicks like her really should not have such deadly choppers.

And this is the problem with dreams, Max thought. He was in the alley, but he could hardly remember how he had gotten there. How had he approached? When had he handed over the message? Moments like this made him long for the security of the waking world. They almost made him feel that, in return for that solidity, even life as a cripple would be better than this.

Almost.

Something large brushed against his leg. He jumped back. A golden, dragon-like creature, larger than a Great Dane but with a slender, sinuous reptilian body, snaked about Max's legs. It had a thick, leonine mane and a handsome spread of wings. Its tail whipped back and forth, expressing its fury.

This must be Jig, Max thought, the witch's celestial dragonne, who had remained loyal to her despite her fall from her previous exalted estate. He eyed the creature nervously.

"Blasphemer! Angelicide!" Lady Puzzledeep cried, waving the scroll that the angel had given Max to pass on to her.

Uh-oh. That did not sound good.

She continued, "For longer than you can imagine—you miserable worm!—I have been seeking my redemption, seeking some way back into the bosom of the higher realm that rejected me when I foolishly dabbled in necromancy. Yet, my progress has been so slow that sometimes, I despair that I have made any at all. To have to watch another bright one fall! You have no idea how that horrifies me...infuriates me!"

"Er...excuse me, mi'lady." He had pulled his hood very, very low. "I'm just the delivery boy. May I go now?"

"Go! You! You shall never go anywhere again! Not until all your hopes and aspirations have been ripped from your soul! Not until your blood has been used to water the Trees of Nightmare! Not until all suns in all skies have grown cold and been forgotten. Look! Heaven has betrayed you!"

She held up the scroll for Max to see. It read:

THE BEARER OF THIS MESSAGE IS
RESPONSIBLE FOR THE FALL OF KADESHIEL.

"Son of a..." Max uttered a short, bitter laugh. "Some chance for redemption!"

"Remove your hood. I would know the face that brought about the doom of my dear one."

"Lady, are you sure? You might not like..."

"Remove it!" She reared back on her sinuous snake tail. "Now!"

He sighed, and—because there was no other choice—he could hardly outrun the golden dragonne—Max removed his hood.

A moment of utter silence followed. Lady Puzzledeep and Jig stared at him.

Max's halo buzzed on. As it grew brighter, its neon light banished the illusion that the Witch of Stolen Hopes wore to make herself look young and fair. Instead of a lovely lillend, he now beheld a withered, ugly, dried-up old hag. The shriek Lady Puzzledeep let out when she realized that her disguise had vanished reminded Max of the cry of the screech owl that calls the names of those about to die.

Might as well have been. His hours were numbered now. Heck, hours. More likely seconds were all he had left.

"So that is how it was done." Her voice was as soft and sharp as death itself. "You found the Cup of Desires and wished yourself to be an angel! To grant your request, the demon Akinshata ripped the halo from the head of Kadeshiel. So horrified was he by his disfigurement that he cast himself from heaven. He fell, crashing into the city of Dylath-leen. Those who were not destroyed by the impact were devoured by the demon he became."

Max sighed again. Suddenly, he gave a short, harsh laugh. Might as well be hanged for stealing a Maserati as hanged for a Ford.

He shrugged off his trench coat—as he had been longing to do for many years. The other two gazed at him, puzzled.

"Not just his halo." Max opened his wings.

With a noise like a hundred doves taking flight, two beautiful arcs of moon-white feathers unfolded to either side of him. They shone with their own unearthly, celestial glow. Unlike the halo, which had to be dingy if he wanted to stay in the Slumbering Plane, the wings were as pure and pristine as the day he got them—the day everything went wrong.

"Seize him!" cried the Witch of Stolen Hopes.

Max writhed in his bonds; a knot in the wood of the post to which he was tied dug into his back. He could hear the *shing* of steel against whetting stone, as the witch prepared the knife with which she intended to take back the wings attached to Max's back. Apparently, she wished to reattatched them to the demon Kadesh. She hoped this reminder of his former angelic nature would motivate him to forsake his depravity and seek the path to redemption.

Max wondered what the loss would do to him. Would his halo work on its own? Or were the wings just intended to allow him to fly through the Slumbering Plane with unerring direction and grace, a use to which he had never put them. A lump formed in his throat. He wished he had been braver. He thought of all the nightmares he could have so easily avoided.

He had never taken even a single flight.

The Witch of Stolen Hopes had wanted to take his halo, too, but when she had grabbed it, it would not budge. The smell of burnt flesh, from where it seared her hands, still hung in the air.

Jig slithered out of the air, snaking in and out around Max and the witch as she worked. His wings opened and closed rhythmically. His tawny mane blended elegantly into his rounded scales, which ran the length of his body before reaching the frippery of his tail, where the scales blended into what was either feathers or fur—Max could not tell.

The beautiful golden dragonne whispered, "Why? Why did you do it?"

"You had the Cup of Desires!" The witch moaned, raising her haggish face. "The most wishing magic on the Slumbering Planes, and you wasted it! You wasted it on something so blasphemous...so trivial! Wishing yourself an angel! You could have done so much! You could have set so many wrongs right. You could have overthrown the Khan of Nightmares. You could have..."

"Returned Lady Puzzledeep to her once-high estate," whispered Jig.

"No," The witch said bitterly. "We see now that is not an option. All that would have happened if I made that wish is that I, rather than this one, would have damned Kadeshiel."

She rose and approached. The gleaming blade in her hand.

"Shall we kill him first, Jig? Before we cut off the wings?"

"It would be the more merciful thing," Jig replied.

She raised the knife and plunged.

Max flinched as the gleaming blade flew at his throat. His last words lacked the zing he had always hoped they would have. All he managed to get out was: "That wasn't what I wished for."

Quick as golden lightning, Jig threw his body between Lady Puzzledeep and Max. Startled, she tried to jerk the blade upward, but she did not entirely succeed. It skidded against his scales, jangling.

"Jig! What are you doing?"

"A moment," Jig growled. "I want to hear about his wish."

"What?"

"He said that he had not wished to be an angel. I wanted to hear exactly what he wished for." When Lady Puzzledeep scowled, Jig added, "It might give us useful information in our own quest for the Cup of Desires."

Lady Puzzledeep took a half step backward, but she did not lower the blade. It remained huge and shining right in front of Max's face.

Jig turned his great eyes toward Max. "Speak."

Max coughed, taken aback by the momentary reprieve. "To be an angel...that's not what I wished for."

Lady Puzzledeep lashed her serpent's tail and brandished the blade. Jig curled around him, his soft cat-like mane brushing Max's fingers.

"What did you wish for?" Jig's voice purred, though Max was sure this noise did not have the same meaning as the purr of a cat.

"I...I wanted to be able to chose whether or not I was awake."

Lady Puzzledeep knife wavered. "Explain."

"I wanted something every child on earth has. The power to stay awake."

Jig curled about him the other way. "Why?"

Max was silent too long. The witch stabbed the first quarter-inch of her knife into his neck. Pain shot through him. He gasped, his throat making a gargling noise.

Jig curled around Lady Puzzledeep now. "Let's not kill him yet. I still believe what he knows may be of use to us."

The witch pulled her blade from his neck. A sharp burst of agony electrified him. He could feel the trickle of blood running down his throat.

Max choked out, "You've heard of half-dreamers? Beings whose fathers are dream creatures, and their mothers are mortals? The girl gets pregnant in her dreams. Some time later, a baby is born here. Most of the mothers never even know it happened."

"Like Captain Starkadder, you mean?" Lady Puzzledeep's face was contorted with hatred directed at Max. Yet, in spite of herself, her eyes glittered with interest. "Isn't he Auberyon's son with one of his mortal floozies?"

"Exactly like…only in my case, something went wrong." Max said. "My mother was one of Dr. LeBerge's assistants at Stanford Sleep Lab, before he started the Lucidity Institute. You've heard of LeBerge, right? No? Well, where I come from, he was the first person to communicate from the Slumbering Plane to those awake. Maybe it was all the lucid dreaming practice, but…her dream baby was born in the waking world."

"You?"

"Yeah…only I wasn't whole. Couldn't stay awake…or asleep. At school, I'd fall into dreamland in class. On the playground, I'd find myself facing waking nightmares. Here on the Slumbering Plane, where no one goes to sleep, I'd nod off. I just wanted…a life."

"For that, you needed to destroy an angel?" Lady Puzzledeep's voice dripped with icy sarcasm, "Why not wish for the Ring of Dreaming or the Chalice of Waking? Why wish for…"

"Cause no one told me about the price," Max replied bitterly.

"What?"

"My companions who helped me win the Cup of Desires—my half-brother and Chimer, the three-headed monster who was my childhood dream friend—They neglected to tell me about *how* Akinshata fulfills the wishes. They didn't mean any harm, they just didn't know I didn't know.

"So, when we finally found the Cup of Desires, I wished to be able to control whether I was awake or asleep. That's all. The demon chose, as he always does, to fulfill my wish in the way that did the most possible harm to others."

Jig hissed, "Which was that he tore the halo and wings off Kadeshiel and gave them to you?"

"Exactly," Max nodded. "Only I didn't know that until later. At the time, I thought he'd just created them *ex nihilo*. It was only after I heard about the fate of Dylath-leen that I began to put two and two together."

The knife at his throat trembled. There was a long moment of tense quiet. The dragonne moved rapidly about them; its length vibrated so quickly it hummed.

The witch's voice was low. "You were the boy. The child on Starkadder's flag."

"That...was me. Once."

Jig nosed the discarded hood. Then he froze suddenly, staring at Max, his absolute stillness as eerie as his constant motion. Finally, he hissed, "You knew that Lady Puzzledeep would slay you if she saw your halo. Why did you agree to deliver this message?"

Max sighed. "The angel said it was a chance for redemption."

The witch snickered. "The redemption of painful death!" With her free hand, she gestured at his halo. "Did it work?"

"Yeah. It worked. Exactly as it should." Max said. "I found I could brighten or dim the halo by an act of will. When it reached a certain level of brightness, I woke up. When I wanted to go to sleep, I'd lay down and dim it a bit. Then, I'd be asleep. No one could see it in the waking world, of course, but I could still tell it was there."

"What went wrong?" sang Jig.

"What do you mean?"

"You bear an air of sorrow."

"Worked like a charm." Max's voice was devoid of emotion. "I had seven good years of life. I could wake when I wished and sleep when I didn't. Just like everyone else."

"What happened?"

"A patch of perfectly ordinary black ice. On the road one morning, coming back from an early soccer practice. A car skid and swerved right into mine." At the witch's blank look, Max waved a hand. "A...chariot, a carriage. Took my wife, my little son, and my infant daughter. Took my legs, too. After that...well, there wasn't much worth staying awake for."

Jig lowered his leonine head. "I am sorry."

"Sorry!" Lady Puzzledeep raged. "Because of him an angel was defiled! So, his motives were good! Does his ignorance excuse his crime? I say nay! Once Kadeshiel was an angel of healing who brought respite to the weary. Now he feasts off the bodies of those killed by his terrible fall. Someone must pay for this!" She raised her knife again. "I say it shall be you."

"Many have made mistakes," Jig curled in and out, around her legs, around Max's, around hers, around Max's. His golden eyes fixed upon her face. "Some were even warned."

The witch wavered. Then she scowled. "Do not cross me in this, Jig!"

She stepped forward again and raised her blade, preparing to strike.

Max met the hag's gaze squarely—no easy feat, especially as he could feel the blood from the wound she had already inflicted dripping down his neck.

He said, "You want to go back up, right? Up where you used to be? Sometimes the path upward begins with a single decision. Such as the decision to spare a life that is rightfully yours to do with as you like."

Lady Puzzledeep froze, knife still on high. Her eyes locked on Max's, and she glared at him. Her haggish face contorted with such hatred that Max feared her gaze alone would slay him.

Suddenly, her face went slack, "I see."

"See what?" Max rasped.

Very slowly she lowered the knife and began cutting Max's bond. "You were not the only one to whom heaven was offering a chance for redemption."

<hr>

Max stalked back across the dream plains. He rotated his shoulders. They felt lighter, unburdened. There was a good side to the strange flow of time. The pain of having his wings shorn had flicked by in a brief nightmarish montage. But it had been worth it.

In return for his willingly giving her his wings, Lady Puzzledeep had promised to return a dream that had been stolen from his half-brother, Captain Starkadder. She had even offered to talk to the Guardian of the Ways about giving his old pal Chimer some well-earned vacation.

His halo buzzed. He gave it a slap. It flickered on, bathing the path around him in a steady neon glow. He smiled. It seemed no quirkier than usual.

As he headed for Sam's, Max glimpsed the Floating Palace of Madam Equinox through the distant haze, still hovering like a vertical egg. He saluted its unseen mistress.

"See." Max grinned. "Some things do change for the better."

Feeding the Mouth that Bites Us

THE COLD WINDS BLEW DOWN FIFTH AVENUE. HANNAH SHIVERED BUT could not find the energy to zip her coat up as she plodded along the sidewalk toward her apartment. It puzzled her that small actions as zipping her coat or adjusting her hat seemed to require such Herculean efforts. It had not used to be that way. Only a year ago, she could recall running across Central Park, laughing as the kite she was trailing behind her became entangled with a bicyclist instead of taking flight. Had it really been only a year ago...seemed like an eternity.

Hannah blinked quickly, hoping to moisten her eyes, but they remained uncomfortably dry. Her mouth was dry as well. She would have liked to believe that the winter wind caused this unpleasant sensation, but it had been with her for months now, even in the most balmy weather of the early fall. Her doctor said it was extreme dehydration, for all the good that information did her. He could not come up with a single explanation of why a recently healthy girl like Hannah would suddenly suffer such symptoms.

She had been tested for every popular disease, chronic, contagious, or sexual, and some less popular as well. She drank huge bottles of Evian and popped iron pills like M&M's yet neither the dry eyes, nor the nausea, nor the anemia improved. Recently, she had become so tired, so drained, that she was beginning to contemplate telling her doctor the truth. But, how did one explain to a modern Jewish doctor that your boyfriend was a vampire?

Having a vampire for a boyfriend had its good points, she mused. The night life was always interesting and being with him was exhilarating. On the other hand, it also had its downsides; like having to put up with him always necking with other girls. Okay, he called it dining. Furthermore, it gave a whole new meaning to the fear that 'he just wanted her for her body.'

Some people, she mused, might think her stupid for allowing someone to suck her blood and then wondering why she felt like shit. Yet, it just did not make sense that the small amount of blood she let Ambroise take could be making her feel so bad. The Red Cross was willing to take a pint every 56 days. Hannah gave Ambroise a half a cup every other week, which over 56 days, came to a pint. So, why should she feel so much worse than other donors? It had to be something else that was making her feel so bad, maybe her doctor had missed some important clue.

As she passed Central Park, she considered raising her head to see if there was still snow on the branches, but could not find the strength for even so simple a task. Frightened by her own weakness, Hannah started to cry, only no tears came. Her body was wracked by the force of her sobs, but her eyes remained dry. What was happening to her? When had things become so bad?

Ahead a group of nuns were handing out bright yellow flyers. The sight of them, in their traditional black robes with their white wimples calmed Hannah's spirits, and she examined them with more interest. On their left breasts, they each wore a pin the shape of a gold cross surrounded by a sun. It was not a denominational logo Hannah recognized, but then she knew very little about Christian denominations.

One of the nuns spotted Hannah, where she leaned against the stone wall separating the Park from the busy street, her face in her hands, her shoulders shaking with self-pity. The nun came forward, smiling kindly, however, when Hannah raised her head and revealed her face, dry-eyed with no trace of tears, the nun's smile died. She thrust a yellow flyer into Hannah's hand and muttered something about how help sometimes comes from unexpected places.

Arriving at her apartment, Hannah sat motionlessly in her living room unable to find the energy to move. Her eyes trailed about the cluttered room. Her cello stood in the corner by the fireplace collecting dust. She had not played it in weeks, maybe months. On her bookshelf, the newest books by her three favorite authors languished unread. The scarf she had started last summer as a birthday present for her mother lay on the coffee table, still a pile of knitting needles and yarn. The scarf for Ambroise, however, she had finished. It sat on the mantle wrapped in shiny red paper, awaiting his visit later that week.

It bothered her that they had so little time together. Once every two weeks hardly seemed like enough, and how empty and lonely were the hours that stretched between his visits. Yet, it could not be helped. Apparently foraging for food in this modern age took so much of Ambroise's time that he could only spare one day out of fourteen for himself. During the long hours she spent alone, too morose and tired to do more than stare blindly at the droning television, she sometimes dreamed that a time would come when they moved in together. Then, she could see him every day and guard him while he slept. Sometimes, she even imagined that she might bring home guests, so that he would not need to go out to forage. Though, she often wondered if such dreams were disloyal to the friends and co-workers she pictured in the role of the guests.

She would have felt more comfortable if Ambroise had been more forthcoming about what exactly he did with the rest of his time. She understood his desire to shield her from the more gruesome aspects of his life, but secretly she felt he should have understood that she was enough of a modern woman to face the graphic truth without flinching...or at least she had been before her malaise began. And why did he shy away from certain restaurants or areas of town? She understood why he would not go to the Full Moon Cafe, the place was wall-to-wall mirrors. But, what did he have against the Golden Bull or Formacetti's?

Yet, when he was with her, all her doubts and fears evaporated. He was so handsome and carefree with his auburn curls and porcelain skin. When they were alone together, he whispered such sweet caressing words in her ear. She recalled his strong arms, his musky smell, his infectious laugh. Sinking deeper into the chair, she contemplated the feel of his hands pinning her down, as he bent his head to kiss her bare stomach. Hannah sighed. No other man made her feel so good. How empty her life would be without him.

Ambroise.

She wet her dry lips.

Ambroise.

Half an hour later, she found the strength to make it to the kitchen and open a can of soup. She sat by her kitchen table, waiting for her soup to warm. Seeing the flyer laying face down, she lackadaisically pushed at it until it flipped over and exposed its print. As she pushed at it, she wondered vaguely what it might be. Most likely, it was an ad for a charity or a church. Hannah did not go to temple very often and she had no interest in becoming a Christian. Still, she felt a mild curiosity as to what brand of poison the nuns had been pushing.

The Flyer read:

Do you suffer from

the following symptoms:

Dry eyes

Bouts of depression

Exhaustion

Anemia

Back or stomach pains

Numbness

Troubling Dreams

If so, there is hope!

Come to the Order of St. George's Clinic

At the bottom was an address in Westchester, a phone number, and an email address.

Hannah pushed back her long black hair, which had always been unruly but which was even worse now that she seldom washed it, and read the flyer again. It listed her symptoms exactly! Not one at a time, as the medical books did, but all together—as if their presence in connection with each other was significant! If these were symptoms others suffered as well, then her condition must have nothing to do with Ambroise after all! With a feeling of buoyancy she had not felt in months, Hannah rose and made toast to go with her soup.

⁂

It took her three days to get up the energy to actually visit the clinic. The only reason she went at all was that Ambroise was coming the next day, and she lived in fear that her lethargy might become so overwhelming that she would be unable to enjoy their time together. Ambroise's bi-weekly visits were the high point of her otherwise dreary life. So far, she had managed to perk up whenever he arrived, but with each visit the effort it took to stir herself to receive him grew. Hannah began to fear that even his presence would soon fail to cheer her. If she was no longer fun to be with, would Ambroise stick around? She doubted it.

The clinic was situated in an old church that was connected by a hall of black glass to a rectangular stone building behind it. Since the flyer had boasted of night hours, Hannah had considered waiting for Ambroise and asking him to go with her. Now she was glad she had not. Ambroise would have been out of there already. He hated walking on holy ground.

Tentatively, she pushed open the heavy oak door and found herself in a mirrored corridor. Compounded reflection of the hall lamps in the many mirrors produced a dazzling glare of lights. Hannah hurried through the hallway and was relieved to escape into the large sunny waiting room beyond.

The soft noise of rushing water greeted her. A tall, three-tiered marble fountain stood in the center of the room. As Hannah entered, a nurse in white nun's robes was filling a pitcher from the fountain, which she then poured into a silver samovar that sat on its rolling stand near an inner door. The blue flame heating the samovar was reflected against the silver wallpaper dancing among its gold foil flowers. Hannah, still cold from the street, found a seat near the samovar, but the lure of the reflected flames proved false, for they offered no warmth.

The Order of St. George was obviously a Christian sect. A golden cross stood atop the fountain and wooden crucifixes hung on the walls. Crucifixes also marked the leather golf bags containing croquet sets sitting in every corner. Hannah thought of the simplicity of her synagogue and felt out of place. She wondered bleakly if the nuns would expect her to convert.

A small garden circled the room, taking up the foot of space closest to the wall, except where the doors opened. It grew with mint and St. John's wart and other herbs Hannah did not recognize. The theme was echoed in the long ropes of dried herbs hung around every window. That and the tea boiling in the samovar gave the clinic a pleasant smell that reminded Hannah of her grandmother's kitchen.

As the chill of the outside air left her, Hannah examined the other prospective patients. They sat on the benches sipping tea from delicate china cups or filling out paperwork. Their faces were uniformly drawn and exhausted. Hannah shivered. What ailment did this clinic treat? Did she have it too? If so, would she end up as bad off as that sunken-eyed man by the hat rack?

In the shiny surface of the wallpaper Hannah could see her reflection. Was that her? So, pale and drawn, with an unruly mop of unkempt hair? What had become of the pretty Jewish American Princess she had been such a short time ago? Hannah thought of her adoring father seeing her like this, so wan, with dark circles under her eyes, and nearly began to cry.

A nun brought Hannah a questionnaire which she proceeded to fill out. Yes, her eyes and mouth were often dry. Yes, she found herself crying a lot. Yes, she often suffered from depressing thoughts and troubling dreams. Despite her gnawing fear of discovering she had some incurable disease, the questions comforted her. There was something reassuring about knowing that others had experienced her same symptoms; especially as it meant the problem had nothing to do with Ambroise.

The next question gave her pause, and her hand stole unconsciously to her neck. "Have you ever noticed a lump or bug bite about the size of quarter? If so, were there two such lumps very close together? Did any numbness or tingling you might have experienced seemed to originate from the location of the lumps?"

Hannah glanced surreptitiously around the waiting room. Previously innocent aspects of the decorum began to take on ominous implications, such as the herbs which she now recognized as braids of garlic, or the polished wood spikes and flat-headed mallets she had taken for croquet sets. Her eyes flew quickly over the walls, but found none of the medical posters usually found in free health clinics. If the Order of St. George treated those suffering from some accepted disease; why didn't the name of the illness appear on any of the wall hangings or literature?

Upon finishing her questionnaire, Hannah was led to a private counseling room. It was a small, comfortable room with firm leather seats and a wide window looking out over the church grounds. A TV and VCR on a wheeled cart sat in one corner, next to a small refrigerator. Behind an old oak desk sat a young man in black with a head of blond curls. He was so youthful that it was not until Hannah took in his calm beneficent expression that she recognized him for a priest.

"Welcome. Come, sit down. I'm Father Joseph," he said kindly, rising to help her with her chair. Hannah handed him her finished questionnaire, then sat mutely as Father Joseph read it over.

"I see," He glanced quickly down at the questionnaire. "...Hannah. You wrote here that you have found lumps such as the ones described. Do you have any now?"

Hannah wanted to lie but felt obscurely uncomfortable because he was a priest. She really did not know much about priests, except for what appeared in movies. But in movies, people were always confessing their innermost thoughts to them. Reluctantly, she nodded.

"Can you show me?"

Trembling, Hannah stood and unbuttoned the top of her shirt, exposing the bites on her neck. The priest glanced briefly at her throat and nodded. Touching an intercom button, he called for a nurse. A young nurse in white with a white wimple came bustling in, carrying a silver pitcher, much like the one Hannah had seen when she first arrived. Father Joseph gestured toward Hannah.

"Hannah, show the nurse," he commanded.

Hannah did so. The bites were nearly two weeks old and had faded to bruised lumps faintly resembling old mosquito bites. The nurse took a swab of cotton from the pocket of her white smock and dipped it into the pitcher.

"Holy water. From the fountain," the nurse explained brightly. Swabbing the cotton over Hannah's neck, she added, "Hold still, this may sting a bit."

The cool water felt good against the numbness in her shoulder. Then, the burning began. Hannah screamed as molten lead ran through her neck and down her veins. The searing pain rapidly approached her heart. *I'm going to die,* Hannah thought, trying to push the nurse's hand away. Behind her, the priest moved deftly to catch her arms, holding her immobile. As the pain entered her heart, feeling like a blowtorch held against her flesh, she prayed that her death might be quick and that her father would not be too sad without her.

Then, just as quickly, the pain was gone, and she felt...better. The priest released her, and she stood a moment, rotating her shoulder and lifting her arm. The numbness, which had troubled her for months, was fading. As the priest returned to his seat, she gave him a shaky smile.

"Thanks...I guess."

The nurse had left. She returned now with a cup of tea. From the pleasant spicy smell, Hannah recognized the scent of the tea bubbling in the samovar. She recalled that it had been made with fountain water too.

"I-is it going to burn?" she asked. The nurse smiled and shook her head.

"No, that's all over now, ma'am." She handed Hannah a bottle of some kind of vitamins. "You'll be wanting to take one of these every day for a month. They'll have you feeling better in no time."

"Will...will I get better?" Hannah asked, experiencing a sudden stab of hope.

"Most certainly," The priest gave her a reassuring smile.

Hannah sat down, and the nurse left the room. Carefully at first, she sipped her tea, but it tasted wonderful and produced no strange side effects. Examining the vitamins, she read the ingredients: 'iron, garlic extract, mandrake root, penny royal, wolfsbane, belladonna,' and underneath 'Made with Holy water.' Hannah shrugged and put the bottle in her purse. She did not believe in holy water, of course. But, hey, if it worked, why fight it? After all, this was the first time she had been able to breathe properly in months!

The priest leaned forward. "From what you say here, I don't believe it's a serious case. However, I still have some questions I must ask you. It is very important that you answer as best you can. Your own health and the health of others depends on your honesty. Please tell me everything you remember about how you received these marks."

Hannah raised her tea cup to hide her blush. "Like what?"

"Do you know what is causing them?"

After a pause, she nodded.

"Can you tell me who it is? A name? A description? An address?"

Hannah hesitated, afraid. Eventually, she mumbled.

"If I tell you, what will you do?"

"Come, I'll show you."

He took her through the old church into the dark glass hallway connecting the church to the rectory. The windows were black, making the corridor dark and gloomy. When they had gone about halfway down the corridor, Father Joseph stopped and touched a switch on the wall. Instantly, the glass cleared. The light of day streamed through the windows, and Hannah felt the sun's soothing warmth touch her face.

"This is all we do," Father Joseph said. His blue eyes sparkling kindly. "It's not so bad, is it?"

At first, Hannah returned his smile cheerfully. Then, understanding came. "But won't the sunlight kill him?" she blurted.

The sparkle in Father Joseph's eyes died.

"So, you do know."

<hr>

Back in the counseling room, the priest and Hannah sipped their tea in momentary silence.

"So, you know about vampires," Hannah said finally, breaking the silence. It felt good to have someone she could discuss the subject with, even if the priest was technically a member of 'the enemy'. "Basically, the Order of St. George runs...what?"

"A vampire victim crisis center," Father Joseph said with a flicker of a smile.

"There are really so many vampire victims?" asked Hannah.

"The number grows every day," replied Father Joseph. He put his teacup down. "You may have heard of the increased incidents of clinical depression over the last decade or so? People blame our modern lifestyle, but much of it is actually caused by vampires. Most of the victims are not like you, Hannah. They don't know. They are hypnotized at the time of feeding and are not aware how they received the marks. Usually, as their condition grows worse, they are treated by psychiatrists, who give them Prozac or Paxil and send them on their way."

"What causes the depression? The lack of blood?"

"The toxin the vampire injects into his victim in order to draw blood painlessly. It is similar to the poison used by mosquitoes. Only, a vampire deposits a great deal more into the nervous system than the average mosquito."

"I don't understand. Are we talking about a real chemical? Something science can study?" asked Hannah, who had expected some mystical mumbo-jumbo explanation.

"Certainly. When we have patients who are less sure of the cause of their troubles, we often draw blood and test for traces of this toxin. It breaks down slowly in the human body. Traces can be found in the blood stream for two to three weeks after the initial bite."

"So, after three weeks, a person would be fine?" asked Hannah.

"Theoretically, but it gets worse. The toxin works by over-stimulating the pleasure receptors in the brain, which is why their victims find vampires so enticing. Over time, traces of the toxin build up on these receptors, damaging them and causing a chemical depression. Eventually, if left unchecked, the receptors burn out altogether. We have a few such patients in our In-House care program in the rectory."

Hannah shivered, inwardly seething at Ambriose for causing her such misery. But, then, he probably had no idea what he was doing. After all, vampires could hardly be expected to visit such crisis centers on fact-finding missions. Besides, she had done everything possible to hide her condition from him. She would not hold her love responsible, she decided. He could not help what he was.

"Now, I must ask you again. Can you give us anything to go on?" asked Father Joseph, and he pushed a card across the table which had multiple places for Vampire's name and address.

Hannah thought of the hall and the sunlight. She tried to imagine Ambroise dead, his beautiful face marred or his perfect breast pierced. The image upset her so she nearly started crying in front of the priest. Silently, she vowed that she would rather die herself than let such a thing happen to Ambroise.

"But, Am-he hasn't done anything wrong! I consented," she cried hastily.

Father Joseph looked at his hands and sighed. His face looked careworn and sad, as if he had been through this scene a hundred times before. Hannah wondered why she had thought he was so young.

"I did not want to have to show you this. I spare all those who I can," he said, rising and moving to his computer. He clicked on the screen, starting a video. "You will excuse me if I don't stay and watch it again myself. Watch the whole thing—to the end. Just press the intercom button when you're done."

<hr>

The video showed a real vampire initiation. The hidden camera gave the scene an odd, warped look, but she could still see the vampires converging on the initiate like vultures on road kill, biting him and, presumably, drinking his blood. She could not see over the press of bodies. The initiate, now pale and trembling, then approached an old man, who had been bound to a stake and gagged. The old man wept as he awaited his fate. Hannah felt a stab of envy at his watery tears. Then, the initiate slit the old man's throat with a ceremonial knife and began sucking up mouthfuls of his spurting blood.

"All vampires are murders," explained the announcer. "Their power to sustain their existence beyond the grave is granted to them by an unholy power. This power will only accept initiates who have proved their loyalty by sullying their soul with the murder of an innocent. All vampires are murderers. They have murdered before and will most likely murder again."

Hannah dismissed some of the explanation as Christian claptrap. Yet, she did believe that what she was seeing was real. The old man's death was not like any special effect she had ever seen. For one thing, there was much more blood than they showed in the movies. Hannah had never seen a real person die before, and the experience rattled her. She tried to console herself with the thought that the sacrificial victim was very old and probably would have died soon anyway, but she could not quite believe it. Her dear father, who adored her so faithfully, was not much younger than that man. The thought of her father perishing so ignominiously filled her with fury.

But, if she ratted on Ambroise, wouldn't that make her a murderer too?

Unexpectedly, she remembered the night she and Ambroise broke into the Central Park Zoo and toured the menagerie together. It was never open during the hours they saw each other. She remembered the raucous monkeys and the sleeping lions. She remembered the cotton candy machine Ambroise had found. How he had laughed when she got the sticky stuff all over her nose. How he had bent his head to lick it off. No. She could not kill him. She loved him.

And yet...much as she loved him, she wanted to play the cello again and to enjoy a good book. She wanted to be able to take a shower or call her mother, without weeping at the terrible effort it took. She wanted to live her life.

Shakily, Hannah acknowledged that her relationship with Ambroise must end. She would go home and explain to him the harm he was causing her. She would explain that under the circumstance it would be wrong for them to continue to see each other. She imagined herself, an old lady, unmarried and alone, still pining for her one true love. Perhaps, they would meet on the street; her old and withered, him still young and vital. Perhaps they would exchange a brief smile or a fond word. The thought made her cry. But, no tears flowed as she turned away and left the priest to face her shaking shoulders.

"I...I can't help you," she said finally.

"Hannah..."

"I love him. I would rather die myself than be party to his murder," Hannah declared valiantly.

The priest frowned. "What about his other victims?"

If she left Ambroise, would it push him into the arms of other women? An image came to her of Ambroise embracing various young women of her acquaintance, whispering to them. She pushed it angrily from her thoughts. No, no one who said the wonderful things Ambroise said would ever hurt her as her no-good, son-of-a-gun ex-fiancé had. Ambroise was a one-woman man, just as she was a one-man women. He might feed off other women to stave his incurable hunger, but he would never love them as he loved her.

Now, if someone had offered to kill Eddie, her two-timing ex, that might have been a different matter!

"I feel sorry for his other victims," Hannah began, "but..."

"But not sorry enough." Father Joseph cut her off. He thrust the card at her again. "Here, carry this. Come. There is someone I would like you to meet."

✦

Father Joseph led her through the glass hallway to the rectory, where patients with more serious aliments were treated. The rectory, or the infirmary, as the priest called it, was a long chamber with thick, white walls and tall, arched windows. Beds extended from the walls, each draped about the head with soft white fabric, forming a short canopy. The room was airy and bright, but smelled heavily of disinfectant.

From each canopied cot, pallid, drawn, and tired faces stared back at Hannah. Their eyes were dull and looked sticky and dry, much like her eyes occasionally looked in the mirror, only worse. Many were on IV's. The nun who had swabbed Hannah's shoulder was with one patient, wetting his lips with a pink mouth stick. She smiled at Hannah and the priest as they passed.

From the last bed on the left, a shrunken, wrinkled woman in a white hospital gown watched the newcomers with a malevolent glare. Hannah recoiled, shocked by the woman's horribly withered appearance.

The woman's dry eyes fixed on Hannah. Her voice was a rasp of scorn. "How old do you think I am?"

"Me? I-I don't know," Hannah stuttered. The woman must be at least in her nineties. Hannah prayed she would never get that old! She decided to flatter the old hag and guess young. "...seventy-six?"

The deaden eyes watched her, unblinking.

"I am thirty eight...surprised you, didn't I?"

Hannah turned to Father Joseph and whispered conspiratorially, "How old is she really?"

The young Father's face was grave. "Clarissa is thirty-eight, my child. She is one of our most difficult cases.

The shrunken woman spoke, her voice contemptuous. "I thought myself so fancy with my vampire lover. I looked down on my friends because I was going to live forever. After all, he loved me *sooo* much. He often said so." She scowled angrily. "Where in Anne Rice does it say that you have to murder someone to become a vampire? I...I couldn't do it." Her eyes drifted, as if her thoughts moved far away.

"Time for your transfusion, miss," said a pretty nun, coming up beside Clarissa. The woman scowled.

Father Joseph inclined his head toward Hannah and said quietly, "Clarissa was seduced by a vampire to the point that she participated in an initiation. However, when it came time to kill the victim, she refused. She can no longer produce her own blood, but at least her soul is her own."

"That's small comfort when the pain starts," the patient grumbled, as the nurse turned her to prepare for her transfusion. "Sometimes, when the pain is very bad at night, I curse myself for not having gone through with it. I could have become deathless. I could have been immortal...but, then I wake to the sunlight and know I've been fooling myself. I could never have withstood that life. Most vampires fade away within the first five years. Did you know that? It's only the rare initiate who actually grows hardened enough to survive that dreadful life."

Her eyes focused on Hannah and she added, "We criticizes the stupidity of dogs who bite the hand that feeds them. But, look how much stupider we women are, when we continue to feed the mouth that bites us."

Hannah shifted uncomfortably, tugging at her unruly hair.

Father Joseph said gently, "Hannah has not yet decided whether or not to help us."

"So you brought her back here to show her the likes of me, hoping to shock her into feeling pity for her lover's other victims?" Clarissa laughed, a short uncomfortable sound. "Priests! They know shit about women. But, don't worry, Father Joe. I'll fix things for you."

She fixed her baleful gaze on Hannah. "Let me ask you a question, honey. When you first met lover boy, did you see him every day?"

"Yes."

"But now, you see him once every two weeks, right? Am I right?"

Hannah nodded reluctantly. Her heart skipped a beat. She understood why the clinic had been able to identify a pattern to her symptoms. But, how could anyone else know the pattern of

Ambroise's behavior?

"You want know why, sweetheart? I bet you don't. But I'm going to tell you, nonetheless. Because the damn bloodsuckers have a feeding cycle. They can't sip from one 'cup' more than once every two weeks. Otherwise, they weaken their victims beyond their usefulness. The average fanghead has between twelve and twenty-five victims, and that's not counting their constant supply of one-time supplements. And, since most of their victims experience the toxic-induced euphoria as sexual pleasure, they usually oblige them."

"I don't understand..."

"Oh, yes you do. Your lover has between twelve and twenty other squeezes he visits the other days of the week, when he's not with you. They all do. Face it, sweetie. To him, you're just a glorified ham sandwich."

"I don't believe it! Ambroise is different!" Hannah said stoutly.

"Ambroise? What him again?" Clarissa raised a faintly scornful eyebrow. "Didn't we have two other girls babbling about Ambroise just this week?" When Father Joseph nodded, she snorted. "Seems this Ambroise is quite the ladies' man. If I remember correctly, one of them vowed to die before anyone laid a hand on her true-love."

"You mean, he's cheating on me?"

"My, how sharp you are," Clarissa's thin lips settled into a malicious grin.

"That bastard!"

Hannah felt as if she had been punched in the solar plexus. She allowed Father Joseph to help her to a chair, where she sat rocking back and forth, as a thousand pleasant memories shattered like tempered glass. After all she had done for him! All she had given up. Her very life's blood! And all the time, Ambroise had been using her like so much cotton candy!

Father Joseph offered her his pen. Hannah stared at it blankly. Then, snatching it, she wrote out the card, describing exactly where Ambroise would be the following evening, and thrust it at the priest, who accepted it gravely.

Wiping an honest-to-goodness wet tear from her cheek with the back of her hand, she sniffed and said.

"Sunlight's too good for him. Couldn't they use a stake?"

Flight of Ideas

THE CROWD IN FRONT OF THE ATLAS BUILDING WAS GROWING THICKER, despite the biting November winds whipping down Fourth Street. They stood with their heads craned up, shifting from side to side, straining to get a better look at the person who stood on the edge of the wooden plank, protruding from the roof, some twenty-two stories above. The sharper-eyed could make out a young woman who stood facing back toward the building. She wore a bulky woolen cloak which billowed wildly in the winds.

"Think she's going to jump?" asked old Mr. MacBrien in his thick Dublin brogue.

"If that cloak of hers doesn't pull her off first," replied another member of the crowd.

"Bet you a hundred bucks, she doesn't jump," Albert Wrigley announced cheerfully elbowing the withered old man in the ribs.

"I'll bet you a hundred that she does," replied a man standing nearby. Under his leather coat, he wore blue overalls. In one hand, he carried a white hard hat.

"Why that's my next door neighbor, Annie Halloway!" a woman's voice said.

"Oh, God, I hope not," Mary Andersen exclaimed. She was trying to hold her squirming thirteen-month-old daughter still in her arms. Her face had gone white as a sheet. "Annie's pregnant."

"The poor little bairn," whispered old MacBrien.

Three days earlier, the Halloways had waited in Dr. Rothberg's office for the results of their Embryo Wellness Tests. Mr. Halloway had hung his London Fog jacket neatly on the coat rack and sat down in one of the plastic waiting room chairs. Rather than waste the idle time before the doctor returned, he had pulled an issue of Engineering Today from his briefcase and was taking notes on an article on modern improvements in lighter than air technology.

His wife, on the other hand, stood by the wide window looking dreamily out, with her hand resting on her newly rounded belly and a little smile on her lips. She still wore her coat, though one side of her scarf had fallen off and trailed onto the floor behind her. A little raspberry knitted hat covered her soft, chestnut hair. Unruly curls escaped all about the rim. She stood watching the birds and wondering what it must be like to live as they lived. Her favorite dreams were always the ones where she could fly.

The door opened to admit Dr. Rothberg. He was young doctor in his mid-thirties and wore a custom-tailored suit under his white doctor's smock. He nodded brusquely and came right to the point in a manner that pleased Mr. Halloway and caused Mrs. Halloway to sigh sadly.

"I'll cut to the chase, Mr. and Mrs. Halloway," he said. "In all respects, except for one, your child is perfectly normal. He lacks the genes thought to lead to three of the major diseases that tend to kill before seventy-five. Barring accidents, he should be in for a long life."

"Expand on this 'one respect,'" Mr. Halloway said, his voice steady and even, as if he were discussing a malfunction in an airplane. "You found the Helsinki Pair, didn't you?"

The doctor inclined his head curtly. "Yes, Mr. Halloway. The results showed that both of the Helsinki chromosomes were present. However, as we have discussed before, the procedure for removing the offending gene is tested and safe. It will require a few day's hospital stay for your wife, but she will be in little danger."

"I'm sorry," Mrs. Halloway interrupted. She did not look at the doctor or at her husband, but at her hands, where she worried the wool of her long scarf between her fingers. "Explain to me again what this Helsinki Pair is?"

"Come, dear, Dr. Rothberg has already explained it to us three times," her husband said, a slight note of exasperation creeping into his voice.

Annabel Halloway glanced up and met her husband's eyes. Her small face remained calm, but her eyes were not entirely focused, as if her thoughts remained elsewhere.

"I wasn't paying attention," she said simply.

Any impatient reply Mr. Halloway might have made was cut off by Dr. Rothberg.

"I would be happy to explain again, Mrs. Halloway," the young doctor said. "Gene alteration is a big step, and no one should go into it without understanding it. The Helsinki Pair are the chromosomes that, when they appear together, are responsible for Bipolar Disorders and other similar chemical imbalances."

"You mean manic-depression and other mental illnesses, don't you," she asked gently.

"Yes. Only we prefer to call this class of disorders chemical imbalances. Modern medicine has shown that they are derived from physical rather than mental causes," Dr. Rothberg said briskly.

"And does everybody who has this Helsinki Pair become manic-depressive?" Annie Halloway asked.

"No. Some are lucky. In some people, the disease never manifests itself," he said.

"And what happens to them?" Annie Halloway asked.

"What do you mean?" the doctor asked

"What happens to them?" Annie repeated.

"Anna, dear, that's enough. Do not pester Dr. Rothberg," her husband said. But Annie remained where she was, looking at the doctor inquiringly.

"What happens to the one's that do not develop the disease," she insisted softly.

"The majority of those people try to become writers, artists, or musicians," Dr. Rothberg stated.

"And are there any well-known writers, artists, or musicians who do not have this Helsinki Pair?" Annie asked, smiling gently as she spoke, as if she felt sorry for the young doctor.

Dr. Rothberg cleared his throat. "Very few....Actually, none that modern medicine is aware of."

"So, if I go ahead with this treatment, I destroy my child's chance of becoming a great man?" Annie asked. Her wide brown eyes had grown weary and sad.

"Will you excuse us for a moment, doctor," Mr. Halloway said. He took his wife by the arm and pulled her away to stand in the corner between the window and the coat rack. "If we don't go through with this treatment, our son could end up like your brother Billy, in and out of an asylum every few months."

"They don't call them that anymore," Annie said quietly, gazing down as if unable to make herself meet her husband's eye.

"When he's not too depressed to function, he's talking your ear off a mile a minute," Mr. Halloway continued, ignoring her remark. "He's unable to be quiet even long enough to hear the answer to his own questions. Then, he yells at you for not listening to him. It's damned annoying, even if he is suffering from...what is it the psychiatrists call it? Racing thoughts?"

"Flight of ideas," Annie said, her eyes downcast.

"Flight of ideas, yes, that's it. You wouldn't want people to talk about our son the way they talk about your brother, would you? You don't want *that*, do you?" he asked.

"No," she said softly.

"Good. It's settled," he said.

"But what if our baby's not going to end up like William, what if he's going to end up like my sister. You never heard Sharri sing, but she had the kind of voice that brought tears to your eyes just to hear it," Annie asked. When she spoke of her sister, it was as if a light had come on within her, illuminating her frail features and giving her delicate face a kind of classical grace.

"I hardly think a suicidal teenager who died driving her car into a tree is a good role-model for our unborn child, whatever kind of voice she had!" Mr. Halloway said.

Annie gasped and pulled away, putting her hand to her cheek as if she had been physically slapped.

"Suicidal? Sharri..." she whispered. "Where ever did you get that?"

Her husband cut her off, "Oh, come, dear! Don't play so naive with me. You must know that the truth has been all over the neighborhood since the beginning. Your sister got hysterical because that Daugherty kid dumped her."

"Is that what they say?" Annie said, her voice wooden.

"Face it, Anna," Mr. Halloway continued. "Our child's chances of benefiting from these genes are about as good as your chance of leaping off the top of the Atlas Building and living."

Dr. Rothberg had been standing with his back politely turned, now he came forward, smiling.

"I don't usually tell patients this, Mrs. Halloway, but, as an embryo, I myself received the treatment you and your husband are considering. My older brother and I both were originally conceived with the Helsinki Pair. At the time, gene alteration technology was not advanced enough to help him. He lives in Newark, New Jersey now. He's a bartender —all his hopes of Broadway forgotten under the strain of real life. I, on the other hand, have always had a very realistic view of life. Consequently, I have prospered."

The young doctor smiled from husband to wife and continued.

"Removing the Helsinki Pair does not interfere with ingenuity. In fact, many fine young engineers and inventors have arisen from the early efforts. When we really get down to it, Mrs. Halloway, what have artists ever done for the betterment of mankind?"

Mr. Halloway was nodding as the young doctor spoke. However, Mrs. Halloway peered at him as if she could not make out what he was saying. Her expression was balanced somewhere between incredulousness and stark pity.

"What of Shakespeare and Rembrandt and Byron. What of Poe? What of Mozart and Beethoven?"

"Exactly my point. How many of those men improved the quality of one's life? They don't build. They don't improve our standard of living. They produce nothing. Not even so much as your husband here does. What field of engineering did you say you were in, Mr. Halloway?" asked Dr. Rothberg.

"He makes those new space planes they use on international flights," Annie replied. "But, surely, you can't be serious about..."

"I had never thought of it that way...I believe Dr. Rothberg is right, Anna," Mr. Halloway said. "Very few artists have been more than useless dreamers."

"Basically," Dr. Rothberg confided, "What modern science has found—with the discovery in Helsinki of the two genes both of which must be present to produce an artistic temperament—is that artistic creativity is not natural to the human animal. As we moved from the instinctive world of emotions to the rational world of man, a mutation developed. Art is a way of dealing with emotions, sharing them with others. But, once we invented language, we no longer needed to encourage ourselves to depart on flights of fancy. We can express ourselves in a more straightforward manner. Imagine the human race of tomorrow, who wastes little or no energy on the creation of television programs or rock music. How productive we will be!”

“Shall we schedule the treatment for Monday?” Dr. Rothberg finished, smiling.

“That will be fine,” Mr. Halloway replied. He smiled the two men shook hands. Annie made no objection, but she stared at her husband as if she were seeing him for the first time in many years.

“Don’t worry, Mrs. Halloway, your son may grow up to be just like me,” Dr. Rothberg said, smiling congenially.

“That is what I am afraid of,” she said softly.

Standing on the plank some careless worker had left atop the building, Annie found that she was not as frightened as she had expected. Mr. Halloway stood on the roof, as near to the edge as he dared. His face was pasty white.

“Just come back, darling. Everything will be okay,” he was saying.

“Then, you agree not to go ahead with the treatment, Christopher?” Annie asked patiently.

“Honey, I can’t promise that,” her husband called, trying to be heard above the wind.

“Why not?” she called. “It was you that said that our child had as much a chance as if I leapt from the Atlas Building.” Annie said calmly. The dreaminess that had characterized her behavior at the doctor’s office was entirely gone. She was awake and resolute. “Do you really believe that? Would you rather I jump than take the chance?”

Annie watched as Dr. Rothberg leaned over and whispered. “Go ahead, promise her anything. You can always change your mind once she’s safe.”

“You’ve got to come back, Mrs. Halloway,” Dr. Rothberg called, straightening. “Think of the child.”

“I am thinking of the child, Dr. Rothberg,” Annie said. “Well, Christopher?”

“But if we don’t have the treatment, dear... Well, look how you’re acting! Climbing up here. Threatening to jump off,” he called. “Without the alteration, the child could end up like...”

"Like me, Christopher?" Annie called. "Is that what you are afraid of?"

Her husband did not answer.

"Christopher, why did you become an engineer?" Annie asked.

"Why? Ah, I like engineering. It's practical, what kind of a question is that?"

"That's not what you told me when we first met," Annie said.

Beside her husband, Annie could see Dr. Rothberg saying, "What did you tell her when you were courting her? Quick, give her the answer she wants!"

"I...I wanted to be an engineer ever since I was a kid. When I read Asimov and Heinlein and Brin...," his voice died off.

Annie smiled joyously.

"In other words, you were inspired...by artists!"

Then, she waited, her fingers crossed under her heavy cloak. To the baby, she whispered, "If he understands now, we stay. If he doesn't....well, then the life he offers would not be worth living. Oh, please, Christopher. Oh, please. Oh, please!"

Mr. Halloway was quiet for a long time. His face twisted by conflicting emotions. For once, Dr. Rothberg remained silent.

"You made your point, darling. You can come in now," he said finally, scowling.

Annie started forward joyously, "Then, no treatment?"

"I...I can't agree to that. We can't risk it, even for an Asimov. What if we got a Billy?"

Annie stopped. She stood very still like a deer frozen in on-coming headlights. Then, slowly, she began to back up, until she was at the very edge of the board.

"I love my brother William," she said, tears in her eyes. "When we were children, he used to make up the most wonderful stories. Stories like those written by the very men your Dr. Rothberg wants to destroy. Stories that inspire men to great things—to build the Atlas Building, to become engineers. Stories that inspire men to fly."

She stepped backward, into the air.

✦

Below, the jocular mood of the crowd became gasps of horror and cries of sorrow. They watched—powerless to help—as the young woman plummet through the air. The force of her fall ripped the cloak from her body, sending it spiraling upward like a crumpled leaf. Mary Andersen fainted. The man in the overalls dropped his construction hat to grab her before she dropped little Maria.

"Hey, what's is that red and blue thing on her back?" asked old MacBrien, pointing up.

Out from Annie shoulders, like the wings of a hawk, spread cherry and royal blue nylon. Aluminum struts snapped into place. The drag of the hang glider slowed Annie's downward plunge. Then, she was flying.

The whisper of hope spread among the crowd, growing into a roar. People cheered and laughed and slapped each other's backs. Someone threw a soda on Mary Anderson to wake her. The construction worker grinned at Albert Wrigley.

"Guess you owe me that hundred," he said.

"Good for Annie," Mary whispered weakly, waking.

Above them, smiling, with the light of her determination burning like a fire in her eyes, Annie Halloway flew off over the financial district toward the sea. She did not look back.

On Rocky Ground

*This story is dedicated to
the Freeman Children*

"Has Monte Musine gotten steeper?" Erasmus Prospero wiped his forehead and paused to catch his breath, leaning over so as to shift his heavy pack. "I don't remember panting so hard when I climbed up here in my youth."

"Seems the same to me," replied his brother, Mephisto, who wore no pack at all. He skipped up the side of the steep Italian Alp, as if it were as flat as a hop-scotch board. As he went, he stopped to poke at rocks and interesting mushrooms with his long, carved staff—a six-foot long collection of figurines, like a slender totem pole.

"Must be misremembering." Erasmus eyed his brother balefully through his dark hair, which hung across his eyes lank with sweat. "After all, it was over four centuries ago. Back when Father was still Duke of Milan. Or, maybe, last time, I wasn't carrying nearly seventy pounds of fertilizer!"

Mab Boreas sighed as he plodded along behind the Prospero brothers, overheated in his trench coat and fedora. He shifted weight to steady the large wooden yoke he carried across his shoulders. An aluminum pail hung from either side of the yoke—the only container they could find capable of holding salamander manure. Steam rose from the pails, along with an unpleasant stench.

When he had agreed to come on this cockamamie outing, the plan had been that Mephisto would carry the yoke. Yet, somehow, here Mab was, schlepping the burden up the side of the steep slope. Shaking his head, he sighed a second time.

"I don't suppose you could bring out that cheer weasel, brother?" Erasmus turned and gazed down the mountain, regarding the Italian countryside below. He slung his pack to the ground and rolled his shoulders.

"Nope, sorry!" chimed Mephisto. "I lent it to Caliban. He's trying to cheer up our grumpy brother Cornelius. But I could bring out Cheery's cousin, the chill weasel."

"Chill weasel?" Mab murmured sardonically. He puffed up his cheeks and blew. A brisk gust of wind came out of his mouth, carrying away the putrid stench issuing from the aluminum pails. "Oh boy, I gotta see this."

Mephisto tapped his staff. The three hikers began to imagine that there was a small creature on the rock beside Mephisto. Then, there it was.

The chill weasel regarded them quizzically. Like its more cheerful counterpart, it was as long as an ordinary weasel but fluffier. It had horizontal stripes of muted color—brick red, butterscotch, burnt ochre, moss green, periwinkle blue, and eggplant. Its nose came to a tiny black button of a point. Its unusually large black eyes were surrounded by additional black fur that came to a stiff point on either side, giving the appearance of a pair of cool sunglasses.

Mephisto picked up the chill weasel by the tail and swung it at his brother. The creature elongated as it swung, as if it were made out of muted-colored pompoms strung together by elastic. It let out a long, low tone like a jazz saxophone. The furry slinky struck Erasmus, who let out a startled noise.

"Want one?" Mephisto turned to Mab and held up the fuzzy weasel enticingly.

"No, thanks." Mab backed away, holding up a halting hand. "Never touch that stuff when I'm on the job. An Aerie One like me? One whack, and I'd be so chilled out, I'd hunker down for days."

"Oh, that feels nice!" Erasmus's eyelids fluttered closed, his shoulders relaxing. "Makes me forget my aching feet. Or that I am hauling—to be precise—sixty-seven pounds of fertilizer up Monte Musine to help my scatter-brained brother pay his debts to a bunch of rocks."

"*Oreads* are not rocks!" Mephisto threw Erasmus an injured look. "They are lovely ladies of the mountains. They just like stuff that's good for the earth. Like bone meal. And flaming salamander poo!" Mephisto patted Mab's arm, jiggling the huge yoke and its stinky burden. "Thanks for carrying that for us, by the way!"

Mab said nothing, but he glared at Mephisto from underneath the rim of his battered fedora.

"And these *oreads* moved my house." Mephisto continued, "Twice! I...just can't remember if I paid them. And we all know that it's not a good idea to leave debts to the supernatural community unpaid!"

"That's why I'm here," Mab muttered. "Miss Miranda—er, I mean Lady Stormwinds—asked me to see that this matter got taken care of while she was on her honeymoon." Looking down at the burden he bore, he muttered. "I didn't realize, when I agreed, that this would involve me becoming a pack mule."

He sighed again. He had not realized it, yet he should have. Best as he recollected, all Lady Stormwind's stories about traveling with her brother Mephisto ended badly.

"We paid them the first time, Mephisto. That was when the Great Hall was moved from Italy," Erasmus waved a hand in the general direction of Milan, "to Scotland, back in the sixteen hundreds. It's your second move...over the Atlantic Ocean...that we are worrying about, right?"

"Don't look at me," muttered Mab. He reached up carefully, so as not to disturb the yoke and pulled the brim of his fedora lower over his face. "I'm just here to carry the flaming poo."

Ahead, the trees thinned. The slope was still steep, but grass lay underfoot now, instead of sharp rocks. Erasmus paused and looked down at the Italian countryside stretching out into the distance, with checkerboard farmland and tiny, toy-like houses.

"We're nearly there!" Mephisto announced. He tossed his staff into the air, did a back flip, and caught it again before it struck the ground.

"That chill weasel is powerful stuff, Brother," Erasmus said with uncharacteristic mildness. "I don't even feel like killing you. Even though I just hauled thirty-five pounds of high-nitrogen fertilizer, twenty-four pounds of bone meal ground from the bones of dead giants, and two bags of Fox Farm Happy Frog Japanese Maple Organic Fertilizer up the side of Monte Musine on what might be a fool's mission."

"What's the last one for, anyway?" asked Mab. "So far as I know, there are no Japanese Maples on the peaks of the Italian Alps. Or is it fertilizer made from Japanese Maples?"

"It's not for the trees," Mephisto chided him cheerfully. "It's for the *oreads.*"

"It's the giants I feel for," Erasmus opined, gazing down the slope at the Italian countryside below. "Just because they claim they'll grind the bones of Englishmen in fairytales, doesn't mean we should harvest them for plant food. Or, in this case, food for spirits of the earth. Where did you get giant bones, anyway?"

"From Brother Theo," answered Mephisto.

Erasmus laughed.

"Why does it not surprise me," grunted Mab, "that Theophrastus the Demonslayer would have giant bones on hand?"

"So..." Erasmus shifted his pack. "We go greet these ladies. We give them our offerings. You make sure that they're satisfied, and we blow this Popsicle stand. Right?"

"Sure." Mephisto nodded happily. "If we're lucky. We can get in and out before the Gnome of Musine even knows we're here."

"Gnome?" Mab looked around warily. "I'm gathering not the garden variety? Are these the kind that can cause earthquakes if they get angry?"

Mephisto spun in a circle, arms spread. "Indeed!"

Erasmus continued to stare out at the view with a wistful smile "Italian Mountain Gnomes are more hands-on than their western kin. Rather like *oread* shepherds."

"I think of them as more like pimps," Mephisto chimed in. "They're obnoxious. And they love their bling!"

"Great example, Mephisto," Erasmus sighed and rubbed his temples. "Only you would think of that particular analogy."

Mephisto spread his arms and spun in a circle. "I tell it like it is!"

"Funny," Erasmus turned toward Milan, about a hundred miles away. "There's our old home. It used to take us days to cover that distance, assuming Father wasn't around to teleport us with the *Staff of Transportation.* Today, we made it in under two hours."

"The modern world is a wondrous place," Mephisto agreed happily.

"It was nice to see the old stomping ground," Erasmus continued, musing, "I mean...without all the giant fungi and with no rivers of blood."

"That was Infernal Milan, Professor Prospero," Mab reminded him with a shiver. He did not care much for that memory himself. "Real Milan never looked like that."

"Good point," Erasmus mused. He sighed. "I'm losing my mellow disposition, Mephisto, hit me again."

"Here," Mephisto draped the creature around Erasmus's shoulders. "You carry it."

Ahead, in the shade of a tall tree, seven large rocks jutted out of the grassy slope, some narrow and tall, some round and squat.

"Hello, girls!" Mephisto shouted at the stones, turning a cartwheel. "I'm here to pay my debts!"

Subtly, the stones changed, until they resembled feminine forms. Wide eyes, like shadowy pits, gazed out at the three travelers.

"Meh-phiiis-tooo," murmured a low voice, as if the earth itself sighed. "How wonderful to see you again."

"Look what I brought!" Mephisto turned a second cartwheel. "Erasmus! Mab! Show them the loot! The loot!"

Like a breeze blowing through rocks, the earth-voices spoke again, huskier now. "What is that wonderful, odiferous aroma?"

"I brought you flaming salamander manure! Your favorite!"

"*Somebody* brought it for her, anyway," muttered Mab. He lowered the pails to the ground and stepped out from under the yoke, rubbing his sore shoulders. Straightening, he tipped his hat to the ladies. Never did to be ungentlemanly.

"Ooooo," murmured the rock-ladies. With a deep grinding noise, they leaned closer to see the goodies Mephisto had brought.

"Remember when you moved my house for me? All the way across the Atlantic? Well...I couldn't remember if I had paid you for your effort or not. So I thought I'd bring..."

The ground in front of them broke open and out popped a gnome. He was a short, fat fellow made of stone, no more than two-and-a-half feet tall. He wore a high-collared purple coat with three large golden nuggets hanging from a chain around his neck.

The gnome strutted forward like he owned the place—which, Mab granted, perhaps he did. "What's going on here?"

"Hello, Grumpy-Gnome!" Mephisto threw out his arms, the tip of his staff sweeping upward. "Don't you recognize me?"

"Sure, I recognize you, you disrespectful punk. You're Stefano Sforza."

The smile on Mephisto's face slid a bit until it was slightly lopsided. Mab had to struggle to keep from chuckling. Witnessing this moment made the whole, horrible trek up the mountain almost seem worth it.

Mephisto put his arms down. "Um...yeah, I am...but nobody calls me that anymore. I use my middle name now, and my family changed our last name when we moved to Scotland." He thrust out his hand toward the gnome. "Hi, I'm Mephistopheles Prospero. Pleased to meet you."

"Get your hand out of my face, Squishy Scum, or I'll show you what a real handshake is like." He clenched and opened his stone hands, making a sound like rock grinding against rock.

Mephisto pulled his arm back. "Ah...yeah....so....right."

"What'cha want?"

"I'm here to see the girls, of course. Hi, girls!" Mephisto waved his fingers.

The rock-ladies giggled and waved back. "Hi, Mephisto."

"I got some goodies for you!" Mephisto gestured at the fertilizers.

"Oooo! Mephie! You didn't have to!" the *oreads* did not move, but they craned their heads to get a better look.

Mab and Erasmus stared at the rock ladies, blinking. They were some fine-looking rocks.

"Those are some...rather chunky ladies," Erasmus said softly.

"Yeah, *oreads* are fat. Round limbs like boulders." Mab lowered the brim of his hat. "Yet, surprisingly lovely all the same though."

"Yeah," Erasmus murmured back, as the rock nymphs gyrated and cooed. "Strangely appealing."

"Wait! What-da-we got there? Huh?" The gnome stomped over and glared down at the offerings. "What's this?" He stuffed his hand into the bag of high-nitrate fertilizer, rupturing the plastic, withdrew some of the white powder within, and tasted it. "This stuff's crap! I hate this high-nitrate stuff! Why didn't you bring..."

"It's not for you. It's for the ladies," Mephisto grabbed the bag and yanked it away from him. He carried it over to where the *oreads* stood and started sprinkling it over their heads, eliciting a burst of rumbly giggles.

The gnome looked after him sourly but then turned his attention to the remaining bags. "What's this one?" He ripped open the next bag, spilling some of the powdery beige substance, and thrust a whole fist of it into his mouth. "Mmm." He munched. "Giant's bones. I like this."

Immediately, he doubled in size. With a greedy, eager leer, he grabbed another fist full and then another. In no time, he was nearly as tall as Mab and Erasmus, and three times as broad. His purple jacket ripped away, until it was nothing but a mere scrap, like a scarf, on his back. His gold nuggets jingled.

"Professor Prospero," Mab murmured to Erasmus in a low voice. "Maybe we should do something."

"No, I'm sure it's fine." Erasmus stroked the chill weasel's soft burnt ocher and periwinkle coat. "What could go wrong?"

"Maybe you should put that thing down, Mr. Erasmus. I think it's going to your head. And we might need our heads about us. Outings with Mr. Mephistopheles seldom go well."

"What makes you say that?" Erasmus asked mildly.

"Er...Miss Mir...Mrs. Stormwind's told me a few stories."

"Like what?"

Mab scratched his stubble. "There was a time they went after a Yeti, where everyone but your brother ended up under an avalanche. Another time involving a mermaid..."

"Oh, yes. I remember that," Erasmus frowned slightly.

For a moment, Mab thought he was going to straighten up, throw off the weasel, and take charge, saving the outing from disaster. But he merely shrugged, smiled, and went on petting the weasel.

"Hey!" Mephisto shouted from where he was chatting up the rock ladies. "Don't let him eat that. That's for the girls!"

Erasmus reached forward and yanked the bag of giant bone meal away from the hulking gnome who now looked a great deal more like an ogre or a troll. "I think you've had enough for one day."

"Do you now?" The gnome shoved his large, bulbous, rocky face into Erasmus's face. "And what if I don't agree?"

Mab tensed, but the ordinarily irascible Erasmus just shrugged and patted the rock spirit on the shoulder.

"Just chill, *paisano mio*." Erasmus gestured casually at the creature's increased bulk. "Look how much you have got out of it already and be grateful."

"I'll take that!" Mephisto snatched the broken bag from Erasmus and carried it over to the *oreads*, spilling a trail of beige powder behind him.

The glowering gnome regarded the last two bags: the Fox Farm Happy Frog Japanese Maple fertilizer. He ripped open the first one and took a bite.

"Hm. Feather meal, kelp meal, bat guano. Organic even. Not bad. Not bad," muttered the gnome.

Mab scratched his ever-present stubble. "What does organic bat guano even mean?"

"One can hardly blame him for his excitement." Erasmus made an airy gesture. "I mean, I, for one, would certainly not want to eat a diet including chemically-reproduced bat guano."

Mab gave Erasmus a sharp glance. "Are you sure you aren't overdoing that mellow mustelid maybe just a little bit, Professor Prospero?"

"No, no," Erasmus replied pleasantly. "This is fine. Much better than me blowing my top and bruising my fist on the sucker's face."

"I see your point." Mab scratched his stubble again, muttering, "Still, I think, if we get out of this in one piece, you might want to think about a visit to Weasels Anonymous."

Meanwhile, the gnome tossed the rest of the entire first bag of Happy Frog fertilizer into his mouth in a single gulp.

"My, that was scrumptious!" He wiped his face, while Erasmus incredulously mouthed '*scrumptious?*' and shrugged. "Hit's the spot. Let's have more."

He picked up the second bag and was in the act of ripping it open directly above his gullet, when Mephisto turned around.

"Hey, give that back. That's for the ladies. They love that!"

"Give 'em the next bag."

"That's all there is. You ate the other one."

"What!" The gnome stomped, and the slopes trembled slightly. "You only brought two tiny, puny bags! How dare you!" Looking around angrily, the gnome spied the yoke and its odiferous burden.

"Alum!" The gnome's face went slack. He ran and knelt beside the aluminum buckets, wringing his rocky hands. "Alum? Is that you? I wondered where you'd gotten to! Al, talk to me!"

Mab shook his head. "Oh, good grief!"

This was not going to go well. He could feel it in his airy bones.

The gnome snarled. "You think this is funny? You think you'd like to find your friends and relatives ground into meal or made into buckets?"

Mab pulled down the rim of his fedora. "No, sir. No disrespect meant."

"Oh yeah? None meant? Not sure I believe that, tough guy. Come on! Let's see what you're made of."

"I'm made of wind. I'm an Aerie One. You can't wrestle the wind."

"What about you?" The gnome turned to Erasmus. "Ready to go around?"

"Not really, *paisano mio*," Erasmus stated. "About Mephisto's debt. Is it discharged now? Or not?"

"Discharged? Discharged?" screamed the gnome. "You bring before me my ground-up relatives, and my melted friends, and you want me to applaud you for that?"

The gnome let out a bellow and stomped his foot. The entire mountain shook. The *oreads* cried in fear. Mephisto turned around annoyed.

"Stop that, you're frightening the ladies!" He stormed over to the gnome.

"Mephisto, let it be," Mab warned nervously. He glanced hopefully at Erasmus, but the professor was still in chill-ville.

"No," Mephisto leaned into the face of the gnome. "I'm not afraid of some rock-headed idiot who's gotten too big for his britches. Or at least for his purple coat! Leave us alone, and stop bullying these wonderful ladies."

"Or what?"

"Or you are going to have to answer to me!"

"Mephisto," warned Erasmus, finally looking faintly alarmed. "Why don't you let the angry stone man be?"

"We'll never forgive your debt now!" shouted the gnome.

"It's not up to you," Mephisto yanked on the remaining bag.

"Oh, yes it is!" The gnome yanked back.

"Give it to me!"

"No. You give it!"

"No, you give it to me. You...stonehead?"

"Yeah, my head is stone, is that the best you can do?" crowed the buffed-up gnome. "At least I got some. You don't got none. You don't got the stones to wrestle a gnome." The rock spirit flexed his rippling stone biceps. "You've got nothing hanging but withered old sacks!"

"Withered!" Mephisto cried fiercely. "Oh, I beg to differ! Just ask the ladies! They'll tell you. They'll tell all. You're the one who has pebbles where you are supposed to have *cojones*!" To emphasize his point, Mephisto swung his staff and rapped the gnome between its rocky legs.

Mab flinched. Erasmus flinched. Even the chill weasel flinched.

The blow could not have done much harm, but the startled rock spirit dropped the bag of Happy Frog fertilizer. Mephisto snatched it up and sprinted back to where the *oreads* waited.

The gnome howled. Again, he stomped his foot. The mountainside bucked.

With a roar of anger, the gnome raised his hands. One of the aluminum buckets shot into the air, spinning. The odiferous, smoldering contents that Mab had so painstakingly carried up the mountain flew out and splashed all over the Aerie One's face and coat. The fiery filth burned. He shouted in alarm.

The gnome raised his hands again, and the other pail flew at Mephisto, who did a back flip and moved handily out of the way.

Unfortunately, Erasmus had been standing behind him. The contents of that pail slopped over his head and shoulders.

"Ye-ow!" Erasmus screamed as the hot manure slid down his body.

"Wait! I got it!" Mephisto shouted, jumping up and down. "I know what to do!"

"You've done enough," shouted Mab.

"Back off, Brother," shouted Erasmus from under the second pail. "You're only making things worse."

"No! I got it this time!" Mephisto called back. "Remember what you said, Mab, about hunkering down? Well, maybe it's time for our gnome friend to CHILL OUT!"

With that, he grabbed the chill weasel from Erasmus's neck and smacked the gnome across the face in a burst of soulful jazz.

***

"Hey! It's okay!" Mephisto ran toward the other two, waving his arms cheerfully. Behind him, the overly-mellow gnome, who had shrunk back to his normal size, chilled among the lovely lady standing stones. "Turns out, I had already paid the *oreads*! Back when they first moved my house!"

Mab and Erasmus looked up from where they stood, dripping with steaming manure. Mab absently patted at a spot where his trench coat had started to smolder. He could feel something unpleasant sliding down the back of his neck.

"You were right, Mab," Erasmus sighed. "This is how it always ends."

"Doesn't have to be that way." Mab pulled his trusty lead pipe from his pocket and slapped it against his palm. "What do you think, Mr. Erasmus? Should we break his kneecaps? For the trouble he's put us to?"

"No point," Erasmus replied wryly, wiping muck from his face. "We'd just end up being the ones who had to carry him down the mountain."

"Yeah, you're right." Mab rotated his sore shoulders. He looked down at his soiled trench coat. "On second thought, think I'll take a whack of that weasel, after all."

The Mirror of Matsuyama

Once upon a time, in the Japanese village of Matsuyama, there lived a good man who had a beautiful wife and an equally beautiful daughter. Yuki, the daughter, was the apple of her parents' eye. She was clever, lively, sweet-tempered, and the spitting image of her mother.

Every morning, Yuki would rise from her straw *futon*, put on her blue *kimono*, and wrap her bright red *obi* about her waist. Then, her mother would come and brush out her long hair, and the two would talk and laugh together. They shared everything, their hopes, their dreams, everything except her mother's secret treasure.

Her mother's treasure had been a gift from Yuki's father. He had brought it back from the great city. Yuki knew that her mother kept it in the sleeve of her kimono, wrapped in a cloth of green silk, but Yuki had never seen what was beneath the cloth.

One day, Yuki's mother grew ill. As her illness grew worse, her beauty faded and was lost. Yuki and her father did all that they could for her, yet every day she grew weaker. Finally, she called Yuki to her side and said, "It will be hard for your father when I am gone. Promise me that you will take care of him."

"Of course, Mother," promised Yuki.

Her mother drew the secret treasure out from her robes. "Daughter, this is my greatest treasure. Take it and let it remind you of my love for you. When you are lonely or glum, look upon it, and it will cheer you."

Without unwrapping the silk cloth, Yuki hid the treasure away in her own sleeve. Soon after, her mother died. Overcome with sorrow, Yuki drew out her mother's treasure and unwrapped it.

Within the cloth lay a wonder. One side of it was etched with pine trees and cranes, symbols of long life and devotion in marriage. The other side was polished and shone like the moon.

When Yuki peered more closely, its shining surface showed her what she most wanted to see—her mother's face.

It was not her mother as she had last seen her, withered and pale from illness, but her mother as she had once been, beautiful as a dove. Yuki exclaimed with delight. So did her mother. Yuki could not hear her mother's words, but she could see that her mother was also overjoyed to see her.

From then on, Yuki spent hours peering into the treasure and talking to her mother. She told her mother of her hopes and her dreams, just as she had done when her mother was alive.

Eventually, Yuki's father remarried. His new wife was very different from Yuki's mother. Yuki's mother had been beautiful and delicate, this woman was plain with a wide, round face. Yuki's mother had been quiet and gentle, this new wife's voice often grew loud and shrill. Yuki did not like her new stepmother. She felt her dear and loving father deserved more.

Yuki's father assured her that she would come to love her new stepmother as he did, but this did not happen. The longer the new woman lived in the house, the more miserable Yuki became. Nothing Yuki did pleased the woman. The rice Yuki cooked was either too wet or too dry. When she braided the other woman's hair, the braid was too tight or too loose. The tea Yuki prepared was too hot or too cold. Yuki began to believe that she could never make her stepmother happy.

Whenever her misery became too great to bear, Yuki would take out her mother's treasure. Sitting cross-legged on the smooth wood floor, she would tell her mother of her troubles. She could not hear the advice her mother gave, but she could see how concerned she was for Yuki. Her sympathy made Yuki feel much better.

Sometimes, Yuki's stepmother walked in while she was talking to her mother. Whenever this happened, Yuki quickly hid the treasure, fearing that her stepmother might take it from her. If her stepmother questioned her, she pretended she did not know what her stepmother meant.

Then, one day, as she was talking to her mother, the paper windows separating her room from the main room of the house suddenly slid open, and her father appeared. Yuki had never seen her father so angry. She drew back, afraid.

"How dare you!" he shouted. "How dare you try to kill your stepmother with sorcery! She works so hard to keep our house, and you repay her with this?"

"What do you mean," Yuki cried, shocked. "I would never try to harm my step mother. For I love you, and I know that she is dear to you."

"But we saw you, through the hole in the paper wall," her father said, though his anger was draining away, for he had been touched by her love for him. "We saw you murmuring spells."

"I was talking to my mother," Yuki said.

"Your mother is dead."

"My mother left me this gift. In it I can see her face. When my heart is heavy, I talk to her, and she comforts me." With trembling hands, Yuki brought out the treasure for her father to see.

"Why that is the mirror I brought your mother from Kyoto!" her father exclaimed. "Let me see it."

When her father leaned over the treasure, to Yuki's great surprise, it did not show her mother's face. Instead, it showed his face. When her stepmother peered at it, it showed her stepmother's face.

"This is just an ordinary mirror," said her father. "How do you see your mother in it?"

"Like this," said Yuki, and she held the treasure before her own face.

Her father and her stepmother began to laugh, but it was a kindly laugh.

"Daughter," asked her father, "that is your face you are seeing, your own reflection."

"But, it looks just like Mother, the way she looked before she grew ill," cried Yuki, who had never thought of herself as beautiful.

"And so do you," said her father. "You look just like your mother when she was young."

Yuki gazed down at the mirror in wonder. Her stepmother now spoke.

"I am greatly ashamed. All this time, I believed you meant me ill. Please forgive me," she finished, bowing to Yuki.

"Of course, I forgive you," Yuki replied kindly.

With those words, trouble departed from that house in Matsuyama, never to return.

'Overheard' on Public School Virtual Band #447

"Hey, are you crying?"

"Are you rude? What kind of question is that? Who is this anyway?"

"Just trying to be nice. I'm Henry—grid mark 42B, level 5. If this was a real lecture hall, I'd be on the same tier as you, but behind you and to the left."

"Okay, I see you. How are you talking to me? What if our proctors see? I don't know about your proctor hall, but mine has a console where the proctors can look in on what all the kids are watching, to make sure we're not playing games or something, instead of paying attention to our classes."

"Don't worry, Julia..."

"It's Jillian. Jillian Marsh."

"Don't worry, Jillian. With equipment like you and I have, we could hold fifty conversations at once and never get caught. Proctors at these public halls are used to dealing with free-issue Datamark baseband vid-sets. It will never occur to them to check for broadband visors. After all, who would be on the public band if they could afford good equipment?"

"If you say so."

"So, Jillian, how did you get Reduced?"

"My father died. We couldn't afford academy bands anymore."

"Sorry. Is that why you were crying?"

"Yeah. How'd you know I'd been Reduced?"

"You're the only one in the room wearing professional V-actor glitz. Everyone else's face looks pale and washed out, like an old silent movie. No one bother's wearing that stuff on public bands. Their equipment isn't good enough for it to make a difference."

"Does that make everyone think I'm a dweeb? Because I wear reflective cream, and they don't, I mean."

"Who cares? The other kids attending this class may technically be our peers, but we don't have to eat lunch with them. What state are you in, anyway?"

"Minnesota. What about you?"

"Seattle—Washington....Look, sorry about your dad."

"I miss him so much. I used to sit in his corporation's study hall. We used to eat lunch together every day. Now, I'm stuck in this smelly room with fifty other kids. None of whom view any of the same classes I view."

"What did your dad do—if you want to talk about it?"

"He wrote software for the United Nations Web Police."

"He worked for the U.N.W.P.? They're the enemy!"

"Don't say that! My dad wasn't the enemy!"

"He was in my book. His software probably helped put many good men in jail. Men like Gunther Jacobson, Mark Anderssen, and Henry Burns III."

"Those men are international criminals, not heroes!"

"Criminals? Look, Miss My-Daddy-Was-A-Fascist-Toady, a man isn't a criminal just because he's in jail."

"Don't talk about my father that way! He was a good man who cared about his work and protecting the people from insidious Black Net influences."

"Insidious Black Net influences? Jacobson and Andessen went to jail for writing software that was too good. Do you call that a crime?"

"Okay, maybe those two weren't so bad. They were just casualties of the Switchover. But, that doesn't apply to HB3! He was arrested for international espionage!

"And I'm the Man in the Moon! Don't believe everything you read on the Supernet, sweetheart. Look, here's the real story. Henry Burns the Third ran a mail-forwarding service that guarantied anonymity. When the police showed up on his doorstep after the UN passed Edict 1001, he erased his records instead of handing them over like 'a good little boy.' They put him in jail for it."

"There had to be more to it than that! That case was all over the news for months. You don't put a guy away for ten years for erasing his own files."

"That was it. Any news media that said differently was lying."

"But My dad used to subscribe to three different Supernet news services. They all told the same story."

"You're a wiped disk, aren't you? The Supernet is censored, stupid. That's what Edict 1001 is all about. Everything goes over the Supernet, and everything on the Supernet has to be read by the Gestapo Gateways. It's all lies."

"Okay, Mr. I-know-it-all, if all the news is censored, how do you know so much about it?"

"Cause I know."

"Yeah, right. I guess that kind of smarmy answer is all I can expect from a dweeb who's dumb enough to have a widow's peak. Yuch! Don't you know that Sampsonair can cause hair to grow on your brain?"

"You really are a real wiped disk, Jillian! That's a myth. Too much Sampsonair can cause weird side effects. But, it won't grow fur on your brain!"

"I am not wiped! I just think having fur on your face is stupid. At least, you don't have a skunk stripe or tiger stripes like some guys. My mom says that widow's peaks and skunk stripes are our generation's contribution to the eternal hair war between youth and the establishment."

"The eternal hair war?"

"When she was young, kids used to get crew cuts and shave stuff into their hair—like swear words and Batman symbols. Next came pierced tongues and tattoos. And we have Sampsonair. She says kids today should develop a little dignity and leave the Sampsonair for the bald men. I can't believe you're such a repro-head as to use that stuff, Henry!"

"To each his own, Jillian."

"Seattle, huh? Boy, that's far away. It's a shame we can't hang out together after school. We just moved. I don't know anyone here."

"We can hang out, Jillian—the same way we are now."

"I can't afford the phone bill."

"That's okay. I can cover it for both of us."

" What are you doing at a public school band, Henry, if you can afford today's long distance prices?....Unless...there is one kind of low life who's short on cash and long on phone credit....You're not one of those are you? You wouldn't dare!"

"One what? Say it."

"A Black Market Router!"

"In the flesh! Or, maybe I should say, in the electronic image."

"How could you! That's almost as bad as drug dealing! You haven't actually been on the Black Net, have you?"

"Sure, all the time."

"Really? You're a jumper? I can't believe it."

"Sure, there's nothing to it. Just plug in and jump. It's not illegal, after all."

"Really? Then, how come so many jumpers get arrested?"

"They don't get arrested for being on the Black Net. They get arrested for sending encrypted info abroad, or routing pornography, or other anti-Edict 1001stuff. Jumpers don't think that much of the UN and its Edicts. I can tell you that!"

"But, isn't that what Black Market Routers do? How they make their money, or their phone time, or whatever they get paid in, I mean."

"Yeah."

"You do that?"

"Yeah, sure."

"Couldn't you get arrested?"

"Yeah—if I got caught."

"But aren't you afraid of the Gestapo Gateways?"

"Look, a Gestapo Gateway is not a doorway somewhere guarded by two jack-booted Nazis. It's just a type of router—a piece of hardware—with extensive search programs, and a program that randomly flags passing programs and displays them to the human censor. If you don't send your information through them, they can't possibly flag you. Not having to use Gestapo Gateways is what makes the Black Net so fast—if you don't run into a virus."

"Faster? But, I saw this editorial said that the Supernet runs at 600.mbps. It said that most of the Black Net still runs at 20 mbps to 100 mbps, at the tops."

"Those liars! Oh, the backbone of the Supernet is fast all right. The packets travel asynchronous transfer and, with the speeds of today's Fire Arrow cable, easily reach 600 mbps. The Supernet routers won't let data travel on without a Gestapo okay bit. Every time a transaction wants to go from a private net to the Supernet, all individual bits of data must arrive simultaneously and in order at the gateway to be scanned and approved. So, it's good-bye packet switching, which means good-bye ATM speeds. Not to mention the additional delay every time your data gets selected to be viewed by a human censor. And the same thing has to be done at the point of arrival. After all, you can get arrested for just *receiving* anti-Edict material. Even with the efficiency of today's censoring software, this reduces the overall speed of a transaction over the Supernet back to the speeds of over twenty years ago, 4 to 20 mbps at the most. It's a racket!"

"My Dad used to say that the problem was that there were too few gateways, so that all the data got bottled up."

"Well, he's somewhat right. Gestapo Gateways are really expensive. It's because they to have that special U.N.W.P.-installed software."

"Cisco and Sun Microsystems are supposed to be coming out with a Gestapo Router that's going to be cheaper than a gateway. I saw a commercial about it."

"More censors won't stop the problem."

"But, if companies didn't use them, they couldn't know if their employees were engaging in Edict violations. They could get huge fines, or kicked off the Supernet, or sent to prison. If a company wants to do business today they need the Supernet. To use the Supernet, they have to have a censor."

"The solution is to get rid of the United Nations Web Police and their Edicts."

"But then who would police the Net?"

"Why police it?"

"You wouldn't want it to be chaotic! What if things went back to being like the old Internet at the turn of the Century! Fortunes ruined, classified secrets released, children viewing pornography? The whole World Wide Web dominated by those Twentieth Century Hacker Barons?"

"There was nothing wrong with the Internet, other than its speed. It was free—unrestricted. Caveat Emptor. In fact, the Black Net is the old Internet, for the most part."

"But, I though the old Internet became the Supernet."

"Depends on how you look at it. You're probably too young to remember when the Supernet came over the telephone, instead of the TV. Well, a lot of those old systems that used the phone lines are still in place. That's what we jumpers use for our net. It's not as reliable as the Supernet, so you really have to know your stuff. But, it's that extra effort that keeps us one jump ahead of the U.N.W.P.."

"Is that why you guys are called jumpers? Because you're always jumping around to avoid the police?"

"No, idiot. The term 'Jumper' comes from a speech Gunther Jacobson made just after the first appearance of the Dead_Again virus—before anyone knew that it had been released by our own government. He said, 'If traversing the Supernet is akin to surfing. Then, traversing the Black Net more like bungie jumping.'

"After he got arrested for releasing his anti-Dead_Again program to foreign markets, we started calling ourselves jumpers in his honor."

"God! The whole thing sounds terrible! I hope I never see the Black Net as long as I live. I hope my dad's software catches all you jumpers!"

"You and I are talking on the Black Net right now, babe. That's how come I know that the proctors won't catch us."

"Oh, my God! Oh, my God! Isn't it dangerous? Can't we get diseases or something? Get me off! Get me off now, or I'll pull my visor off!"

"Calm down. You are such a wiped disk! Humans can't get sick from computer viruses. You're perfectly safe. Geesh!"

"Are you sure?"

I'm positive. You can't catch a disease from the Black Net. It's like cats and humans. We can't catch their diseases, they can't get ours."

"We can get rabies from animals! And cats can so catch a few of our illnesses!"

"Well, this is different. How could a virus that is made of software get into you? And even if it did, what could it do?"

"Well, in Jumper's Revenge, the bad guy…"

"Give me a break! Real life isn't like a Damian Harley movie, Okay? The Black Net is perfectly safe for humans. It's safe for computers too, as long as you're careful. It just doesn't provide its own anti-virus ware, like the Supernet does. That's all."

"We're really on the Black Net? You mean we can say anything we want...even swear words?"

"Yup! Go ahead. Try it."

"Really? Fu...no, I can't."

"Sissy wimp."

"I can't believe you've hooked us up to the Black Net in a public school!"

"It's not like we're snorting coke or shooting up. The Black Net is just a computer network. It would be a perfectly good computer network, if dweebs like your dear old deceased daddy didn't write viruses for the U.N.W.P. to release."

"How dare you talk about my dad that way! That's it, you Bastage! I'm turning you in! Lecturer! What's your last name, anyway, Henry? ...Come on, you might as well tell me. It will only take me a second to look it up! Okay, I'll look it up....Burns? Your name is Henry Burns? No wonder you're a fan of that criminal."

"Look, just for your information, I'm Henry Burns the Fourth, and my dad is not a criminal."

"HBIII is your *dad*?"

"STUDENT 53F LEVEL 5, THIS IS THE LECTURER, MRS. HARRIS. YOU SEEM DISTRESSED. IS SOMETHING THE MATTER?"

"Yes, something's the matter all right. I'd like to report that..."

"THAT WHAT, MY DEAR? ...YES...I'M WAITING. I MUST GET BACK TO LEADING THE CLASS IF I CAN'T HELP YOU."

"...That student 42B level 5 is..."

"YES?"

"Making fun of my dead father."

"I'M SORRY, MY CHILD. I WILL TELL HIM TO LEAVE YOU ALONE. PERHAPS YOU SHOULDN'T WEAR SO MUCH REFLEC-TIVE CREAM, MY DEAR. THE INFRARED IMAGER IS PICKING UP YOUR TEARS, YOUR IMAGE IS TERRIBLY STREAKED. YOU HAVE MY LEAVE TO GO WASH YOUR FACE, IF YOU LIKE."

"No thank you, ma'am. I'll stay."

"VERY WELL. MRS. HARRIS OVER AND OUT."

"...Henry?"

"Ffew, that was close! I thought you were going to turn me in. What happen?"

"Well…I realized that in this whole virtual hall, you're the only one, including the lecturer, who would notice if tomorrow, someone else was 52F level 5."

"Hey, thanks. It means a lot to me. It would kill my mom to have me and my dad both in jail."

"Were you there when the U.N.W.P. came for your dad? Did the scarlet logo flash across his screen with that cool alarm noise?"

"Don't be such a vid-potato! Is that all you ever do? Watch Damian Harley movies? No, it wasn't like in the movies. My dad wasn't tracked down by Agent Damian Harley, and the FCC policeman who came to the door didn't look anything like Christopher Barrymore."

"Too bad. I love him. My mom says he has dream-boat eyes."

"Yeah? Well, I got dream-boat eyes too, babe—you just can't tell from my virtual face."

"Likely excuse."

"So, can I call you tonight? We'll chat online? I'll even spend my hard-earned phone credit on the kabillion-dollars-a-minute Supernet if it makes you feel safer."

"Yeah, I guess so…Okay. Well, class is ending. I've got to go. I'll talk to you tonight."

"Oh, and, Jillian? Don't listen to anyone who tells you to wear less V-actor cream. It shows off your expressions. It makes you the prettiest girl in the room."

"Thanks, Henry."

"Besides, you're not the only one who cares about how they look over the imagers."

"What do you mean?"

There was a pause. "I don't really have a widow's peak."

Knight's Mate

"D AMN Tarot! They've forked us!" said Officer Demetri Rangacheck-Seven to his partner. The two of them stood in a back alley in the worst part of Metachronopolis, the city beyond time, staring down at their own dead bodies.

"Forked? I am not familiar with the term," said Delling-Two. His baby-fresh skin acquired a greenish tinge as he continued to stare down at the burnt remains of his once-handsome face and his once-spiffy black-and-gold uniform. However, he took it well. His voice was steady and even.

"It means we're screwed," said Rangacheck.

The older cop kneeled and ran his chronoscope around the perimeter of the murder scene. Tiny images flickered by on the viewing screen. At first the image showed only the empty alley with the two corpses sprawled on the wet pavement. Then, Press Gang punks flickered across the silvery screen, moving backward, like a film seen in reverse. There were twelve of them in all. Three pushed cam-carts loaded with Evening News quality equipment. Four carried the giant spots which they positioned to illuminate the shot. The rest carried the cheap, illegal sineguns which they used to blow away the two cops. After the blast sucked back into the gun, and the two officers stood up, the scene ended.

"Crime just happened to occur at the early side of our twenty minute range, my foot! You get to be as old as I am, you stop believing in coincidences," grumbled Rangacheck. He slipped the chronoscope into the pocket of his trench cape, pausing to shake out the smooth pink-skinned hand that had been holding the scope. "You know what I hate the most about getting blown away? Having to grow new calluses."

"I still don't understand. How are we disaccommodated?" Delling asked. "This is the first time I've had to use a spare, and I admit that it was disconcerting. But, as far as the crime goes, it looks like an open-and-shut case."

"Disaccommodated? Kid, you crack me up," Rangacheck smirked. Then he leaned back on his heels and tipped up the rim of his slouch hat. "Open and shut...how?"

"The last thing I recall before waking up in the hatchery was that you and I were about two blocks from here—on the corner of Windswept and Westerly. Just ahead of us, two civilian policemen were being hassled by a Press Gang. Apparently, the Press Gang was either overly exuberant, or unusually short for news. They though the death of Causality Police would make for a better news bite than that of an ordinary street cop. The chronoscope backs me up. If we reversed the image we just saw, we would see our-selves walk up, and the Press punks shoot us. The bodies at our feet have burn marks in the corresponding places to those we saw in the chronoscope. Close of case," Delling stated. He spoke into the recording head of his omnipad as he recited his findings. Once finished, he depressed the 'end of file' button and put the device back in his pocket.

"Close of case? Don't you see a few holes blue whales could swim through in that story? No?" Rangacheck snorted. Then, he shrugged. "I guess that's not a bad try for a rookie who had just gone under for the first time. But let me set you straight on a few points.

"First of all, Press Gangs might kill Civy cops—sometimes, but they never kill Causality Police, okay? 'Cause they know we can hunt them down like dogs. Besides, cack enough Causality Police, and you might piss off their bosses. Having a real live Time Ar-chon breathing down your back is not the kind of attention that looks good on the Evening News. You could wake up one morn-ing to discover some Historic fluke has wiped out your whole fam-ily tree.

"Secondly, they were firing sineguns. Not even good ones, at that. Our randomizers should be able to soak up that kind of damage easy, not to mention our body armor. Besides, even if one Causality officer could be taken out that way, they certainly couldn't take out two of us! Without even losing a man? Geesh!

"Thirdly, no Causality officer worth his salt would walk into a setup like we just saw in the viewer. I mean they had their cameras and their spotlights blazing, for Christ's sake! You might be able to take out a Civy, or a rookie, with a maneuver like that. But, an old-timer like me?" He thumbed his chest with his new white thumb. "I'd never fall for it."

"What's your theory then?" Delling asked politely.

Rangacheck pushed his corpse with his toe until it rolled over. Then, he stooped down and pointed at its back.

"Here. What do you see?"

Delling knelt and examined the black fabric of the trench cape and the salt-and-pepper hair, much grayer than the new jet-black locks of the young-looking Rangacheck who squatted beside him. In among the fabric and the hair, he noticed green-gold glints of some grass or fiber. Locating a piece about a half an inch long, he pulled it carefully from the body, sniffed it, and rubbed it between his fingers.

"Synthetic grass. All over the back...but none on the front. From the placement of the fibers against the weave of the cape, I'd say this body was dragged along a synthetic lawn," Delling said. He turned and examined his corpse. "Both of them were dragged!"

"Good boy. Now, what about the wound, notice anything strange?"

Delling got out his medic stick and took a series of measurements. Rangacheck pulled a box of cigarettes from his front pocket, along with a thin electric lighter. With a sneer of disgust, he tossed the lighter away and began rummaging through the pockets of his corpse, until he came away with a box of wooden matches. One side of the box was soggy with blood. Rangacheck struck a match against the other side of the box and lit his cigarette with a satisfied sigh.

"God, Demetri! How can you! That's hardly sanitary!" Delling shuddered involuntarily as he watched his partner salvage bloody matches from a corpse.

"This job can be Hell, but it's got its perks. For me, wooden matches is one of those perks. They remind me of something I don't want to forget," he said. "Besides, it's only my own blood, for Christ's sakes."

Delling remained kneeling a moment longer looking up at his partner. "You're not from Metachronopolis, are you?" he asked.

"Nah, recruited. From a Period called the 1930's. Heard of it?" Rangacheck asked. Delling shook his head. Rangacheck scowled.

"Where do they get rookies from now days? What's History coming to when even the Causality Police can't place a thing in time....So, what did ya find?"

Delling stood up. His handsome, youthful face was grim. He showed his partner the medic stick findings.

"Look at the way the blood has pooled, and how rigor mortis has set in. These bodies have been dead nearly two hours. From the nature of the burns, I'd guess they had been dead over an hour and a half when they received the sinegun wounds."

"Good boy," said Rangacheck.

Delling pulled out his watch, a device the size of a cigar case with fifteen different faces, each with hands moving at different rates.

"According to absolute time, we've only been dead twenty minutes—the same time accounted for by the chronoscope. How could that be?" he said.

"You tell me, kid."

"...a paradox? Here, in Metachronopolis?"

Rangacheck nodded, scowling. Both men were silent a moment while Delling contemplated the ramifications of his statement.

"But how does that make us...what was the word you used?"

"Forked? It's a chess term. It's when you use one piece to threaten two pieces at the same time. Imagine our enemy has a piece... a bishop would probably be most appropriate—after all, the Tarot are religious, cause-and-effect-breaking, magic-invoking scum. In the next move of our hypothetical game, that bishop can either capture our knight—that's us, you and me—or another piece, say our king or our queen—something important. Either we let them carry off the prize, or we die. That's a fork."

"Die how? Didn't we just die? I would not choose to go through it for entertainment, but it is certainly better than being dead-dead. What did our 'enemy'—and I use the word lightly for I can't believe there is really a Tarot operating in Metachronopolis. What did our 'enemy' gain by his move?"

"He hasn't moved yet," said Rangacheck grimly. He gestured toward the corpses with a nod of his head. "Take another look at that synthetic grass. Notice the color, that particular glint of gold among the green? That's real gold. Check it with the medic stick if you doubt me. Where is the only place in this city that would have real gold in the lawn?"

Delling frowned thoughtfully, then looked up, startled. "The Chronodome? But the Chronodome is insulated. If we died in there, our responders would not be able to transmit our brain information back to the hatchery. We really would be dead."

"Dead-dead," said Rangacheck, nodding.

"I...I don't understand," Delling said softly. "Why aren't we dead? Dead-dead?"

"Because someone used a paradox to make it so we died out here when we really died in there. Now, we've got a choice. We can betray everything we stand for and look the other way, and let them get away with whatever else they stole or killed or changed at the same time, or we can collapse the paradox..."

"And kill ourselves?"

"Yeah, kid, that's right. There is a war on, after all," said Rangacheck softly. He took his cigarette from his mouth and blew a long plume of smoke into the muggy evening air.

Delling straightened his back. From his hip, he unhooked his Blue Lantern, a huge, heavy, black flashlight over a foot and a half in length. Through the smoky lens, a tiny spark of dancing azure fire could be seen deep within.

"Very well," he said sternly. His gaze met Rangacheck's as if daring the older man to try and object. "I swore an oath when I joined this force. That oath is more important than my life! I will not break it."

"I knew I could count on you, kid," Rangacheck said, a gleam like pride glinting in his blue eyes. "I knew when I chose you as my partner that you were the kind of fellow who would never let our principles down." Then, he reached forward and gently put a restraining hand on the younger man's wrist. "But let's not go commiting suicide yet, okay? There still might be a way out."

"How so? If we live, a paradox is perpetrated. If we live more than three hours, the false time stem starts grafting onto the main trunk, causing causal fraying. Not to mention whatever additional damage is being sustained by our continued existence. In your words, if we save the knight, we lose the queen." Delling asked, his voice breaking slightly as he spoke.

Rangacheck grinned, a large craggy grin that lit his face as a single ray of sunlight illuminates a rain-shrouded mountain.

"Not if we can capture the bishop! You see, if this sucker had to use even one paradox, anywhere, in any line of cause and effect that leads to his cacking us in the Chronodome in the first place—and we can collapse that paradox—we're home free."

"Great! We got this far in just over two hours and thirty-two minutes. That gives us about twenty-five minutes to bag this creep before 3rd-hour-fraying begins. Now, you're sure about the red meat?" Rangacheck asked, snapping shut his watch.

The two officers crouched behind a buttress near the junction of the Zephyr causeway and the golden Chronodome, on the third level of the city. Below, pedestrians and hopper cars milled about like ants. Above, the fat, puffy, cumulous clouds obscured the tops of the spired towers.

"My source assured me that the Lieutenant Cosmic-General has undergone a change in diet and installed a meditation chamber, all since he came back from a recent trip into History. He's basically our only suspect. All the other high officials checked out, and no one else would have access without their palm codes being recorded. Do you think he will come?"

"If your source is right about that boar dinner at The Golden Hind, he'll come all right. I addressed my note to 'His Heinousness,'" Rangacheck said with of grim satisfaction.

"You think we're up against the Devil?" Delling choked. "Out of 22 archetypes, why pick that one?"

"Only the Devil, the Magician, and the Charioteer have the gumption to pull off a stunt like this—sneaking into the enemy stronghold right under their enemies' noses. Of those three, the Charioteer's archetype is too impetuous to have the patience for a subtle chess trap like this one. And, the Magician is a vegetarian. That leaves Mr. Niceguy as the Tarot possessing our buddy, the Lieutenant Cosmic-Governor," explained Rangacheck.

"I hope you're mistaken," Delling said grimly.

"But, you know I'm not," replied his partner.

With a rush of footsteps, a squadron of civilian police ran by, deliberately running out of step so as not to shatter the airborne causeway. Ahead, where the causeway met the balcony of the Chronodome, another squadron of police moved in, accompanied by two Causality Police, their black and gold visible against the drab gray of the civilian uniforms. Higher above, the swallow craft of the Time Archon Wellerand could be seen diving like a jeweled hawk between the tall towers of the city.

"Jimminy Christmas! Has all Hell broke loose?"

"Didn't you hear?" Delling asked, surprised. "The Causal Flame is gone. Someone stole the whole Source Lantern."

Rangacheck growled, "That's our queen piece! That's what you and I died protecting."

"No wonder they went to so much trouble!" said Delling.

"I told ya it had to be something important, for them to bother with something as subtle as a fork. But the Source Flame? Jesus H. Christ! What I don't get is what does a bunch of reality-denying Tarot want with pure causality?"

"Without that flame to recharge our Blue Lanterns, you and I will soon be no better than glorified Civies with a lot of useless skills," said Delling. His blue eyes clouded and serious. "Without the Causality Police to stop the proliferation of paradoxes, it will only be a short time until the main time trunk starts to fray. We'll be back at the primitive level of slash-and-burn agriculture that the Tarot so favor in no time."

"In other words, all they got to do is sit on that flame, and we're screwed? Great! Isn't there any more of that stuff anywhere?" Rangacheck asked.

"Nowhere. The Causality Flame is what keeps Metachronopolis 'beyond time'," said Delling. He frowned, staring at the rushing police ahead of them. "I wonder why 'His Heinousness' wanted to meet here? I'm trying to recall my Tarot Psychology classes from the Academy, but I confess that was not my best subject. Stealth and shadowing were my forte. Does the Devil have any known weaknesses?"

"Weaknesses? Him? Yeah, sure. Once, every hundred blue moons or so, he accidentally tries to hit too many birds with the same stone. Other than that? He's never been beat. Not the sort of odds you want to bet on."

"Perhaps we should call for backup," said Delling.

Rangacheck shook his head. "No point. Anyone we called would just get sucked into the paradox. If we have to bail out, their whole time stem could be weakened. Just talking to someone who's 'doxed can weaken your causal relations. Heck, I didn't even go to see my little girl, for fear my presence in the house would compromise her somehow," Rangacheck said, his voice low. Then, he straightened and slid a soft, baby-pink hand through his jet black hair. "No, kid, it's just you and me. I'm the front man. You're the backup."

"I'm backup? No, Demetri, I'm going with you," stated Delling.

Rangacheck shook his head. "Nah, you gotta watch my back. Someone's got to be there to shine the blue light if we can't find any paradoxes in this joker's timeline. You rather go take on the Devil, and I watch? No? Good. Now, you got the bag?"

Delling held up a crystal-paper bag. Within were fibers of the green-gold synthetic grass, mud from the back alley where they found the corpses, a vial containing a blood sample, and the readout tape from the medic stick. Rangacheck squinted at it, then nodded, satisfied.

"Yup, there's enough evidence here to substantiate the paradox. First sign of trouble, you blue flash that bag! If we fail, at least our deaths should also undo the paradox that allowed for the theft in the first place. Collapsing the paradox should return the Source Lantern to the Chronodome."

. "And if the time runs out?" Delling asked.

"If I'm not back in twenty-five minutes, collapse the paradox, regardless! We can't afford to risk damaging causality; particularly now, when the flame is missing. Okay?" said Rangacheck.

"Yes, sir," said Delling

"Good, kid. I'm counting on you. Now, fall back. Here he comes!" Rangacheck said.

With that, he slapped Delling on the shoulder and, stepping from behind the buttress, headed down the causeway toward an approaching set of footsteps.

Still hidden behind the buttress, Delling looked from the evidence bag to the Blue Lantern secured at his waist. Grimly, he straightened his shoulders, stepped deeper into the shadows of the buttress, and prepared to put his years of Academy training to the test—for what might be the last time.

✦

Rangacheck, shoulders hunched and hat pulled forward, followed the Lieutenant Cosmic-Governor through the phosphorescent hallways of the Chronodome into the surveillance booth overlooking the indoor amphitheater where the Lantern had been kept. Once inside, he pretended to wait meekly, leaning casually against one of the tall, glowing, golden wall panels that lit the booth. Actually, however, he was watching the Lieutenant Cosmic-Governor like a hawk. He passed his observations along to Delling by tapping his fingers against two keys of his omnipad, spelling out what he saw in a kind of fancy Morse code. The omnipad also transmitted spoken comments.

The Lieutenant Cosmic-General was a small, pudgy, balding man, with puffy cheeks and a weak chin, dressed in the formal scarlet and yellow robes of his office. His demonic expression, and the gleam of maniacal intelligence in his eye, were completely at odds with his soft bureaucratic features.

As Rangacheck had walked behind him, he had got a good look at the bottoms of the Lieutenant Cosmic-General's shoes. They were a gray cork, the kind that stuff sticks to. Yet, there was not a single fleck of synthetic grass, nor even so much as a glitter of gold. Now, leaning against the light panel, he tapped his observations out against the pad in his pocket.

Rangacheck wrote to Delling: "This joker has not been anywhere near the Chronoscope lawn in the last three hours. That means—from his subjective time stem, this crime has not happened yet. Am examining each item on his person. One must be the chronogyrator he plans to use to travel back in time in order to steal the lantern and cack us in the past. Chronogyrators used by Tarot usually look like watches or other time icons. No sign yet. Will stay on suspect until acquire target for blue lantern."

They had reached the surveillance booth across from the amphitheater where the Lantern was kept. The place was crawling with civies and techs. The Lieutenant Cosmic-Governor made a brief announcement requiring everyone else to leave, then left it to Rangacheck to enforce his order.

'He's sure certain of his hold over me,' Rangacheck thought. 'I wonder why?'

"So, what now?" growled Rangacheck. He pulled a cigarette from his front pocket and lit it with a match from the now-dry, blood-soaked matchbox.

"I see we all have our little sins. Wooden matches, tsk, tsk. So, my invitation today is not your first foray into the paradoxical, hmm?" The Lieutenant Cosmic-General's voice was smooth and soothing to the ear. Rangacheck, however, was not soothed.

"Listen, mister, anachronistic is not the same as paradoxical. Wooden matches may be anachronistic around Metachronopolis, but they do have a record of the technology for making them. It's not a paradox," he said.

"Ah, my mistake," said the Lieutenant Cosmic-General.

The Lieutenant Cosmic-General pointed to the controls for the security chronoscope.

"Now, please recalibrate these time spying machines so that they will not record any events happening approximately three hours ago," he said, pointing to the controls for the security chronoscope.

Rangacheck moved reluctantly toward the equipment. Time was running out quickly. He had to get Mr. Niceguy talking, had to get him to show off his chronogyrator, or give him the paradoxical object he could collapse. But, what to say?

"Your Heinousness," Rangacheck asked, "Why did you pick me? What made you think I'd go on the take?"

"I'm so glad you asked," said the Lieutenant Cosmic-General smiling graciously. "Two reasons. Firstly, I needed an officer who was sharp enough that he would catch my little trick. A dull-witted officer would not have noticed that the evidence at the crime scene was misleading. I suspect your young partner did not notice. The young man probably has no idea that his very existence is a paradox.

"Secondly, there is no point in going to all this trouble just for this one caper. I want a man who will also be helpful to me for years to come. So, I needed a man who had a reason to want to buck the system. Most Causality police are too clean. But, you....you have something to gain by betraying your old masters and throwing in with me," he finished graciously.

"And just what is that?" Rangacheck asked sarcastically. To Delling, he tapped out, "This kook has got the wrong guy. Think he's mistaken me for someone else."

The Lieutenant Cosmic-Governor pulled an old black-and-white photograph out of his voluminous sleeve and held it up. It showed a pretty young woman wearing a wide-shouldered coat and a long scarf. Her short hair curled about her pretty ears. She was laughing.

Rangacheck stared at the photograph, his expression unreadable. Then, he switched off the omnipad and took his hand out of his pockets.

"Okay," he said gruffly. "You got my attention."

"It must trouble you, Officer Rangacheck, that your 'benevolent' bosses gallivant around History, making changes wherever they see fit. Yet, they refuse to take the ten minutes necessary to save your wife."

"Yeah. It troubles me," Rangacheck admitted slowly.

Rangacheck thought back to the day that a stray bullet had ended the life of his beloved Polly, the mother of his little girl. A thousand times, a million times, he had imagined how he would save her if he were a time traveler. Only he was not. He was the guy who kept other guys from going back and saving their wives. He was the guy who made certain that History did not collapse upon itself, so there would be some place for the little daughters of dead wives to grow up.

"I don't get you guys," Rangacheck asked. "Why do you do what you do? Why are you trying to bring about the downfall of civilization? Aren't men screwed up enough without you? The Archons and the Causality Police have their hands full just undoing what you guys do. Then, all of a sudden, we'll find out you took some action on our side—in favor of progress, like helping the guy who invented steel get a patent. Why? How can you guys justify what you do?"

"Because it is we, not your Archons, who know the secret nature of time," said the Lieutenant Cosmic-Governor. "Do you want to know the secret?"

"Not really," growled Rangacheck. He took a puff on his cigarette and blew out a plume of smoke.

"I will tell you anyway," said the Lieutenant Cosmic-Governor politely. "Time is cyclical. That is the whole secret. But that is what the Archon's, with their push for progress, do not understand. Nature is cyclical. Seasons are cyclical. Animals, their mating seasons and birthing seasons, are cyclical. Everything is cyclical—except for Man.

"In becoming self-aware," the Lieutenant Cosmic-Governor

continued, "Man thought he could rid himself of cycles. However, his departure from them did not change the nature of the universe. Without progress, there can be no failure. Without failure, progress slows and becomes stagnant. When men are in darkness, civilization must grow. When society becomes bloated, stagnant and decedent, civilization must fall. We who know the secret of time call ourselves the Tarot to remind ourselves that Man travels the cycle from the Fool to the World, and then back again to the Fool.

"Imagine the fate of a farmer who builds a greenhouse to protect his corn plants from the bitterness of winter," he continued. "After the corn brought forth their ears, the adult plants continued to live. They continue to drain the nutrients from the soil, but giving nothing in return—neither fertilizer nor corn. The farmer might celebrate the success of his technical improvement— his corn plants are still alive. However, by the next harvest, when the old plants grew no new corn, he would starve. If a well-meaning stranger broke the farmer's greenhouse and let the winter cold kill the corn—the farmer might see it as a harm, but the stranger would actually be doing the farmer a favor.

"The Time Archons are like the defenders of the greenhouse. They want to protect anything men make, just because men made it. We Tarot are like the good stranger. Our actions cause short term strife—but come next harvest time, our actions are vindicated a thousand fold."

Rangacheck stared at the photograph the Lieutenant Cosmic-Governor still held in his hand. He thought back to the rundown section of his old town. Sure a few old fogies had complained about the destruction of certain landmarks. But after the renovation, it had been one spiffy neighborhood. He and Polly used to wish they could afford to move there. Maybe there was something to the Tarot's argument after all. Maybe he had been on the wrong side all along.

"All right, I'll help you," Rangacheck said. He started to move toward the control board, then he hesitated. He turned back to face the Lieutenant Cosmic-Governor, frowning. "But what about Kristopolis? I mean, that's what we Causality Police are fighting for."

"Kristopolis?" asked the Lieutenant Cosmic-Governor.

"You know, the Golden City. 'The city of Man's greatest hour, where the spirit of Man has triumphed,' as the poets say. If the timelines you help grow greater with each cycle, how come none of the timelines you mess with ever lead to the Golden City?" Rangacheck asked.

"Ah, the Golden City," the Lieutenant Cosmic-Governor purred. "I'm surprised at you, Rangacheck, a skeptical man like you! Haven't you guessed? The Golden City is a myth. It's a story made by the Archons to inspire their servants. Good men like you enjoy believing their efforts are protecting some utopian perfect city at the end of time. So, the Archons tell them it is so. The Archons lie."

"Is that so," said Rangacheck savagely. He turned his back on the Lieutenant Cosmic-Governor and the photograph in his hand. "Okay, mister, I'll calibrate your machine."

"The truth is there is no such place. There is no 'end of time' only more cycles," said the Lieutenant Cosmic-Governor.

Rangacheck ground his cigarette out against his shoe and leaned over the controls. He squinted speculatively at the chrono-scope then began flipping switches and tapping kinetic dials. In his pocket, his omnipad vibrated against his hip, indicating that Delling was trying to reach him. Rangacheck ignored it. Eventually, he straightened, wiped his brow, and said.

"Okay, It's done."

"Very well. Then the time has come," the Lieutenant Cosmic-Governor replied, smiling pleasantly. "We shall travel three hours into the past, steal the Lantern, jump sideways to the timeline where you were attacked by the Press Gang so that we can carry the Lantern off in a timeline where it has not been stolen and no one is looking for it—then, it's off to 1932 to save your precious wife."

The Lieutenant Cosmic-Governor reached into his robes and pulled out an intricate, blown-glass, hourglass—the chronogyrator.

"Funny, how these paradoxes work," the Lieutenant Cosmic-Governor observed. "Normally, a dignitary of the rank of Lieutenant Cosmic-Governor would not be allowed to wander through the august Chronodome escorted merely by one Causality Policeman. It is the very commotion caused by my crime that shall give me the ability to commit it."

"Is that so?" Rangacheck said slowly. A glint came into his eye, and he grinned until his teeth showed. "Funny how even the cleverest man can get tripped up by the same flaw again and again. Mister, you just tried to hit too many birds."

Rangacheck reached for his Blue Lantern. The Lieutenant Cosmic-Governor was armed, but Rangacheck knew he could draw and fire before the Lieutenant Cosmic-Governor could begin to react. He had the reflexes of a master.

His fingers closed rapidly about the heavy lantern and yanked. Only he no longer had the well-callused hand of a master. The fresh, soft flesh of his hand scraped against the rough, grip-improving surface of the bulky handle. The lantern flew from his stinging fingers and clattered harmlessly against a vertical light panel across the booth. As a startled Rangacheck leapt for his lantern, the Lieutenant Cosmic-Governor drew a deadly Rholler pistol and fired. A razor-bullet sliced through Rangacheck's body armor, piercing his lung.

"Damn," choked Rangacheck, staggering.

"What a pity," sighed the Lieutenant Cosmic-Governor. "And I so hoped we'd have a long future together."

Rangacheck spat in the Devil's face as he fell.

The Lieutenant Cosmic-Governor walked to stand over the dying officer. Looking down with a sad smile, he asked, "Why? I could have given you your wife back."

Rangacheck's face was contorted with pain. He was choking on his own blood as it burbled up from his lungs. However, somehow, he managed to whisper a reply.

"I've seen it," he whispered, "When I was very young."

"Seen what?" asked his killer

"The Golden City....I've been there. It's like noth...it's worth dying for."

"Worth more than your wife?" the Lieutenant Cosmic-Governor asked softly.

"You fool..." Rangacheck whispered back. "The Golden City had the technology... to bring the dead back to life. Not a paradox if men have...invented the process. It's...like the matches."

Blood gurgled from his mouth, and he could not continue. With his last strength, he switched on the omnipad and typed out. "Kid...do it now. Shoot the bag!"

One of the glowing light panels fell away from the wall. Officer Delling stepped out and fired. A beam of azure Blue Lantern light struck the hourglass. The surveillance booth, the fallen golden panel, the Lieutenant Cosmic-Governor, and everything else associated with the timeline arising from the paradoxical theft of the Lantern began to fray apart, dissolving.

Just before he blacked out, Rangacheck heard the Devil's voice mutter softly, "It really exists?"

※

Afterward, two hours and fifty-six minutes earlier, Officers Rangacheck-Six and Delling-Original stood on the corner of Windswept and Westerly Boulevard. Delling's handsome face covered in the skin with which he had been born. Rangacheck, grizzly-haired and weather-beaten, kissed the heavy calluses on his rough palms and fingers.

Ahead, a Press Gang, decked out in leather and glow belts, harried a pair of civilian policemen. The Frontmen fired their sineguns, singeing the air to either side of the street cops in an effort to fence in their prey. The Backcrew set up the cameras and positioned the giant spots, preparing to catch the kill on film.

"You doubted for a minute, didn't you?" Rangacheck asked, grinning like a wolf.

Delling shook his head, his blue eyes glinting merrily.

"Never," he said.

"Good for you, kid. Now, we've got to go arrest the Devil before he can try anything else. But, as long as we're going that way—you didn't believe me when I said a Press Gang would never cross Causality Police, did you? No? Well, watch this!"

The two Causality Police officers strode down the boulevard side by side with their trench capes snapping smartly in the wind. At the sight of them, twelve gangly Press punks panicked, grabbed their gear, and fled, scattering like flies before a coming storm.

HMS Mangled Treasure: The Rescue of Mr. Spaghetti

⚓

P IRATES, YOU SAY?" ASKED THE DETECTIVE WHO STOOD ON CLARA'S front stoop. At least Clara thought he was a detective, since he wore a fedora and a trench coat and looked disturbingly like a Humphrey Bogart clone. He could have been the claims adjuster, however. She had talked to so many people, she had lost track.

Clara put her fists on her hips. "Listen here, Buster. Maybe you want me to lie to you—like that punk of an ex of mine did last time this happen. Tell you some comfortable story about car thieves and let it go at that. But that ain't gonna happened!" She shook her head for emphasis, sending her many cornrows flying and wagged a finger at him. "I'm one woman who respects the truth, and that. Is. Not. Going. To. Change!"

Usually, this was the place where they shot her the "you should be locked away" look. This guy just nodded calmly, like he was on the set of *Dragnet* or something. Cool as a cucumber, he was.

"Pirates towed your car, ma'am. Is that right?" he asked again. He spoke with a Bronx drawl, so that his 'that' sounded like 'dat'. Clara had never heard a Bronx accent in real life. She kept expecting him to drop it and talk like a real human being.

"Yes!" she snapped.

"That's all right, ma'am. I believe you."

"You...you do?"

"Sure thing, ma'am. These pirates have been towing cars all over town."

Clara sighed. It felt good to have someone believe her for a change. It had been a while since anyone had believed her about anything. Still, it took all the fight out of her.

"Any idea who's behind it?" she asked as nicely as she was able.

The detective nodded solemnly. "A pack of the worst supernatural scum in Faeriedom."

Just great. It would be that the guy who finally believed her was three crayons short of a box. Clara cocked her head and fixed him with the look that her miserable excuse of an ex used to call the Hairy Eye.

"Faeries towed my car?"

The detective met her gaze square on, completely unfazed by the Hairy Eye. That in itself was amazing.

"Ma'am," he drawled. "You just told me that Pirates stole your car and sailed away—in the middle of Chicago, and I believed you. Common etiquette dictates you should extend to me the same courtesy."

Clara frowned. The guy seemed calm and reasonable. Not what she expected from a crazy, but then she had been an ER doc, not a psychiatrist. Maybe real crazies were as cool as cucumbers. It would certainly explain why he dressed and talked as if he had walked out of a 1940s movie.

"Look here, Mr. Spade-wanna-be. Pirates is one thing…" Clara froze, her mouth wide open, because at that moment, she remembered something.

A terrible sensation spread through her body, much like what she imagined it might feel like to be stung by scorpions. Tears pricked threateningly at her eyes. She let out a low warble of a moan.

"Mr. Spaghetti!" she wailed. "He's locked in the car!"

"Is that your dog, ma'am?" the detective asked.

Clara shook her head, nearly whipping him with her cornrows. Next time, she would stand a little closer and wap him good.

"No. A doll. My son's favorite doll." It shamed her that her voice broke. "He's going to be inconsolable."

"Children lose dolls all the time, ma'am. Part of life."

Clara turned on the poor man, showing her teeth like a wolf. "Is that so? Why don't you come home and explain it to my son. He's eight years old, weighs nearly seventy pounds, and has the language capacity of a delayed two year old. You come over to my house tonight, and you explain to Sammy what happened to his Mr. Spaghetti!"

The detective lowered the brim of his fedora. "I'll get your car back, ma'am."

Clara lay on her stomach among the trees at the Lincoln Park Zoo and peered through her binoculars. The ground was damp and cold under her shirt. She hoped this would not take too long. Behind her, she could hear the voices of laughing children as a school group toured the exhibits. This caused a pang of maternal longing, as she suddenly missed her own two kids.

According to her research into recent car thefts—she had called her sister's hunky friend at the police department—the roadside parking area she had under surveillance was a likely spot for the car thieves to hit and just after morning rush hour was a likely time. Pre-dawn would have been better, but she had been forced to wait until after Sari and Sammy had left for school.

Twelve cars had disappeared from this parking area alone in the last week. Like hers, they had all been parked off by themselves, with no one behind them. Of course, that did not mean one would disappear today, while she was watching, but she could hope.

And hope she did! It had taken a whole boatload of effort to rearrange her schedule so she could have today off. It would be weeks before she could arrange another free day. She had to horde her precious time off for when Sammy was home. It was hard enough to arrange things so that she did not have to work weekends.

To judge from last night's reaction, her household would not survive another day without Mr. Spaghetti, much less weeks!

Clara rubbed the bump on the bridge of her nose from where it had broken during the fit Sammy threw the last time Mr. Spaghetti went missing two years ago, the time they had accidentally left the rag-doll at the grocery store. She used to have a beautiful nose. People on the street would stop her and tell her how she could be a model. Of course, that was ten years and forty pounds ago. Today, she had more important things to worry about whether her looks could make strangers gawk.

Besides, what had her looks ever gotten her except her good-for-nothing ex?

Clara lowered her head, resting it on her hands. How had her life come to this? Ten years ago, it had been filled with such promise!

She had grown up in the slums, no one in her family had ever finished high school. No one in her family had ever amounted to much of anything, until Clara came along.

Clara had finished high school. She had finished college. She had gone all the way through seven years of medical school! Clara had become a doctor! When her mamma was young, women did not become doctors, much less women of color. Yet, Mamma's little girl had become one of the top physicians in the Mercy Hospital Emergency Room. She had saved lives!

She still had a vase of dried flowers on her mantelpiece, the remnants of the first bouquet given to her by someone whose life she saved.

She had given all this up for Sammy.

Clara recalled back to when Sammy was a baby. He had been the sweetest thing in the early months, even happier and less troublesome than his older sister, Sari. Even the Second Coming of Christ Himself could not have been sweeter!

But by two, he still was not talking, and he had started doing things with his hands, odd things that made him stand out from other children, holding them funny and waving them in front of his face. By five, he still was not talking, he still did weird things with his hands, and he was still throwing fits—the kind of fits her friends' children had stopped throwing at three or four. Then, her so-called-friends stopped bring their children over to play with Sammy.

And the screaming! Bright lights set him off. Cleaning products in the air set him off. Dyes in the food set him off. And not being allowed to eat the brightly colored candies the other children ate? That set him off the worst of all.

At first, Stan went into denial. He tried to cover for Sammy, when the boy was young, to hide it. But by the time he had a six-year-old who was still in diapers and who bent over and gestured oddly while moaning in public, even Stan, Master of De Nile himself, could not hide it anymore. He started saying that Sammy was not his son, even accused Clara of having an affair!

Her, Clara, the ultimate good girl! Boy, she let him have it for that one!

Of course, it had not always been like that. Once, Stan had been the husband she was so proud of, so handsome and buff. She gave the tear on her cheek a vicious wipe. Did no good to focus on the past. Just made a girl feel sad. Had to stay focused on the present.

It had been her decision to leave the ER and stay home full time to take care of Sammy that had really ruined things. Stan did not like losing the status of his doctor wife, and he did not like losing her six digit paycheck, not one bit. He tried to have Sammy put in an institution. When Clara would not go along, he bugged out. Took his sorry ass and ran.

Well, good riddance to him! She didn't need a man like that anyhow.

Stan sent money, but it was never enough. He spent most of what he made on his new wife and their perfect little girl. Clara was reduced to working at Smarty-Mart.

Smarty-Mart! From a top Emergency Room physician to the manager at a Smarty-Mart. It was enough to make a lesser woman cry.

But Clara was not a lesser woman. She was a survivor. If sacrificing her hard-won career to become a manager at the Smarty-Mart was what God required in order to give her son a good life, that was what she was going to do!

It did not mean that she did not break down and bawl like a baby now and then—usually at night when no one was awake to see. But she sure as heck did not sit around grousing about what life had thrown her way, like some people she knew.

By and large, now that she thought about it, that was true of all the mothers of "Special Needs" children she knew. Being active on her son's behalf had led her to meet a lot of other mothers of children with problems "in the spectrum." They were a surprisingly resilient lot—not counting the one or two who could not hack it. There was a reason that their mutual support group was called Mothers From Hell!

These mamas were not going to let anyone keep their children from having the best life possible to them!

And it was all worth it of course. Sammy might not be like other children. He might not talk clearly. He might flail his limbs when he got upset, sometimes even hurting his mother or sister. All that vanished, however, when she looked at him and saw his steady, shining eyes gazing back at her with such love, such trust.

It was like gazing directly at his soul, like looking into the eyes of an angel!

One smile from Sammy made all the crap worth it!

From somewhere above the tree tops came a very strange sound. Clara stiffened and listened. Voices, she thought, like a chorus. Only the voices were cold and eerie and soulless and filled with a harsh glee that had nothing to do with gladness.

> "The crew of the Mangled Treasure are we
> Fearless and peerless and wicked and free!
> Deathless and pitiless robbers are we
> Our hearts be as restless and cold as the sea!
>
> We do not bleed blood and we cannot weep tears!
> Our hearts are as empty and deep as our years!
>
> Sing yo ho, me bullies, and heave with a will
> We sail over ocean and hamlet and hill
> Cold iron, man's iron, our plunder-holds fill
> For men are our cattle and we wish them ill!"

"This one will do, lads!" called out a deep gravelly voice.

Clara's blood turned to ice in her veins. It was the middle of the morning! A God-fearing woman like her should be at work. What was she doing out hunting demented car thieves?

Her thoughts turned one last time to Sammy. To the look of hurt desperation that had come over his dear face when his beloved Mr. Spaghetti had not been in his proper comforting place last night. She had to get that doll back!

Clara brought the binoculars up to her eyes and stared. Her jaw gaped. Even though she had caught a glimpse of these thieves twice before, it had not prepared her for what she saw now.

A huge, square-rigger with sails the color of swamp fog mist sailed down out of the cloudy sky. The mainmast bore the symbol of a bleeding moon and a Jolly Roger flew from the foremast. Aboard the vessel was a crew of pirates, but not like the pirates in any book or movie!

Short, squat men in long jackets and boots with crimson sailors' hats, served as powder monkeys. They toiled to and fro carrying rocks to the cannons. Huge, hulking creatures manned the guns, their tri-cornered hats, vests, and breeches were of bark and dead leaves. Tiny, winged pixies, no bigger than Clara's finger, swarmed about the lookout. They were not cute, pretty creatures, like from a story book, but cruel, nasty, little things with ugly, distorted faces. In their hands, they held shiny copper cutlasses.

At the helm stood a leering old man with a long white beard. He was covered in barnacles and seaweed and wore a conch shell for a hat. To his left stood a horrifyingly ugly creature with an enormous nose and no mouth at all. It leaned precariously over the railing, holding what appeared to be a pistol made of wood.

The captain and his officers were of another cut. Clara trained her binoculars upon them in fascination. These tall, haughty faeries, as handsome as sin, were decked out in pirates' garb of capes, jackets, blousy shirts, bright sashes, and high boots. Only the capes were tattered and flowing, the blousy shirts were diaphanous, and the wide sleeves of their jackets hung down like the specter's shroud. The whole ensemble looked not so much like pirates as masqueraders at an eerie Venetian ball impersonating pirates.

On the side of the hull, scripted in flowery loops, was *The Mangled Treasure*.

Redcaps threw down copper hooks, green with patina, that caught on a tree and a bicycle rack.

"Heave! Heave!" the crew shouted harshly. Three large, burley trolls winched the ship down to the ground. The tree swayed wildly. Atop, redcaps and pixies reefed the mainsail and the foresail. With a rusty creak, the stern of the ship opened outward, descending until it touched the ground where it formed a ramp.

The harsh crack of a whip made Clara jump. A huge creature, muscle-bound and awkward, stumbled forward; one big, red eye peered out from the middle of its head. It was bound in chains. A huge, spiked, bronze collar surrounded its neck and similar rings encircled each wrist and ankle. The greenish chains were held by many redcaps, each anchored by a troll.

That was a cyclops, from Greek mythology! What was it doing on a ship run by nightmares out of the Brothers Grimm?

The horrible creature with the ghoulish, mouthless face held the whip. It drove the cyclops down the ramp. Shuffling slowly, the one-eyed brute moved to the red Chevy parked by itself and secured the vehicle with the hooks. Then, it shuffled up the ramp again, grunting under the onslaught of lashes when it paused, and began turning a crank. Slowly, with jerks and stops, the car was winched up onto the deck.

Then, the captain gave the signal. An unseen mechanism hoisted up the stern ramp and the faerie square-rigger floated eerily upward. Atop, the pixies raised the sails, and the ship shot off over the buildings, straight up into the cloudy night sky.

Clara lowered her binoculars and stared after the departing faerie ship, her body trembling. That detective guy had been right. She owed him an apology.

She stared after the ship for a long time, fear warring with determination. Then she stood up, shook herself, and headed across town to wait for the library to open.

By the time Clara scrunched down on the floor of her rental car and spread the blanket over her head, it was already dark. It was cold down here and the rug smelled faintly of vomit; she had not thought to check that when she rented the vehicle.

She rested her head against her old gym bag—from the days when she had time for things like going to the gym. The bag was stuffed with the goodies she had bought after her trip to the library, things the books at the library had suggested she might need. Of course the gym bag did not smell that great either, but even old musty sweat was preferable to vomit.

As she waited in the dark, under the blanket, in the chilly, smelly car, she prayed. Her great faith in God had never wavered, not through all the curve-balls life had thrown her. She just no longer trusted that God would answer her prayers. Still, it did no harm to ask him. He was a God of Mercy, maybe he would take pity on her plight.

More likely, of course, he was laughing his Divine rear off.

The car lurched and bumped. Clara's stomach tensed. Was it them? Maybe her prayers had been heard after all.

She grabbed her gym bag tight with one hand and braced herself against the seat with the other. There was a moment of stillness accompanied by a low clanking sound. Then the car began to move. As it swayed in the air, Clara snorted with sad amusement: first prayer answered in eight years, and God picks her request to be kidnapped by faerie pirates.

Clara lay very still, listening for the sound of retreating feet. The ride on the faerie square-rigger took about half an hour, according to her cell phone. Then the car had been lowered again into its current location. There had been some banging around, some muffled voices, and a loud scraping sound. Then, everything went quiet.

Very slowly, Clara pushed the blanket aside and sat up. She crawled onto the back seat and peered through the window. Another car sat next to hers, and then another and another and another. She sat up higher and peered farther. No one seemed to be about. Opening the door, she climbed out and shimmied up on to the roof of the rental, shading her eyes to help her see in the pale moonlight.

There were cars as far as she could see.

The sea of cars spread out from her current position in all directions except to the left, where a tall building stood. In the other direction, toward the edge of her vision, she saw a couple of boats standing among the vehicles. To the right of that, near what might be a road, was that...a plane?

How would she ever find Mr. Spaghetti?

Jumping down, Clara gave the rental car a fond goodbye pat. With the loss of this car went her very last credit card, the one she had been keeping for emergencies, in case one of the kids got really sick and needed more doctoring than their mother could provide.

She shrugged and threw the strap of the gym bag over her shoulder. No point crying over spilled milk, after all, or spilled credit. No point in berating herself for not thinking to take one of the kids' backpacks instead of a bag that merely had a strap either. She just hoped she would not have to run. Otherwise, her carefully compiled gear was a going to give her a spanking with every step.

She crept quietly forward, peering into each car as she went, shivering a little despite her inside-out sweatshirt—that was one of the tricks she had picked up during her time in the library. Wearing your clothes inside out was supposed to keep faeries at bay. From time to time, she stopped and listened, but she could hear nothing except the hum of a freeway in the distance. She soon realized that her current efforts were futile. The gibbous moon was not bright enough to let her distinguish the details of individual cars at a distance. There was no way to spot her car from afar and there were far too many cars to search individually.

Setting off for the huge building she had glimpsed to the left, Clara swore solemnly that if she ever got her car back, she would buy one of those little Disney figures at Smarty-Mart that snapped onto the antenna to help you find your car in a crowded parking lot. A new electronic opener—something she could point and click, and her car would light up—would be even better, but those cost a pretty penny. More pennies than were in her piggy bank.

◆

The bay door led into some kind of warehouse or factory. She could not see much, stumbling around in the dark, but it must have been a large place, because every object she accidentally knocked or kicked echoed eerily. She needed to find a light switch. She flicked her gym bag in annoyance and snorted. All this clever gear, and she had not thought to bring a flashlight. And her piece-of-crap, pay-as-you-go cellphone didn't have a large enough screen to illuminate anything but her foot.

Of course, in her defense, it had been two o'clock in the afternoon when she came up with this plan. Only she had not been able to find anyone who would baby sit her kids while they were awake. So she had been forced to wait until after their bedtime. Even as it was, she had been forced to promise to do her sister's laundry for a month. Candice was smart enough to know that a night without Mr. Spaghetti would be no picnic.

After bashing her head on some hanging thingamajig, Clara finally found a door leading to another room. On the far side of the door, she found a light switch, only now she no longer needed it.

Before her stretched a foundry. It was dimly lit, but the bright orangey glow of molten metal illuminated the vast area, making it look like a nightmare about the fourth circle of Hell. The place smelled of hot metal and was warm, a welcome change from the chill of the night. Clara moved forward cautiously, glad she had paused before flicking the switch. She was obscured by shadows that would have vanished had she blunderingly flicked on a new light source.

From her position, she could not see the work force. They must be too small in relation to the gigantic cylindrical vats. However, work force there must have been, because huge cranes were lowering cars—full size sedans and SUVs—into the molten vats. Far above the factory floor, a wooden command center hung out over the work area, supported by buttresses. Clara stopped beneath it and gave the structure the Hairy Eye. Who would be kooky enough to use burnable materials, instead of steel or glass, in an environment so filled with fiery sparks?

Faeries, of course, who cannot touch cold iron—and apparently not hot iron either.

If the faerie overlords were not willing to come onto the factory floor, of what did the work force consist? More enslaved cyclopes?

With a loud grinding creak, one of the vats tipped. A stream of hot yellow liquid poured into some kind of long trough, illuminating more of the building. Shadows fled from the corner around her. Clara saw something pale dangling on the wall to her right. She moved to investigate.

"Dear God!" She pressed her hand against her mouth, hard.

Hanging suspended by a rope was the detective who had questioned her the previous day, the one who had promised to get her car back. He hung by his wrists, dangling above a circle of toadstools that grew directly from the cement. His face had been beaten. He had a black eye and an ugly purple-and-green bruise on one cheek. He did not seem to be breathing. "Is he...are you dead?"

"Nah, it's okay, ma'am." The voice came from some place to the left of the body. It sounded as if a pair of cymbals had been granted a voice and were speaking with a Bronx accent. "That's just my body. Normally, I stay in there. I kinda got out of it, on account as I did not like the way they was treating it."

"What...what are you?" Clara's hand was already in the gym bag, reaching around for some kind of weapon. She pulled something out at random and found herself holding a bell and a carton of salt. Would that work? The faerie tales had not been very specific on the subject of what worked on who.

"Ever read *The Tempest*, by that Speareshaker guy?" His voice now issued from the air above the closest point of the toadstool circle When Clara nodded, he continued. "Remember Ariel? Well, I'm his...you'd call it a brother. Only I spend my time in this body here, on account of how Mr. Prospero wanting me to be able to help you humans. He's the one who decided I was to be a detective. Name is Mab, by the way."

"Mab?" Clara looked to and fro, but could see no sign of the speaker, which made sense, she supposed, if he was some kind of spirit of air. She crossed her arms. "I thought that was the Faerie Queen's name?"

"Nah, her name was Maeve. Spencer got a little confused."

"I see. Can I get you down?" Clara took a step forward, eyeing the toadstools dubiously. "I brought some herbicide."

"Herbicide? Clever! A girl after my own heart. You'll probably need it, but don't use it here. There are other spells, you might get hurt."

"What can I do?"

The voice was silent for a moment. Then, with a sigh, he said. "Ma'am, I'm going to ask you a favor. I realize you might not be able to grant it, but I...I gotta ask."

"Go ahead," Clara eyed the air suspiciously. "Worst I can do is say no."

"In order to get anything out of here, you're going to have to face the faeries. Faeries don't got free will—well not in the way that a creature with a soul does. They are constrained to obey certain rules."

"Like them leaving a poor soul alone if his clothes are inside out, or not crossing a circle of salt?" Clara asked. What had seemed warm when she first stepped in from outside was now growing uncomfortably hot. She wiped sweat from her brow.

"Right! And they have to stick to the rules under which they operate, whether they like it or not. And they're tricky. Comes from having no hope of Heaven, you know; no reason to behave. If you survive whatever they throw at you, they'll let you pick one thing to take away with you. Pick me."

Clara drew her head back and stared at him like he was bonkers. "Pick you, not my car with Mr. Spaghetti?"

"Pick me, ma'am, 'cause once I get out of here, I can shut this place down. Shut it down forever. Put...let's just say I can put everything back where it goes—I could do it now, if I could get to my danged cell phone, but I can't work it in this form, and you can't cross the magic circle to get it for me.

Mab's voice became more serious. "If you pick something else, ma'am, you'll get to leave with it, but everything else will stay here. Until...some other mortal happens upon me, I guess. I could be here a very long time. Not that that's your problem."

"What's the number? I could call them," Clara offered, pulling out her phone.

The voice sounded truly embarrassed. "No one commits numbers to memory anymore."

"That won't help, then." Clara slipped her phone back into her pocket. Then, she put her hands on her hips and snorted. "You think I'm going to be tempted by some stupid, shiny, lesser offer, Detective Mab? On one hand, I get a doll or a car. On the other hand, I get both the doll, my car, the rental, and I save you, another human be...another living being. And you think I'm going to find this decision hard?" She waggled her head at him. "You have another thing coming."

The detective's voice was low and sad. "Ma'am, you have no idea. If you chose to ask for me, I swear I will do everything in my power to return...everything here that is yours. But if you do not, I'll understand. Mortals can only bear so much."

"You're crazy," Clara took a step back, unnerved. "You may have believed me and be an airy spirit without a body and all, but you're still as kooky as a...kooky thing!"

"Just sayin', ma'am. That's all," replied the detective.

Clara held up her hand, as if she were saying the Pledge of Allegiance. "I give you my solemn word I will ask for you. There. How's that! I am a woman of integrity. I. Do. Not. Break. My. Word."

"You shouldn't have done that, ma'am...but thank you."

She slipped around the wall and was about to head up the stairs to the command room when she saw it. Her car! It sat in the line of cars waiting to be turned into slag. Clara flew down the stairs that led to the waiting area. She hunkered down and ran between the vehicles like a spy in the movies. Reaching hers, she fumbled with her keys, breathing hard. Then, she had the door open.

A lunge into the back, and Mr. Spaghetti was in her hands!

Clara shut the door and sat down, leaning against the tires of the next car over, a huge green van. She hugged the stupid, tattered rag-doll to her chest, its fingerprint-stained, spaghetti-like hair flopped against her shoulder.

"You caused me a whole whopper of trouble, Buddy O!" she whispered to the silly thing. "I don't know what my son sees in you, but he loves you."

But that was the way of love, was it not? Heck, she would probably feel the same way about whatever goofy boy Sari eventually picked for a husband.

She blew her nose on an old tissue she found in her pocket and toyed with her cell phone as she thought about calling home to check on the kids. Reluctantly, she decided not to. The last thing Candice needed was for the phone to wake Sammy.

He had cried himself to sleep, the poor baby.

She felt bad about imposing upon her sister, who had her own family to worry about. Back when Sari was little, she would have asked her neighbor. That neighbor no longer talked to her, though, ever since Sammy peed on their front door. Clara tried to reprimand him at the time, to show that she understood their concern, but Sammy just laughed, his white teeth flashing in his silly dark head.

Clara could call him silly, because she had earned the right through sweat and tears, but the Lord help anyone else who dared call her son names!

She did not know if the neighbors blamed Sammy for urinating with malicious intent or blamed her for letting him out to play—For pete's sake, she could not keep an eye on him every single minute! She was only human!—Either way, they just had not understood.

Of course, her sister's children had a daddy to watch them when their mama was out; so maybe she should not feel so bad about imposing on Candi.

Clara gave the rag doll a last fierce hug and shoved it in her bag. She wiped the sweat from her face again. What to do now? If it were not for the detective, she would just leave now. Forget the car, forget that she had ever seen anything like this. Just get the doll back to Sammy and life could go back to normal…without a car or a credit card. But she felt bad just abandoning the guy. Maybe she should try the herbicide on the toadstools after all.

Wiping a stray tear from her eye that had crept out when she was hugging the doll, she rose to her feet. As she did so, she glanced toward the factory floor.

Where had all the children come from?

Clara's feet did not move toward the door. Instead, they crept closer to the factory floor.

It was like walking into a Dickensian nightmare. Children, from tiny three year olds to burley teens, worked the factory, moving levers, throwing switches, changing the molds into which the molten metal poured. Dirty children, dressed in rags, with bruises and open sores. Sweaty children, working in all that heat. Dull-eyed children, who went through their routines without any sign of that spark that made a child well…a child.

Human children. Enslaved by faeries. Here in the modern day, in the country of freedom!

In all her years of medical school and ER work, Clara had never chucked her cookies. She had been proud of that. Her Stomach of Iron failed her now. She vomited behind the tire of a white BMW. Crouching down, she grabbed her knees and stayed there until her legs stopped shaking. Then, slowly she stood up and made herself look again.

Children. Little children, like Sammy. Like Sari. One of the little dark boys even reminded her of Sammy.

Despite the heat, an icy, cold chill traveled own her spine.

No, not reminded her—this boy looked like Sammy. *Exactly* like Sammy. Except, he looked like what Sammy would look if he were an ordinary child—without that sometimes stupid, sometimes benefic expression the real Sammy usually wore. Like what Sammy looked like when he concentrated hard, and you could not tell that there was anything amiss with him. Like what Sammy would look like with a festering wound on his cheek and forehead.

That boy out there, with burn marks on his wrist where molten sparks had caught him—the bastards did not even give the children leather gloves—looked *exactly* like her son.

How could that be?

Clara examined the rest of the children she could see. Her heart nearly stopped. There! That little girl was a splitting image of Jillian, the sole little girl in the ABA program at Sammy's school. And behind the giant crane! The boy who was missing an arm. He looked like the twin brother of Nicholas, from that Special Need's exercise class she used to drag Sammy to.

Slowly, her legs gave way. Clara sank to the cold cement floor and bowed her head.

She knew how it could be. She had only just read all those faeries stories.

Hot tears splashed from her cheeks to the floor. Her life, her wonderful career, the lives she might have saved, the husband she had—yes, she would admit it now, she had loved Stan before it all went wrong, and the coward ran out on her—all thrown away so she could raise a faerie imposture, who had been left in place of her real son.

Her Sammy was a changeling.

Now that she knew, her life finally made sense. Laughing in the face of discipline. Weird behaviors. Lack of empathy with human beings. Was that so different from laughing at funerals and the other bizarre things faeries were wont to do in tales?

And modern chemicals? Bright lights? Of course, her son could not tolerate them! He was a freaking faerie! In retrospect, she wondered why she had not figured it out sooner.

Were they all changelings? Over a million autistic children in America alone. Had they all been stolen by faeries?

She thought of her friend Jenna, patiently enduring the screaming and fits of her three autistic boys. She thought of Martha, who spent her days driving from one doctor to another, determined to find the illusive missing cure. She thought of Mrs. O'Conner, whose daughter had bugged out, leaving her to raise her two autistic grandchildren.

All these women, all that labor and love, wasted on changelings—while their own children suffered as slaves.

"Samuel!" she took off at a run, sprinting across the factory floor. "Samuel!"

The little boy turned as she approached. His eyes grew large. Staring up at her in wonder, he asked in a small voice. "Are you...my mama?"

Clara grabbed him and clasped him to her heart. "I am! I am your Mama! And I'm never going to leave you again!"

She knelt and hugged him, her missing son, her long-lost, beloved child. He smelt like metal fumes and smoke, but under that was a scent that reminded her of hugging Sari. This little boy smelt like her daughter! Any doubts Clara might have had evaporated. The two of them hugged and cried and cried and cried.

A scrabbling noise startled Clara, just as a redcap lunged for her. Screaming, Clara threw her body between the redcap and her son. Frantically, she stuck her hand into the gym bag, feeling around for something of use. The redcap let out a squeal of frustration. His hands clawed at her but did not touch her.

Her clothes! The inside-out clothes! They had worked! Losing no time, Clara grabbed her son, pulled off his soiled shirt, and turned it inside out. Putting it on him again, she took off, sprinting toward the cars and the stairs and door out beyond.

More redcaps appeared. One wore a cutlass. One swung a copper rope. Another held two wooden belaying pins like daggers. Soon three chased her, then four. As she neared the automobiles, she saw a fifth redcap standing straight ahead of her, grinning. Clara ground to a stop, hugging her boy tight. She had deliberately looked up redcaps in the library. What had that big black book claimed countered them? She rooted around in her bag for her cheat sheet.

Oh, right! Bible verses. Made them stop and lose a tooth or some such rot. Clara blurted out the only Bible passage she could bring to mind.

"Give us this day our daily bread!"

The five advancing redcaps stopped cold. Moaning, they grabbed their jaws and writhed. A moment later, a tooth popped from each of their mouths. The teeth shot across the room, bouncing off of the floor and ricocheting off of vats. From the additional moans and pings she heard beyond the range of her sight, she assumed more redcaps had been on the way.

During all this, Clara had not been idle. She grabbed the Morton Salt carton and spun in a circle, letting the salt pour out liberally. Then, she spun around again, to make sure she had not missed a spot. She had to pour salt on the two gaps she found, but, finally, she had a closed circle.

The redcaps rushed up and crowded around the circle. They were short, bearded men in dark sailor's suits, wearing red sailor's caps and each missing a tooth. They shuffled around the circum-ference, as if searching for a weakness.

"Hey, little men?" Clara called. When they gathered around to hear her, she shouted, "Boo!" and gave them the Hairy Eye, the real deal, with the full force of her scorn.

The redcaps scattered like leaves before a leaf blower.

"Now that's how it's supposed to work!" Clara hooted tri-umphantly, her confidence returned. "God only knows what was up with that detective. He didn't even blink!"

From the far side of the factory came a curtain of sparkling lights. This glittering pixy dust sprinkled like rain onto any children that got in its way. These children slowed and stood still. Some staring blankly, others slumping and falling to the ground, asleep. Clara grabbed her frightened son close and murmured, "Salt, don't fail me now!"

As the curtain of sleepy sand approached, Clara saw that a platoon of pixies flew above, dropping the pixy dust from little pouches they carried on their belts. The pixies flew directly toward her. There was nowhere to run. Clara gritted her teeth and stood tall.

The glittering wall of golden dust struck the circle of salt and curved, until Clara and Samuel seemed to be surrounded by a semi-circular curtain of shimmering light. But neither the pixies nor the dust crossed the salt.

"Hot dang!" Clara grinned widely. "Those books at the library *rock*!"

The pixy dust hung in the air for a time, like motes in a beam of light, then it slowly sank to the ground, forming a sparkly, golden semi-circle around her white circle.

Samuel looked up from where Clara had pushed him against her body, his eyes wide. "What happens now, Mama?"

"Don't know, Pumpkin. We wait."

"I'm scared, Mama."

"I'm here with you, baby." She smoothed his curly hair. "I'm not gonna leave you!"

A door opened in the wooden command center, and the captain of *The Mangled Treasure* emerged. He began floating down. Clara scowled. The ship's name had seemed kind of amusing when she read it in the park. It did not seem amusing now.

The captain was tall and fae, with silver-dark eyes and pale translucent skin. His long coat fluttered about him like wings as he descended. His features were godlike and easy on the eye; his expression was distant and cruel. As he came closer, Clara saw that the captain had lost a limb at the knee. In its place was a silver peg leg inscribed with Celtic knotwork.

A tiny pixy sat on his shoulder. The pixy, too, was in pirate garb: tri-corned hat, blousy white shirt, black, half-open vest, red sash, blue pantaloons, black boots and a copper cutlass—the whole works.

"What you think you doin'?" Clara always reverted to the language of her youth when she got really angry. "Takin' advantage of these po', defenseless children?"

The captain smiled. His teeth were all sharp; two were made of silver. "My! Aren't you a feisty one, me beauty! But yer days of wreaking havoc here are over. Hand over the boy and go, before we find more appealing uses for ye. Arrgh!"

He spoke like a pirate using all the correct words and intonations, but his voice was languid and insolent, entirely out of keeping with his words. It was creepy.

"Appeal this, you POS!" Clara snarled, as she rooted around in the gym bag. Lord, she had better get out more. She had spent so much time around children, she had forgotten how to swear properly. "You let these children go, or you're going to be sorry you ever drew air!"

"Begging your pardon, me beauty, but are ye referring to me crew?" The captain gestured lazily toward the factory floor. His fingernails were long and crowned with slender caps from which long needles protruded. He saw her looking and held them up, wiggling them. "The better to claw out the eyes of disrespectful ship hands," adding languidly, "Arrgh."

"Arrgh!" growled the pixy on his shoulder. "Those scurvy louts!"

"They are CHILDREN!" Clara shouted. "They are supposed to be out playing and running around."

"On the contrary," the faerie pirate captain drawled. "When children are left to their own devices, they are prone to cause havoc. We put a stop to that." He leaned back his head and stroked his non-existent beard with a black-gloved hand. Airily, he added, "Me thinks ye should be thankin' us for the service!"

"Arrgh!" repeated the pixy on his shoulder. "Otherwise, you'd be swabbing up the mess."

Clara glared at the little bugger. What was he supposed to be, the parrot?

"I ain't even dignifying that with a comment," she grumbled, as she searched her bag.

Her hand came away with a handful of powdered chalk and a pile of red thread. She threw the stuff down with a grunt of disgust. They were no use! She plunged her hand back into the bag again. It had to be here somewhere!

"These wee ones are our weaponsmiths. They make pistols and spears, for use against our enemies, the Unseelie Court. Or are we the Unseelie Court?" The captain cocked his head to address the pixy. "So hard to keep these trivialities straight. The Servelings make weapons now. When they get bigger, we give in to their pathetic mewling and let them wield the things. They're given the honor of cutting down our enemies, Arrgh! Fine bully boys, they make, all hot with anger. We cannot make or hold iron weapons ourselves, of course."

"Arrgh!" declared the pixy. "Melts us like slag." It grinned nastily. "Melts our enemies like slag, too, and they don't got themselves a Serveling army!"

"Servelings! The word you are looking for is *Slaves*!" Clara spat. "You've enslaved children to make weapons?"

The captain of the *Mangled Treasure* chuckled deeply. "Aye, the blackbirdy has spunk, do she not? Look at her bristle like a vixen defending her kit. If we had mothers, lads, we would know how mothers get, wouldn't we?"

There was muttering laughter from the redcap pirates, answered by tinkling giggles from the little floating pixies. Clara glanced around, unnerved. She had not realized they had an audience.

The captain continued, "Besides, me fierce beauty, the little powder-monkeys do more than just forge weapons. Some are lucky enough to become cabin boys, or personal servants to other fae. They serve many uses, quite versatile, really."

"Very useful, Arrgh!" the pixy leered, "Especially the saucy little wenches!"

"If they are useful," Clara asked through clenched teeth. "Why do you treat them so badly?"

"Treat them badly?" The captain turned to regard the children, puzzled. "I see no harm upon them. They are given food, water, and a mat to sleep upon, same as crewman. What more would ye have us do?"

Clara glared at him, but the captain merely looked confused. Her blood ran cold. Great Mother of Heaven, he was serious. The faeries were so callous, so alien to human kind, they did not even know the children were being harmed.

Finally! Clara's shaking hand—shaking more with wrath than fear now—closed upon her *piece de resistance*. She held it tightly but did not yet pull it from the gym bag.

"Listen here, Faerie Face, I'm leaving and I'm taking my son!" she declared.

"Arrgh! I think not. Pirates never relinquish their loot," The faerie pirate smiled, showing his sharpened silver teeth. "However, Ancient Law, far older than the ways of pirates, require that we must let ye go—with a single object of yer choice—if you can successfully answer a riddle."

"Listen here, you Jack Sparrow wanna-be!" Clara drew the sawed off shotgun from her gym bag and aimed it at the faerie captain. "I ain't playing any of your pixy games! I am a lady of principle! I. Do. Not. Make. Deals. With. Slavers."

"I fear ye have no choice, me saucy lass, yer in our territory now. Our territory, our rules!" The captain seemed totally unworried. Behind her the redcaps and trolls cheered loudly.

"See this shotgun?" Clara trained it on the faerie pirate captain's chest. "It's packed with rock salt and iron filings. Iron hurts you guys, doesn't it? Of course it does, or you wouldn't bother kidnapping helpless babies! Do you know what these filings are gonna do to you when they hit you? Suppurating lung wounds. Ripped aorta. Perforated stomach wall.

"Don't you mess with no MD, punks!" Clara chortled, jabbing the gun at him. "When it comes to knowing how to hurt, we can open up a whole can of whup on your sorry ass!"

"Arrgh! Tradition requires that we…" the faerie pirate captain began.

Clara aimed the gun at his head and set her feet.

"Or we can declare the riddle answered and move on," the faerie captain amended. "Oh, very well, ye may ask for one thing, and one thing alone to take away with ye. Anything ye likes out of our booty. Cars. Pieces of eight. Magic rings. Whatsoever ye please."

Clara opened her mouth to tell them that it was sure as Hell going to be her son. Only she stopped. Behind her, laboring in the factory, were the other children, hundreds of other children, thousands of other children.

"What if I want to take them all?" She asked. "Do you need me to remind you of what is gonna happen to you and your punk pixy mini-me if I pull this trigger?"

"Now don't do anything hasty, me feisty one!" The captain urged. "We of the Old Lineage are bound by yer circle, but them thar human Servelings are not. Children love shooting pistols, ye know, and we have many here. What a tragedy t'would be if ye and yer little boy were gunned down by yer own kind. Poets would write ballads about it."

"Cut the act!" Clara snarled. "You can't possibly really talk like a pirate."

"Aye, most likely not, me beauty, but you wouldn't want to see me out O' my pirate guise. I give you me word on that!"

The captain began to grow, taller and darker. Shadows gathered about him like a shroud. Antlers sprouted from his brow, and his eyes began to glow with a reddish light. Behind her, Clara could hear the redcaps and trolls stealthily retreating. The little pixy on his shoulder gave a cry of horror and fled.

"*You would not like me without my pirate guise, creature who smells of mortal blood,*" came the eerie, rasping words.

"Okay, okay! Do the pirate thing already!" Clara cried out, her voice shrill.

All that bulk and shadow might be posturing, especially if he still could not get through the circle of salt, but she would not take any chances. Beside that big, black, glowing-eyes, horned thingy gave her the creeps!

The captain shrank again and donned his fallen tri-corner hat. "'Tis all right, me hearties. Yer captain has returned. Fer the moment, anyways."

There was a hardy cheer, and the redcaps, trolls, and pixies slowly returned back. The little one circled cautiously two or three times before landing again on the captain's shoulder.

"All right, me hearties!" it sang out. "The captain won't eat us today!"

The captain turned and leered at Clara. "What be yer decision, me beauty?"

Clara paused, torn. She looked across the factory floor at all the other little damaged souls. Someone else would have to rescue them. Or maybe she could come back with the police. If the police believed her. If they knew enough to use chalk circles and not just get enchanted.

On the other hand, what if this Mab person could not actually help? What if his promise was a trap?

Clara closed her eyes and prayed. Then, she knelt beside her son. "Samuel, honey. I love you more than air itself. But I promised someone who can save all the children that I would ask the faeries to let me take him out with me. It's very important to keep your word, and we want to save all your friends. I'm going to have to leave you here and come back for you. Is that okay?"

In the best of worlds, Samuel would have smiled at her and said, "That's all right, Mama." But, Clara's life had never been in the best of worlds.

Samuel's bottom lip began to quiver, the way her daughter Sari's did when she was about to cry. He grabbed her leg with both hands and held on.

"No! Mama, no! What about your promise to me?" he cried, his voice heart piercingly shrill. "You told me you would never leave me again! Mama! They hurt me here, Mama! Don't leave! Don't leave me!"

Clara felt as if she had been pierced to the very center of her soul. If someone had shoved a hot poker through her spine and into her heart, it could not have hurt as much as this.

But when the leering faerie captain insisted she, herself, tear her son from her and leave him, weeping, on the factory floor—that hurt more.

❦

Outside on the chilly street, Clara knelt beneath a street lamp, pounding her fists on the pavement and weeping. Detective Mab walked up beside her. He looked bruised and beaten.

"Blow me to the North Pole, you chose me!" he whistled. He looked stunned.

He pulled out his cell phone. Clara shook her head, whipping her slender braids about yet again. She was sitting next to an airy spirit who was using a cell phone. What had the world come to?

"What happens now?" she asked dully when he folded his phone again.

"We wait for the cavalry."

"The cavalry?

"The *Orbis Suleimani,*" he growled.

"The Circle of Solomon?" Clara translated. She had taken Latin to help her with her medical work.

"Organization set up by King Solomon to protect humans from the supernatural." Mab explained. "Nowadays, Mr. Prospero's in charge. We've been looking for these pirate jokers for a long time, but we were having trouble locating 'em." A look of disgust came over Mab's features. "Stealing from humans! Enslaving children! Those punks had to go down!"

"They can't be responsible for all autistic children. There weren't enough children there," Clara murmured, more to herself.

Mab looked grim. "They aren't the only ring of slavers, ma'am, but we'll get 'em. We'll get 'em all!"

"Why children?" her voice sounded unnaturally shrill. "Why not just kidnap adults? Adults would be infinitely more useful for fighting a war."

Mab shrugged. "One of those rules, like why they can't cross salt. They are allowed to take children before their second birthday. After that, all sorts of restrictions kick in. Free will, and all that."

"How long has this been going on?" Clara asked. "Them stealing so many children?"

Mab shrugged both shoulders. "Don't rightly know, ma'am, but I can hazard a guess that it's probably a modern thing. It's only recently, in this age of so-called science, that people have stopped following the old ways, protecting their thresholds, and doing the other things that would keep the faerie folk away. Apparently, the faeries figured this out, too."

Ahead, perhaps a dozen dark figures carrying tall staffs approached the factory building. Just before the door, they halted. Soon, they were joined by more figures in wide hoods and long flowing cloaks. When what appeared to Clara to be a small army of SCA members had assembled, they moved, streaming into the building. Clara lowered her head and prayed that, whatever happened, no one would hurt the children.

As she glanced up again, her gaze fell on the gym bag. Mr. Spaghetti's head stuck out of the open top. Clara grabbed the doll and hugged it. Then, she flung it away from her.

Mab raised an eyebrow. He walked over and picked up the discarded rag doll, examining it front and back. "Begging your pardon, ma'am, but isn't that what you came here to find?"

Clara glared at him and snarled. "My life, my health, my marriage, all the sacrifices I made—I thought I was doing the right thing! The good thing! But that...monster is not my son, not even a human being. Just some kind of..." tears threatened to spill over her lashes again, "some kind of soulless monster."

It was the pain, the humiliation, of not having noticed that hurt the most—of having loved him so much. It was worse, even, than having wasted her beauty and her youth on Stan.

Mab took off his hand. "Ma'am, you must be a praying woman."

Clara glared at him suspiciously. "What makes you say that?"

"'Cause only the Almighty could arrange a coincidence like this one. Less than a dozen beings on this world who could tell you what I'm about to say, and only one of those who has actually been through it happens to be me." He paused and pushed up the brim of his hat. "Before I go on, let me ask you—truthfully, using your own judgment. Do you really believe your son—your other son, I mean, Sammy, I think you call him—has no soul?"

Clara closed her eyes and pictured the thing she used to think of as her son—that moaning, bobbing freak who had broken her nose. But what she saw in her mind's eye was not the screaming, thrashing Sammy, but his beneficent smile, that open clear look in his eyes—like gazing into the eye of an angel.

Suddenly, Clara knew, from the crown of her head to the bottoms of her sneakers, that Sammy had a soul. She had seen that soul gazing back at her. Sammy might not be the son she had given birth to, but he loved her!

Wordlessly, Clara nodded. Somehow, the detective seemed to know what she meant.

"You clearly know something about faeries. Have you ever come upon the story of St. Patrick and the mermaid?" asked Mab.

Clara shook head.

"Well, the short version is that St. Patrick once got a mermaid a soul. It can happen. Mr. Prospero, my boss, he investigated it. Found out that the easiest way to grant a supernatural creature a soul is to put it in a human body and let 'em live with humans, interact and communicate with humans, learn decency and love.

"Ma'am," Mab put his hat back on and handed her Mr. Spaghetti. "Before Mr. Prospero gave me this body, I was as soulless as the rest of my fellow airy spirits. But then I started hanging out with Mr. Prospero's daughter, Miss Miranda—you may remember her from the play—and learning stuff about humans. To make a long story short, I came upon this little silver star that only people with souls could hold...and it didn't fall through my hand and it didn't burn me. I held it just like any other human...I've won me a soul!

Clara clenched the doll. "Wait. Sammy might not have had a soul when I got him, but he might have one now?"

Mab stuck his hands in the pocket of his trench coat. "Bodies change the way we think. Faeries going into a child's body becomes a child the same way immortal souls conceived by the Almighty sent into a child's body becomes a child. That faerie who impersonated your son had never known motherly love. He'd never known courage or sacrifice or any of those things you've been doing for him. Do you think soulessness can hold out against the power of a mother's love?"

Clara lifted her chin. "You mean, in return for giving up my cushy life and the lives I might have saved...I helped a soulless creature gain a soul?"

"Exactly, ma'am."

Clara stood there, flabbergasted. "Did...did the faeries do this on purpose? Is that why they left us changelings?"

Mab shook his head. "Nope. They haven't got a clue. Don't know it happens."

"But what...what is a soul, Mab?"

Mab gave a tired weathered smile. "The key to the Pearly Gates, ma'am. That little boy you're raising? The one who loves that goofy rag-doll you're strangling?" Mab looked her straight in the eye. "Thanks to you, the gates of Heaven just opened for him."

Children began to pour out of the building into the faint moonlight. Clara saw Samuel right away. He paused looking for her and then came running as fast as his feet could go. Clara's heart leapt. She had feared he would never trust her again. She ran to him, lifted him up, and swung him around in the air. He laughed, but hearing it squeezed Clara's heart, it was a hesitant, rusty sound, a sound a child might make if he had never laughed before.

Children mulled everywhere, shivering in the chilled night. In the midst of them, Clara saw the cyclops. His collar still on his neck, and his copper chains dragging behind him. He stopped and stood, blinking his single red eye, as he gazed at the street around him. Then, a tall figure carrying a staff came and gestured for the creature to follow him.

Mab came over to join her. Clara hugged Samuel fiercely, holding him to her chest, and surveyed the crowd. There had to be thousands of children here.

"How is anyone ever going to find their parents?" she mused.

Mab rotated his shoulders. "Not sure how I'd do it myself, but I know a fella who might be able to help. He's got a list with their names on it, watches 'em when they're naughty and nice. Maybe he could deliver them on his rounds this year, like Christmas presents."

"Santa's real, too," Clara gave a short laugh. "Lordy, that's too much for me! I'm taking my son and going home!"

So, now Clara had three children. She had to change her real son's name. Could not have two boys in the house both called Samuel, and it made sense to change the name of the one who had only just learned he was a Samuel. She called him Stanley, she thought his good for nothing father would have liked that.

It was not an easy life, but Clara would not have traded it for anything—not even to have been the head ER physician at Mercy Hospital, married to the most handsome man in the county.

She kept an eye on the news, tracking the stories about the "foundlings." Children arrived in homes far and wide—apparently these *Orbis Suleiman* guys made the faeries give back all their changelings, all over the world.

It was not an easy time. These battered children went to homes that were already dealing with problems. Some families had two or three such children. Her friend Jenna was suddenly the mother of six!

Some families rejected the new children, who was then shunted off into the foster system. Some rejected their changeling in favor of their flesh and blood. But, for the most part, they did what families always have done since the dawn of time, they made do. They found room. They loved them all.

In America alone, over a million faeries had gained souls.

EQUINOX

THE LONG, SLANTING RAYS OF THE SETTING SUN LIT THE NARROW cobblestone street. In the wide bay window overlooking the road, the red lights came on, shining luridly through the lacy curtains. A set of stairs led to an underground basement. Garish, glowing posters showed silhouettes of unclad females. At the top of the stairs stood a heavy-set man in a leather jacket. He whispered in breathy, conspiratorial tones to passersby, repeating his message in Dutch, English, and German. He called, "Girls! Girls! Pretty girls! Come see! Three marks a peek! One dollar a peek! Come see! Pretty girls!" Unsuspecting tourists who took the huckster up on his offer soon learned that a peep may be cheap, but a longer stay costs a pretty penny.

In one window, across the street from a thrift shop which closed its doors as the night clients arrived, a young woman leaned against a wall and brought her bare leg up to rest seductively on the window seat. The red light washed out the pale green of her teddy, which clung wisp-like to her rounded hips and narrow waist; its lacy silk barely concealing her voluptuous bosom. A braid of midnight-black hair stretched down her back. She licked her lips and stared with sultry gaze at each man who passed her window, be he a balding Dutch business man, or a young American cyclist on his first trip to Amsterdam.

As she gazed steadily at her perspective clients, her mind wandered elsewhere. She worried about her daughter's babysitter, the attempt of the local organization of Mothers Against Opium to further regulated the red-light district, the bill before the Hague to unionize prostitutes, and whether she would ever make enough to pay back her bloodsucking manager.

Sukey leaned against the wall and lit a cigarette, of the long 'ladies' variety, which she smoked from a slim black holder—some clients found the holder a turn-on. She blew a long, thin trail of smoke into the air and watched it gather into a cloud. It was the twenty-second of September. The summer tourists had returned to their snug, foreign homes. The night's business would be slow.

On the street outside, a man walked briskly, glancing over his shoulder as he went. The brim of a beige felt hat obscured his face, and the collar of his tan overcoat had been turned up. He stopped just before Sukey's window and glanced about as if unsure where to go. Sukey leaned forward, beckoning. She could see his lips curl wryly beneath the brim of his hat. With a final glance over his shoulder, he stepped quickly up the two stairs leading to the outer door of Sukey's building.

As he knocked on the door to her apartment, Sukey drew the heavy canvas drapes into place behind the flimsy lace curtains. She straightened the satin sheets on the brass bed and called for him to enter. In the same low, husky voice, she quoted him her rates: for the quarter hour, for the half-hour, for the hour.

The man in the overcoat stepped inside. He looked around the narrow, dingy room. His eyes rested on the shiny brass headboard, the worn oak standing wardrobe, and the full-length mirror on the back of the door leading to Sukey's private W.C.. There was a soft carpet underfoot, its color indistinguishable in the lurid red light.

Now that he stood in her apartment, Sukey saw that the gentleman was much taller than she had first taken him to be. His eyes watched her intently from under the rim of his hat. Sukey took her cigarette from her mouth and extinguished it, crushing the tip against the crystal ash tray that rested in the corner of the window seat.

"You still haven't paid me," she said coming toward him. Her hips swayed as she walked.

"Will these do?" he asked. He took what appeared to be a Rollex watch from his wrist and reached up his sleeves to produce a pair of cufflinks. He held both out toward her. The wristband glinted of gold. The cufflinks appeared to be studded with onyx and diamonds. Sukey's eyes locked onto his outstretched hand. Her voice trembled slightly.

"How long are you planning to stay, mister?" she asked.

If this guy is for real, she thought, *the trinkets he is offering are worth a fortune.* Her cut alone would go a long way toward paying off her debts. In the glimmer of the watchband, she saw an image of her little daughter playing among rose bushes instead of broken bottles and overturned trash cans. *If he is for real....*

"I had hoped to stay all night," he said.

Sukey reached out toward what he offered. She jerked her hand back.

"No...No. I don't think so, mister. Those could be fakes. Then I'd be out a night's wages. How could I tell?" Sukey asked.

"You have my word," he said.

A shiver went down Sukey's spine. She laughed nervously.

"Sorry, mister. That only works in the fairytales. Find the cash, or find another girl."

"I beg you reconsider, miss," he said calmly. "Someone is following me...to kill me."

Sukey stepped over next to the door. Her slim fingers rested on the buzzer that called the bouncer.

"You're leaving right now, mister. I have heard about such things. They happen in the newspaper, or to other girls. I keep my hands clean," said Sukey.

Her heart pounded in her ears. She was familiar with hard crimes, but not in her own familiar, dingy apartment. She felt strangely unreal.

"My life is in your hands," he said simply.

"I have a little daughter," Sukey said. "Without me, she has no one."

"Many more children than yours will suffer if I die tonight," the man in the overcoat replied.

"Who are you that you're so important?" Sukey asked hostilely.

He stepped forward and tipped up her chin, turning it this way and that while he examined her face.

Sukey drew in a breath. He was close enough now that she could see his face beneath the hat, and he was handsome! Sukey had entertained men with boyish good looks and those with oily charm, but this man was truly handsome, like a Grecian statue or a fairy book knight.

Every girl's dream is to meet a man like this one, Sukey thought. For some girls in her line of work, it was only this dream that made it possible for them to go on night after night. Sukey was more realistic. She had learned young that life was no fairy tale. She had put aside her hopes for a dream man along with other dreams, once held dear. Now, the sight of this man's face filled her with a sinking horror. If there were men like this one in the world, what other mistakes might she have made in her judgment?

"You must not spend much time in the sun," he said finally.

He stepped back and released her. Shaken out of her private thoughts, Sukey glanced about as if to note her place of work and the hour of the night.

"What makes you think so?" she snapped sarcastically

"I do not recognize you," he said.

Unsure of what to make of this, Sukey changed the subject.

"Who's trying to kill you, anyway?" she asked, turning away and walking over sit on the window seat. When he did not answer, she looked up at him inquiringly.

"I am pursued by the king of the vampires," The man in the overcoat said. Then, "Please do not open the drapes, he may be without."

"Yeah! I'm sure he is! Hovering above the eaves, most likely! And you're the world's greatest vampire hunter, I suppose?" Sukey asked.

"What do vampires fear more than vampire hunters?" he asked.

Sukey considered.

"The sun?" she guessed.

He nodded.

"What do you mean?" she said uneasily. "Are you the sun?"

"I'm its charioteer," he answered.

He must be mad, Sukey told herself, staring at his profile; enthralled by the perfection that was his nose and chin. She had lured the most handsome man in the universe into her dingy little parlor, and he was lunatic. But as she looked into his eyes, she found that she could not quite believe that he was mad.

Yet, one of the two of them must be. Her world did not allow for vampire kings and charioteers of the sun. One of them must be mad, she was certain. Yet, if it was not he...

"Are you saying that if you get killed tonight, the sun won't rise tomorrow?" she asked.

"The sun will rise, but it will no longer harm vampires," he said.

"Then what will happen?"

"The vampires will rise and conquer the earth. They will enslave mankind, your young daughter among them. Even if she could escape, she would live in a world peopled by the undead. Life on earth as we know it would come to an end, forever."

Sukey was quiet a time, unsure of how to respond.

"There must be some other way of killing vampires," she said finally. "Can't you put stakes in their hearts, or not let them over your threshold?"

"There are two other ways to deal with a vampire," he replied. "The first is difficult. One must find the vampire in its sleep and stab it through the heart with a wooden stake. The other way is simple, however, men seem not to find it so."

"And that is?"

"Turn your back and walk away," he said.

"That's all?" Sukey asked dubiously. "Just walk away?"

"Vampires feed on fear. Where there is no fear, there is nothing they want," he said. Then, he gazed across the room at her. "May I stay?"

Sukey found that she was shaking. He was clearly mad, and his jewelry was probably fake. Yet, he was so handsome! Just gazing at him made her legs weak. The thought of turning a creature like that out and spending the rest of the night entertaining overweight bank clerks and pimply-faced teenagers made her feel sick to her stomach. *Even if the jewelry is fake,* she thought, *I could do worse than spending a night with the god Apollo or whomever he thinks he is.*

"All right. You can stay, Mister Sun. Take your coat off and make yourself comfortable," Sukey said.

She rose and took the watch and cufflinks from his outstretched hand and brought them over to the wardrobe where she locked them in her jewelry box.

The man took off his hat and overcoat and hung them neatly on the coat rack. Then, he sat down on a chair. Without his coat, he was dressed in a loose white shirt and dusky beige trousers.

Sukey walked to the bed. She sat down and slowly loosened her hair in the lurid semi-darkness. Then she stretched out languidly on her side and patted the smooth satin sheets beside her.

"What should I call you?" she asked, her voice soft and sultry.

"You may call me Belius," he said. He did not rise. "You need not trouble yourself. I only wish sanctuary."

Sukey sat up and hugged her legs. She knew she should be pleased. Her time to herself was so rare. She could sleep now and spend all day tomorrow with her daughter. Yet, perversely, she felt a burst of anger. Of all the men to come to her, that this one would turn her down. It was unjust! She should not give up without a fight.

She rose to her feet and came forward to stand beside his shoulder, gazing down. Her voice low and husky, she asked, "What's the matter? Don't you like women?"

"I admire women," he said, "who admire themselves."

Sukey drew back as if she had been stung.

"What do you mean?"

"Would you call yourself happy?" he asked.

"Of course, I'm not proud of what I do!" Sukey snapped. She spun on her heels and went to sit on the window seat, hugging her knees to her chest. "Do you think anyone wants to live this way?"

"Then cease."

"Who are you to preach, fugitive? If I did as you said, I'd be dead," Sukey said. "Better to be ashamed and alive."

"Is it?" he said.

Sukey started to sneer at him, but when she saw that he was serious, she stopped. She looked away and drew the drape back to look out at the darkened street, she said.

"Yeah, and I bet you think that all I have to do is turn my back on the vampires that are leeching my life dry, and they'll let me walk away."

Outside the window, a large, dark shape fluttered.

"Shut the drapes!" Belius shouted.

He leapt from his chair and crossed the distance to the window in two strides, knocking Sukey's hand aside. The drape fell shut, blocking the view of the street. Outside, Sukey heard a soft shuffling sound.

"He has found me. I am undone," Belius said. "I will go now. You have done enough."

Turning his back on her, he crossed to the coat hanger and picked up his coat and hat. Sukey watched him as he dressed. He did not glance her direction. As he put on his hat, Sukey felt her heart swelling in her throat, until she wondered how she could still breathe. She was suddenly certain that if he left, everything precious in life would leave with him. Desperately, she threw herself between him and the door.

"No! Please! Don't go! Hide in there." She gestured toward the W.C.. "I'll...I'll protect you."

Belius stared down at her. His striking face was stern and inflexible. Sukey thought she caught a trace of disgust.

"Will you?" he said coldly.

Sukey wavered. He pushed her aside. She watched him reach for the doorknob. The thought of him leaving to be slaughtered was unbearable. She stepped in front of him again and met his harsh gaze.

"I give you my word," she said.

Belius nodded. Then, he turned without another word and walked across the room to the W.C..

Sukey perched on the edge of the bed and waited. Her clock ticked. Muted laughter drifted down from the floor above, where her manager entertained guests. From the street, she heard only the raucous sounds of potential clients passing.

From the far end of the room, her reflection stared back at her, pale in spite of the red glow. She smoothed out her wisp of a teddy and fought the desire to laugh. Here she was, sensible Sukey, waiting for the king of the vampires to invade her chambers. The whole idea was insane. How had she allowed herself to believe it?

There came a sound at the outside door.

Sukey leapt up and slid the bolt to lock the door. She heard one of the other girls invite the caller in. The doorknob of her apartment rattled.

"Sorry, mister, I'm busy with a customer," she called. "Can't you see the drapes are drawn?"

The doorknob rattled again. She felt suddenly vulnerable and looked about her room in search of something that could be used as a weapon. She regretted that she had never tried to acquire a gun on the black market. She was glad, though, that she had made a fuss about getting her lock fixed.

"Go away," Sukey said again.

"Excuse me, I can't seem to hear you," a cold soft voice spoke. "Would you mind if I come in?"

"No! I mean, yes!" Sukey said. "Yes, I do mind!"

"Too late," The voice replied calmly.

The bolt began to tremble. All by itself, it slid back and unlocked. The door swung silently open. Outside, a tall man stood. He wore a well-tailored black suit, with a white ascot at the neck. Black sunglasses hid his eyes. Both his white-gloved hands rested on a white cane. He was not touching the door.

"Good evening, Belius," the stranger said mildly.

He stepped over the threshold and shut the door behind him.

"Can't you see he's not here?" Sukey said rapidly, gesturing about. "There's no one here, mister."

"As it happens, I cannot see. But, then, what need have creatures of the night for eyes?" the stranger said, and he drew back his lips, opening wide his mouth.

Sukey gasped. Two shiny, knife-like teeth protruded from his upper jaw. The lurid light dyed them blood red. As he turned his head from side to side, Sukey thought she heard a thin, high-pitched noise. He stood motionless for a moment, tilting his head as if to listen.

"I don't hear him. Where is he?" The vampire said.

Though petrified, Sukey remembered Belius's words about defending oneself against vampires. She crossed to stand beside the bed and turned her back on him. Her heart beat thundered repeatedly in her ears. Behind her, the stranger stepped closer. His icy fingers caressed her bare shoulder. Sukey shuddered.

"I see he has been here. You participate in his peculiar brand of protest." Sukey trembled, but she said nothing. He sighed. "Very well, if you shan't tell me, I shall find him myself." The vampire was silent a moment, perhaps listening.

"Is that you, Belius? I can hear a second heart beat," The vampire said. Sukey heard him laugh softly and step toward the W.C..

"No!" Sukey cried.

She dodged around the vampire and threw herself against the door leading to the W.C.. The vampire rested his gloved hands upon his white cane. He leered down at her. The door trembled, but did not open.

"This door," he asked, frowning, "it leads to a private room?"

"Yeah! I don't share it. If you're desperate, use the head in the hall." Sukey said.

The glass of the mirror on the back of the door was cold against the bare skin of her shoulders and legs. She shivered.

"But, I may use the facilities in this building?" The vampire asked.

"You can't trick me, mister," Sukey said. "I know you can't cross that threshold without my permission, and I'm not giving it."

"Not so quickly, my dear," he said. "We haven't talked business. I can pay handsomely."

"I don't want your money," Sukey said.

"No money then. What of immortal life?"

"As a vampire? No thank you!"

"I offer you immunity for you and your family. When the vampires rule the earth, you will be permitted to live unmolested. We will leave you alone, as long as you give us the same courtesy."

"And raise my little girl amidst a world of vampires?" asked Sukey.

"Your little girl is already surrounded by vampires, my dear. Every man or woman who indulges in pleasures that suck away their life has already yielded to me. Cocaine, crack, whiskey; all these are my agents. Those who use them, my subjects."

"I'm clean!" Sukey said. "I went straight five years ago, when I found out I was pregnant. I've been clean ever since!"

"You may be clean, as you put it, my dear; but what of your associates? As we speak, your manager is upstairs entertaining dignitaries and important guests. How do you think he pays for his handsome suite?"

"Black Rik? What of him?" Sukey asked.

"He is mine. I have only to ask, and his own fear and loathing will force him to obey my will," the king of the vampires said.

"Go-go ask him to help you, then," Sukey said.

"By the time I return, you will have allowed that glorified cart driver to escape," he said, nodding toward the door behind Sukey. "No, you help me now. Otherwise, I shall have a word with your manager. You would not want your life made less comfortable than it presently is, would you?"

"You can't threaten me," Sukey said, lifting her head haughtily. "I've already mortgaged my soul. There's nothing worse he could do."

The vampire played with the head of his cane, which Sukey now saw resembled a snarling wolf.

"No, perhaps not. But what of your daughter, your little girl? Wendi is her name, is it not? You see, I know a great deal. How well protected is she in that house on Vier Straat? I have only to breathe the word, and my minions will be upon her. Can her babysitter protect her from men with long sharp knives?"

"No! You wouldn't!" Sukey whispered, pressing her hand against her mouth.

"Wouldn't I? My dear, for myself and my race to continue, we must destroy the man cowering behind your skirts, or lack there of... What does the death of one little girl mean compared to this?"

Sukey felt suddenly helpless. A picture of her little Wendi, with her long, dark curls and her happy blue eyes, arose in her mind's eye. The picture warped and twisted, as the tiny child changed to resemble photos from the crime pages.

"Why me? Why today? Why can't you two fight in someone else's room?" she said.

She feared that she might cry or scream.

"Do you know what today is, my dear?" The king of the vampires asked.

"September Twenty-second...Ah...Your birthday?" Sukey asked wildly.

"The Equinox, my dear, the Fall Equinox. The one day in the year when the powers of light and the powers of darkness are equally matched; only, unlike during the spring equinox, the powers of darkness are growing. During the summer, he is too strong for me. During the winter, he knows his weakness and hides. Only today can I catch him.

"Now," the vampire said. "I tire of waiting. Invite me across, or I shall give the word. Your daughter shall perish horribly, and her innocent blood shall fill our cups."

Sukey was frightened. She thought of Belius, with his glorious face and upright bearing. She had never met a man such as him before, never even seen one, except, perhaps, in her dreams. She would give her life to protect him, she decided, without a second thought. But could she give her daughter's life?

In her mind, she saw the ghost of her daughter looking up at her with doleful eyes, accusing her.

It would be so easy just to let the king of the vampires take Belius, she thought, *so terribly easy*. A single word was all it would take. He would be dead. There would be no one to reproach her.

"Are you trembling, my dear?" the vampire asked, looming over her. His icy fingers caressed her cheek. "I can smell your fear. Fear acts as an invitation to our kind, you know. That is why we will eventually rule the earth. All feel fear and guilt. All are doomed."

"Not him," Sukey said, biting back tears. She gestured with her head toward the W.C. behind her.

"Yes, but we can never hope to be like him," the vampire said softly.

"Can't we? Perhaps, you can't. I, at least, can try," said Sukey.

And she turned her back on the vampire.

In the full-length mirror on back of the door, Sukey could see the wardrobe, the bed, and the window seat. There was no sign of the king of the vampires.

Sukey's heart swelled with hope. The vampire was gone. Belius had been right. It was simple!

Behind her, she heard the vampire's cold laughter.

Her heart sank. It had not worked. Of course, she could not see him. Vampires did not cast reflections.

Yet, Belius had told her that it was simple, and she believed him. One had to put aside fear, he had said. Hardening her resolve, Sukey raised her trembling hands, stuck her thumbs into her ears, and shaded her eyes so that she could see only the mirror. Silently, she began to pray.

It had been a long time since she had last prayed. At first, she could not remember how. Softly, she promised her God that, should he help her live through the night, she would live such a life as would make her worthy of a man such as Belius.

There came a soft hiss. Cold icy air touched her neck. Sukey started, but refused to turn and look behind her. She concentrated on the empty mirror. *Why is it that vampires cast no reflections?* she wondered. Could it be that they actually were not real? If so, of what was she afraid? As she thought this, the words of the Lord's Prayer returned to her. She repeated them silently to herself, again and again and again.

It seemed as if hours passed.

When she finally felt calm, she turned around. The room was empty. She was alone.

"He's gone!" she exclaimed.

The door behind her opened. Bright light spilled out onto the mulberry-colored rug. Belius stood in doorway, running a hand through his golden curls. Light from the incandescent bulb behind him lit his coat and hair. To Sukey, it seemed that the light came from Belius himself.

"Indeed, he has!" Belius smile was brighter even than the light. "You have kept your word. I thank you."

"It was that easy?" she asked, her voice shaking.

"It was that easy," he said.

He smiled at her and his beauty struck Sukey like a physical blow.

"Will all this happen again next Equinox?" she asked, gazing at his face in naked admiration.

Belius shook his head. "Now that I am aware of his intentions, I will prepare myself."

"Then you are safe?" Sukey asked.

Belius nodded and smiled at her again. Sukey glanced up toward the ceiling and her manager beyond.

She sighed. "If only it were as easy to banish the vampires who suck away my life."

"That is the gift of men," Belius said. "They are always at equinox. At any moment, they may confront the darkness in their soul. Only their own fear holds them back."

Sukey began to protest that he had misunderstood her. Then, she wondered.

Had he?

Was it Black Rik who kept her where she was, or was it fear? Fear of confronting Black Rik? Fear of facing the unknown? However bad this life was, it was her life. She was familiar with it.

Yet, as she remembered the promise she had made while she prayed, she thought familiarity and fear were hardly a good reason to continue living like this. Slowly, her eyes turned upward again, toward the ceiling above her.

"Wish me luck," Sukey said, as she crossed the room and opened the outer door.

"A blessing upon you, Sukey," said the charioteer of the sun.

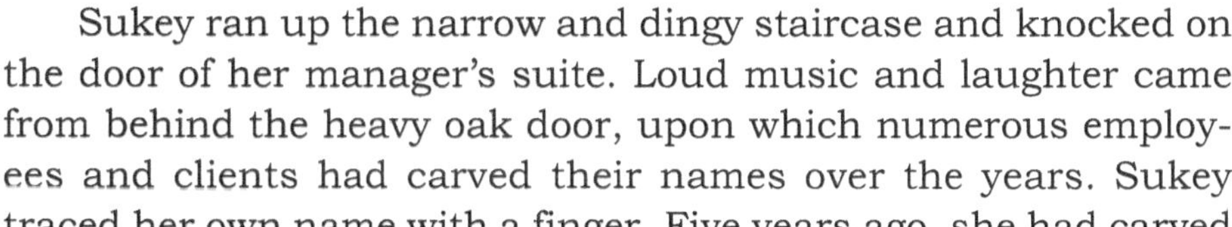

Sukey ran up the narrow and dingy staircase and knocked on the door of her manager's suite. Loud music and laughter came from behind the heavy oak door, upon which numerous employees and clients had carved their names over the years. Sukey traced her own name with a finger. Five years ago, she had carved this. Had it really been so long? She pounded on the door with both fists.

"Black Rik! Black Rik Boulten!" she called.

The door opened. Black Rik stuck his head out. He had bloodshot eyes and an unkempt beard. Over his bloodshot eyes, he wore a pair of small, round glasses. He stepped out and shut the door behind him, frowning down at Sukey in her flimsy teddy.

"Yeah? It better be quick," he said. "We're busy in here."

"It's quick, Rik," Sukey said. "I quit."

Rik scowled and reached into his ear as if to clean it. He tilted the ear toward Sukey.

"What was that? I'm afraid I didn't quite hear you," he sneered.

"I quit."

"Oh, you quit. What about my money?" He asked softly.

"You'll get it. Eventually." Sukey said.

"Eventually isn't good enough for me. Now, go back downstairs and get back on your back. Okay, sweety?" Rik said. "Otherwise, I might have to get angry."

Sukey's legs trembled. She had seen Black Rik angry before. He had struck her once and dislocated her jaw. And that was before he called his bully boys to help. She did not think she could stand up to that again. She nodded meekly and began to turn away.

As she did so, she thought of facing Belius below. He had been willing to walk out into certain death. How would she be able to justify why she backed down? He would regard her with disgust, as he did when she offered to protect him. Suddenly, Sukey felt calm. Nothing Black Rik could do seemed frightening when compared with the thought of facing Belius with her failure.

She turned back to her manager.

"It's no good to threaten me, Rik. I quit," she said. "You can kill me, or let me go. But, if I'm dead, you'll never get your money."

Black Rik scowled at her again. This time she did not back down.

"You owe me a lot of money, sweetheart," he said menacingly.

"I'll get it back to you," Sukey said. She drew herself up and met his eyes. "I give you my word."

Black Rik frowned and scratched his neck.

"For what that's worth," he muttered. Then, he shrugged. "Yeah, okay. Just keep the money coming in regular amounts. And clear out of here by morning. I want to put Matilde in that room."

Sukey was so amazed that for a moment she could neither speak nor move. She had won. It had been that easy. And she could have done it at any time.

"Thank you, Rik," Sukey said.

She turned her back and walked away. As she reached the stairs, however, she looked over her shoulder. He was standing in the doorway, staring after her, a funny sort of puzzled sneer on his face.

"It's been good working with you, Rik," she said.

"Yeah, you too kid," said Black Rik Boulten.

Then, he went back to his party and closed the door.

⁂

Sukey rushed downstairs, bursting into her room with a triumphant cry. Once inside, she spun, laughing, eager to share her joy. However, no returning laughter met her ears. The room was empty. He was gone.

A great sense of loss filled her. She had so longed to see the light in his eyes when she told him of her victory. Even this sorrow, however, could not overcome her joy. She had earned her own freedom. She did not know what she would do or how she would live, but those things seemed less important now. She was free!

She packed her few personal belonging in her green knapsack and changed into her street clothes. Then, she turned the red light out and went to sit on the window seat one last time.

Drawing back the canvas drapes, she looked out. The street was empty. Only two windows still glowed red. Even the huckster with the peep show had called it a night. The eastern sky was alight with a soft peach glow.

She fished out her black, enameled jewelry box from the knapsack and unlocked it. Inside gleamed the Rollex watch and the diamond-and-onyx cuff links. Sukey laughed; tears rising to her eyes again. She no longer doubted that they were real. Once sold, they would bring in money enough to keep Black Rik happy for a couple of months, and still have enough left to get her and her daughter out of Amsterdam.

They could go to Bergen-an-Zee, Sukey thought—she had always wanted to live by the sea—or maybe Germany, or even France. As the dawn grew brighter, Sukey let glorious horizons unfold before her. It seemed amazing that only a few hours ago she had had no hope at all. She wiped her eyes and stood up.

"Who could have guessed that fairytales were real?" she said, her voice trembling.

Returning the jewelry box to her knapsack, she swung it over her shoulder. Without looking back, she left the room, stepped over a drunken client, and came out onto the street. As she walked toward her daughter and home, she felt the first ray of the early morning sun kiss her cheek.

Four Funerals and a Wedding

*This story is dedicated to
Matthew and Eugie Foster,
Who deserved better*

CASSANDRA LEANED AGAINST THE SHOVEL AND WIPED HER BROW AS A flock of geese flew across the face of the moon. Beside her, Archie dug steadily, unearthing the grave dirt above his fiancée's coffin.

"You know," the young woman picked up her shovel again, "this was not where I had expected this to end."

"Let's just hope it doesn't end here," he grunted back. "Or worse, with us both in jail."

For the first funeral, Cassandra wore her sunglasses. They were huge and dark and made her look like a blind owl, but they covered her high cheekbones and her eyes. Nothing showed but the nose and chin she had inherited from her Jewish father—not unattractive but unremarkable. No one ever gave the lower half of her face a second glance.

She chose a slim black dress and low black suede boots. The silver and turquoise cat necklace she had worn whenever she left the house for four years now—Jeremy's last present to her on her last mother's day—was a bit cheery for the occasion, but she could not bear to leave it home. She tucked it inside her dress.

Seated in the back pew of St. Timothy's, she gazed surreptitiously at the crowd. Ahead, the family paraded slowly by the open casket, saying their last goodbyes. An old woman in black and a middle-aged man were crying loudly, but the dead man's wife sat with her back straight, a look of desperate hope in her eyes.

Maybe she read the newspapers.

Cassandra pulled Nicholas's old handkerchief from her purse and pressed it against the corner of her eyes. After four years, it embarrassed her that she still cried. But they had been four lonely years—without Nicholas, without her little Jeremy.

No one understood what it was like to have been a mother and then not be one anymore. The worst was when her friends commented on her having the freedom to spend her hours how she pleased. She would give anything to trade her freedom, her prestigious career as a photographer, and her hobbies for the mess and toil of having her family back.

The door opened and the reporter from Channel 9 evening news came in, his cameraman beside him. Cassandra jerked her head away. If he saw her, he would know. He had been at the last funeral, too.

Should she leave? Her eyes flickered to the face of the widow.

Steepling her fingers and pressing them against her lips, she closed her eyes and quieted her heart. *Life. It was eternal. Nothing could be put to it or be taken away from it.*

The lately-deceased man sat up in his open coffin, blinking. The rafters of the small church echoed with screams of terror and then with screams of joy.

⸻ ✦ ⸻

For the second funeral, she wore her hair down. It fell midway down her back, like a solid black waterfall. She hid Jeremy's necklace beneath her black silk blouse, which she wore over gray slacks. Her sunglasses still hid her eyes.

This one was held at the Presbyterian Church outside of town. Calhoun from Channel 9 was there before her, a big, heavy, scowling man. Cassandra shuddered and averted her face. She had been reading his columns, and they were vile. The man poured out vitriol and bile on every subject he covered.

It made her heart ache for humanity that people paid to read such poison.

Beneath Jeremy's necklace, her heart beat rapidly. Would he recognize her? If he did, what would happen?

It was not herself she was worried about. What did she have to lose? It was the folks who she could help if everyone left her alone.

She had tried going to the hospital, but she felt like a harpy, waiting around for people to die. Besides, hospitals made her nervous—too many bad memories. And when she was nervous, nothing happened. Same thing if she bragged or allowed even the slightest hint of pride.

If she wanted to help grieving families and lives cut short, she had to do it quietly, privately.

If Calhoun from Channel 9 outed her—put her in the public limelight—would she ever be able to help anyone again?

For the third funeral, she wore a very large black and white hat. Its large brim dipped down, making it easy to hide behind. Between that and her sunglasses, her face was hardly visible. This was a good thing because the despicable Calhoun looked right at her as she left the church. His assistant pivoted the camera and pointed the blank, black lens right at her. She had only enough time to duck her head and block her face with the hat.

By the time she arrived home, her whole body was shaking.

For the fourth funeral, she left her sunglasses home. Without them, she became a whole new person. All heads turned when she walked into the funeral parlor as people stared at the young Asian woman, so lovely she could be a model. But no one, not even Calhoun, who was hunched like a vulture at the door, recognized her as the same woman with the upper part of her face covered.

It was a disguise she could only use once.

She also took her work camera with its zoom lens.

There was a lone chair against the wall. Cassandra pushed it into a back corner, behind a large urn containing a palm. The smell of smoke and chemicals made it hard to concentrate. Her heart was beating so loudly, she could not hear herself pray.

She closed her eyes and tried to quiet her thoughts, but the angry, leering image of Calhoun kept imposing on her peace. His latest piece on the mysterious "zombie-maker" had been so hateful that it had made her sick to her stomach to read it.

Who hated a person for resurrecting the dead?

In her imagination, she kept picturing the moment when he found her out, the finger pointing, the clammy hands grabbing her by the arm and yanking her in front of everyone. She felt lightheaded.

Only the sight of the two children weeping beside the casket kept her from fleeing the premises.

She closed her eyes and breathed, but she could not clear her thoughts.

What was it with this man? Why was he so angry? Why...

Why had she not prayed for him?

The funeral proceeded. A preacher gave a blessing. A brother gave a eulogy. Children wept. Cassandra tried to pray for the bloated, angry reporter, but her words were empty. In her heart, she did not wish him well.

There must be something about him, something that could break the spell of disgust he had cast over her, some quality, however small, that she could admire.

Nothing.

The gathering was beginning to break up. People were rising, milling, laying a silent hand on the shoulder of the sobbing widower. And Calhoun still stood there, scouring the gathering, scowling at each person, as if they were personally guilty of having murdered the dead woman. Did he never give up?

Ah, that was a quality Cassandra admired. She had to give Calhoun that.

He was dogged.

Like a spell breaking, Cassandra looked at the reporter as if for the first time. How tired he looked, how bitter, his eyes were bloodshot. He looked...like a very miserable soul indeed.

That was enough. Her thoughts calmed. She closed her eyes. She kept them shut until the children began to shout.

Outside, the Channel 9 man was standing by the front walk, interviewing the happy family. People were crying and laughing and hugging. The woman's husband, no longer a widower, clung to her, weeping with joy and relief.

The camera was pointed right at the door.

She should have worn her sunglasses after all.

Cassandra looked around. Did she dare cut through the vestibule to find another way out? Her hand brushed against her camera. Raising her head, she walked over to the loathsome toad from Channel 9, whom she really could not think quite as badly of as she had before, and stuck out her hand.

Heads turned as she walked. But neither the toad nor the no-longer-a-widower paid attention to her appearance.

"Hi there, Cassandra King Crossing." She patted her camera bag, where it hung at her hip. "I do some freelance work for the Mystic River Press and The Westerly Sun, among other places."

His hand was big and meaty. "Archibald Calhoun. Channel 9."

Despite her nervousness, she flashed a big smile and gestured at the crowd. "I gather we're looking for the same thing? Maybe we could compare notes?"

"You mean the person responsible for this circus?" he snarled. "Yeah, I'd like to find that bastard."

"What would you do if you did?" she asked casually.

"Punch the S.O.B. in the face. Repeatedly."

"For resurrecting the dead?" Her voice rose so high it broke.

"What kind of low human being hides the fact that they can resurrect the dead? Where was this bastard when my Effie..." His voice broke.

"O-oh," breathed Cassandra.

His face had taken on a haggard dullness that she knew as well as she knew her own name. It struck her like a blow to her solar plexus.

"I've been looking for him for weeks. Thought maybe he could save...s-she'd been so healthy just three months ago. We thought the cancer had been beat. Then, wham." The big, ugly brute, who was beginning to look dear to her, rubbed at his eyes with the back of his sleeve. "Our wedding was set for tomorrow. She had bought a lovely dress—the nurses had promised to help her put it on—and her brother was going to fly in from Chicago. But things took a sudden turn for the worse. And Effie...." He swallowed, his big Adam's apple jiggling. "Her brother ended up flying in a few days earlier, for the funeral."

Cassandra could hear the man speaking, but she could not see him. All she could see was the glare of headlights from a car coming directly at her on a slick rainy night. She felt, again, the lurch of the car as Nicholas put the driver's side between the danger and his family. In the heat of the moment, he forgot that Jeremy, so recently free of his booster seat, had moved over to sit behind the driver, so he could talk to his father.

If only...if only Nicholas had swerved the other way.

Cassandra yanked out the silly silver and turquoise cat from inside her dress and gripped it tightly. Her life was hard enough but... Not to have ever been Nicolas's wife? Not to have ever held Jeremy, or see him take his first step, or win his first soccer game? Even this, even all the pain and agony of loss, was better than that.

Tears streaming down her cheeks, Cassandra grabbed the reporter's arm. "Your fiancée, where did they put her body?"

⁂

For the wedding, she wore a wide straw hat with flowers tucked in the band. She even went up into the attic and took out a blue and green dress she had not worn since the last time she and Nicolas went out to dinner. The silver and blue cat looked lovely resting against the silky material.

She also left her sunglasses home.

The ceremony was held at St. Timothy's. The press was there, not just Channel 9, but all the local stations and a few national ones as well. She could already foresee the running caption: *Revenant Woman Weds.*

Effie looked lovely in her white gown, her face aglow. Archie Calhoun stood beside her, proud as a bridegroom could be in his handsome tux. Looking at his round, beaming face, Cassandra could not remember why she had thought it anything but kindly and dear. The bridegroom turned his head. Across the crowded church, their eyes met.

Archie Calhoun winked.

Cassandra winked back—which never could have happened had she still been hiding behind her sunglasses.

L. Jagi Lamplighter is the author of the YA fantasy series the *Books of Unexpected Enlightenment*. She is also the author of the *Prospero's Children* (formerly Daughter) series. She has published numerous articles on Japanese animation and appears in several short story anthologies, including *Best Of Dreams Of Decadence, No Longer Dreams, Coliseum Morpheuon, Bad-Ass Faeries* Anthologies (where she is also an assistant editor) and the Science Fiction Book Club's *Don't Open This Book.*

When not writing, she switches to her secret identity as wife and stay-home mom in Centreville, VA, where she lives with her dashing husband, author John C. Wright, and their four darling children, Orville, Ping-Ping Eve, Roland Wilbur, and Justinian Oberon.

Her website is: http://www.ljagilamplighter.com/
On Twitter: @lampwright4